ONE DARK NIGHT

BLAIR HOWARD

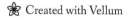

For my beloved daughter Mallory on her birthday.

PROLOGUE

It was late, long after sunset, dark but for the light of a quarter moon that turned the leaves and blades of grass into glistening silver spears. Tall trees on either side of the narrow road cast shadows that pooled like black liquid at their bases as the killer walked slowly on, trying to steady a racing heart.

It had to be done. Everything was riding on what happened that night.

Something splashed in the nearby Tennessee River. A large fish? Probably, but it startled the killer. Getting caught wasn't an option. Neither was chickening out, going home to late-night TV and hoping for the best. They had to die.

Up ahead, two figures were visible in the rear window of a pickup truck parked on the left, on the grass verge, almost inside the tree line. They were embracing, kissing. The killer, rage burning deep inside, revolver in hand, stepped to the edge of the road, deeper into the shadows.

Close now, the truck hadn't been there long. The engine

clicked and snapped as it cooled. The light of the moon was just enough to see that the door was unlocked.

Quick and easy... Quick and... Bitch!

The killer circled around to the passenger side. Samantha Goodkind had her back to the window, her head resting on her boyfriend's chest. Hunter Flagg had his arm around her, rubbing her shoulder. He stared out through the windshield, his eyes alert.

He's heard something? No, no! He can't have. He would have reacted.

The killer stepped forward, grabbed the passenger side door handle. It clicked. The door opened. Hunter turned his head, startled. His eyes widened in recognition and confusion. Surprise turned to fear as the killer leveled the heavy revolver, holding the weapon with both hands to keep it steady.

There was a moment of complete silence. It lasted no longer than a heartbeat, but, years later, thinking back to this moment, this defining moment that would forever alter the killer's trajectory in life, the murderer would remember the stillness, the silence that lasted for what seemed like an eternity.

Samantha tensed, paralyzed with fear. Hunter's arm tightened around her. His eyes locked on the killer's...

The first bullet ripped through Hunter's neck, just above the collarbone. The driver's-side window shattered as the shot passed through him in an explosion of blood and bone.

Samantha screamed, her face covered with the blood.

Slowly, she turned, looked at the killer, pain, fear, and anger merging as their eyes locked in a final, desperate, defiant stare.

She screamed again. The killer leaned inside and pulled the trigger. The blast from the revolver burst her eardrums. A small hole appeared in her chest, then the blood. The stain spread rapidly, turning her white T-shirt into a thing of horror.

Neither Hunter nor Samantha were very heavy, but dead weight is always heavier than you think. The killer grunted, cursed, and dragged the bodies out of the truck and across the road into the shadows among the trees.

Somewhere, far off, a dog barked. The killer paused, listened, but heard nothing more, then continued with the task at hand. There was little time. It had to be finished.

It wasn't easy, and the thick work gloves only made it that much harder as the murderer removed Hunter's clothes and then Samantha's.

The moon disappeared behind the clouds. The night turned black.

1

There was a time, back in '08, when I left the Chattanooga Police Department and began working on my own, that I dreamed of having more time to myself. You know, time to relax, to read a good book, maybe take up a hobby, play a little more golf. Unfortunately, that dream went the way of the dodo in a hurry.

Running Harry Starke Investigations was a full-time job right from the get-go, and then some. Business began with a bang, literally, and continued to grow. Apparently, I was the attorney's dream of an investigator. The phone, so it seemed, never stopped ringing. So, no, I didn't get to take it easy, but I did get to play golf with my father most Sunday mornings.

And so it was on a fine Sunday morning in the spring of 2012 I found myself out on the course with my father and a couple of his buddies, enjoying the crisp fresh air and bemoaning the sad state of my game. It was becoming painfully obvious that I was indeed busier than I wanted to be.

We were on the tee of the second hole, a par three of a hundred and eighty yards, and planned on playing the first nine and then enjoying a couple of drinks before lunch. It was a gorgeous day and the course was in beautiful condition: the fairways had never been greener.

My father, August Starke, a millionaire and legendary tort lawyer, was paired with Henry Strange, a federal judge. I was partnered with Senior Assistant District Attorney Larry Spruce.

August, having birdied the first, had the honor and had hammered his ball onto the green some thirty feet from the pin. His Honor played next to within six feet and was mightily pleased with himself. Then it was my turn. I took my 4-iron from the bag, teed my ball, stood back, lined it up with a divot some three feet in front, then stepped up and took a couple of practice swings... But something didn't feel quite right so I stepped away and took another look downrange. The three older men looked at me expectantly.

And here's where I make my point, I promise. I stepped up again, positioned my feet, waggled my hips back and forth, readjusted my grip on the club, took two deep breaths, re-positioned my feet a little and...

"Damn it, Harry," Larry Spruce said. "Are you planning to hit the ball any time soon? I was hoping to get all nine holes in and a drink before lunch. At the rate you're going, we'll be out here 'til dark."

I turned and glared at the DA. "I'll go sooner if you stop interrupting me."

I focused on the ball and swung.

There was a moment as the ball left the tee when I thought I'd made it to the green. But that hope died as the ball faded right and dropped into a sand trap a good sixty feet from the hole.

August stepped forward, slapped me on the back and said, "Good try, son. Better luck next time."

I frowned at him.

Meanwhile, Larry teed up, took only a second to set up his swing, knocked the ball to the front edge of the green, then turned to me and smirked. "That's how you do it, kid."

And see? This is what I mean. All four of us were working men. Judge Strange and Larry Spruce had full schedules. And my father was always looking for a new, juicy case to win and become even wealthier. Even so, they all had time enough to spare to work on their game.

Me? I was lucky to be able to play on Sunday mornings. Business was booming, but I hadn't yet begun taking on more staff. And with no time to practice, I was as rusty as an old bucket and these three old men, decades my senior, were kicking my rear. But, hey, it was good for business. I worked regularly for both Larry and my father, and Judge Strange was always helpful and usually turned a blind eye whenever I might... shall we say step over the bounds between the legal and the necessary.

August and Henry were riding a golf cart while Larry and I were pulling two-wheelers—the theory being that the walk was good exercise, which it usually was. But my game being what it was... Oh, never mind. Anyway, as I slammed my 4-iron into my bag, grabbed the handle and was about to stride away, Larry joined me and said, "I'll walk with you, Harry. I have a little proposition for you."

"Oh yeah? What's that?"

"Do you know what day it is?"

"Sunday."

"Sunday. Right, but what's the date?"

I looked at my watch. "April first."

Oh no, I thought. *April Fool's day.*

Larry must have seen the look on my face. Because he

smiled and said, "Don't worry, Harry. I'm not setting you up. I really do have a job for you, if you're interested."

"What sort of job? I'm kind of busy... slammed would be a better way to put it."

We'd just finished a long and difficult investigation for my father and things were piling up. I was going to have to find more people soon, and maybe even an intern. But, as I've already mentioned, maintaining a good relationship with the likes of Larry Spruce was always a priority.

"Sure, I'm interested."

"Good. This is... Well, it's not a priority case, Harry, far from it. Oh, don't worry. I'm not looking for a discount. I have some money left in the budget."

I grinned. "You got it, Larry. But April Fool's day? Don't tell me someone's been jerkin' your chain and you're looking for payback."

"No, no," Larry said. "It's nothing like that... Look, April first is... kind of special to me. You see, there was this case I was involved in... It was never solved. You may remember it. The bodies of two kids were found the morning of the second. They'd been shot the night before, April first, out on Sailmaker Circle."

Now I like to keep my finger on the pulse of the city, but I couldn't recall that case.

"I don't remember a double homicide on April first in the last couple of years. How far back are we talking?"

"Fourteen years."

By then we'd reached the edge of my bunker, so I stopped walking, turned to face him and said, "Fourteen years? That's a long time to be thinking about a cold case, Larry. Why haven't you asked me to look into it before?"

He shrugged. "No real reason. I just haven't gotten around to it, is all. But this morning, while I was reading the paper, it all came back to me. I knew you'd be joining us today so I figured I'd run it by you, see what you thought... What *do* you think?"

"Wow," was all I could manage. I pulled my sand wedge from my bag, stepped down into the trap and, without even thinking about it, swung, swept the ball neatly off the surface of the sand and watched it land softly on the green and roll to within five feet of the pin.

I grinned at my father who was standing beside the pin with his mouth hanging open, then at Larry and said, "Seems like your cold case may be just what I need."

"You'll take it then?"

"I didn't say that. Let me think about it."

I'd investigated old cases before, some even older than this one, and they're always a bear. Witnesses die or move away. Memories cloud. Statements change. Evidence gets lost.

Fourteen years? Where would I even begin? Of course, as soon as I thought those words, my instincts kicked in, and before I'd even stepped out of the bunker, I'd already begun to cook up a plan.

I threw my wedge out onto the grass, grabbed the rake, smoothed the sand, then stepped out, grabbed the wedge, slid it into the bag, grabbed my putter and walked to my ball. By the time I got there, Larry had already putted up to within three feet, August had made his par, and Henry had made his birdie. I sank my five-footer, grabbed the ball out of the hole, tossed it high in the air, caught it and then turned again to Larry.

"Okay," I said, grinning at him. "I thought about it. I'm in."

"Terrific," he replied happily. "Come on. Let's get these nine holes knocked out and I'll buy you lunch at the clubhouse." He patted my shoulder and we walked together to the next tee. "I'm sure you'll have plenty of questions for me."

And I did!

2

I t was a little after eleven-thirty when we finished our nine holes and retired to the clubhouse. I won't embarrass myself by telling you my score. Let's just say it was... somewhat over par. My father allowed me to buy him a gin and tonic, as did Judge Strange, and then they both left; my father to join Rose for Sunday lunch at home and Strange... well, I don't remember where he went. On any other weekend, Rose would have joined August at the club, but that Sunday afternoon he planned to work. He had all the intel Bob and I had gathered for him and a case to build for next week. If he won it —and we all knew that he would—he'd walk away with several million dollars, courtesy of a home security company whose system was a little too easy to hack.

Larry and I retired to my favorite table in the great bay window overlooking the ninth hole and ordered coffee and sandwiches.

"So," I said, taking out my pocket notepad—old police habits die hard. "Talk to me, Larry. Tell me about the case."

And he did.

"On the morning of April second, 1998," he began, "the bodies of two high school seniors were found in the woods off Sailmaker Circle. They were identified as Hunter Flagg... that's Flagg with two G's, and Samantha Goodkind."

"Goodkind?" I said, a little too loudly, and then looked around to make sure no one else had heard me. "As in Walter Goodkind? The insurance mogul?"

Larry nodded. "Owner and Founder of Legacy Life and Health, one of the biggest insurance companies on the East Coast. The company's sphere of influence covers from Memphis to Miami and all states in between."

I scribbled rapidly, taking notes. I know, I know. Why didn't I just use my phone? I had an iPhone 4s Plus, sitting right there on the table, arguably the most advanced smartphone of the time, but I still preferred pen and paper. Call me old-school, if you like. But it gets the job done, doesn't it? And, as a bonus, my notepad never needs charging and all the info is always right there at my fingertips.

"Both victims were eighteen at the time, just a couple months from graduating from high school," Larry continued. "They were shot with a .45, one shot each, at close range. There were no casings, so Mike Willis figured the murder weapon was probably a revolver. It was never found.

"Both bodies were stripped and then dumped among the trees. I have the exact location pinpointed. I'll have someone deliver the files for you tomorrow morning." And then he went on to describe the exact location. "Go two tenths—"

I looked up from my notes. "They were stripped?" I asked, interrupting him.

He nodded, looked at me as he chewed a bite of his ham and cheese. "I know what you're thinking, but there was no evidence of sexual abuse... not on either of them. No finger or shoe prints. It hadn't rained in more than a week, if I remember rightly, so the ground was dry, dusty in fact, so there were some tire tracks. I'll see if I can get CPD to give you some more info on that."

"Why remove their clothes?" I said with my pen to my lips, thinking out loud.

"Damned if I know, Harry. Some psycho's twisted fantasy? Part of a cult? Were they shot while engaged in some sort of teenage lovemaking? They certainly weren't engaged in sexual activity."

"Any suspects?" I asked.

He nodded, then said, "I was sure it was the girl's father... either that or he paid for someone to do it. I'm telling you, Harry, I was positive it was him. But we never had enough evidence to make anything stick. Walter Goodkind never even saw a pair of handcuffs."

"No? Why would you suspect him? He might kill the boyfriend, maybe. But what kind of twisted man would shoot his own daughter?"

Larry smiled, but there was a distant sadness in his eyes. "Talk to Flagg's family, and you'll see why. The Goodkinds are rich. Walter owns a house up on The Mountain. The boy? He was trailer trash, through and through. I'm talking hill-country redneck. Needless to say, Walter wasn't happy about the romance."

I added that to my notes and said, "I bet. Who did the autopsies?"

"Doc Sheddon. Who else?" he replied with a smile.

"And who ran the investigation?"

"Charlie Monk was the lead investigator. Do you know him?" He looked at me with eyebrows raised.

I shook my head. "I know of him, and that, my friend, doesn't fill me with confidence."

I didn't know Charlie all that well. He was old school—

fedora hat and a stogie—and he'd been retired for more than ten years.

"Anything else?" I asked.

"I don't know what else to tell you, Harry. It's all in the files. Give me a call if you have questions. I'll call you if I remember anything else. I'll get the files to you in the morning."

I closed my notebook. "Okay, Larry. I'll see what we can dig up. I'm not going to make any promises, though. Fourteen years is a long time, but you know that, and I'm sure you and Monk did all you could at the time. I'm not going to walk out into the woods and find a piece of cloth on a branch and crack this cold case wide open."

Larry Spruce waved the thought away. "Oh, I know that, Harry. I've been around this game long enough to understand how it works. Trust me on that. But there's always that one that got away, you know? Seeing the photos of those kids, dead and naked in the woods... It never left me. It'll get to you, too, I'm sure. I'll pay you for your time, of course, and if after a day or two you decide the trail's too cold, I'll be fine with it. I just figured I should finally put it to rest. Give myself some closure, you know?"

And I did. I had a few cases like that left over from my days as a cop. Sometimes the bad guy gets away, and you have to look the victim's family in the eyes, an evidence bag in your hand and a face burned into your brain, and admit you weren't able to solve the case. That moment stays with you for... forever.

If I could give Larry some closure, I would. Bob and I could go poke the bushes and interview some friends and relatives.

What could possibly go wrong?

3

It was a little after three that afternoon when Larry left me sitting there at the table, deep in thought with a cold cup of coffee in my hand. Already, in my mind's eye, I could see those two kids lying there in the dark. And I knew I was hooked. There wasn't much I could do until I got the files, but I called Bob Ryan anyway. I had an itch, and I couldn't wait to scratch it.

"Bob? We have a new case. Can you meet me at the office so we can talk it over?"

"On a frickin' Sunday? Wow, boss. That's cold." Bob paused. He knew I hated it when he called me boss, but I didn't take the bait.

"Come on, Ryan, you know you live for it, the thrill of the chase, the temptation of a mystery unsolved. You're probably as bored at home as I was playing golf this morning."

I meant what I said, too. We needed a new rabbit to chase, and one had just fallen into my lap, thumping its tail and begging for a good run.

"Golf?" Bob said with a laugh. "Geez, Harry. I never could see anything in it. No wonder you're ready to get back to work. Okay. I'll meet you at the office in half an hour." And he hung up.

Next, I called Tim and Ronnie. As it turned out they were both at the office already.

Ronnie Hall handled the financial side of my business. You know, all the money-related stuff. And, occasionally, he did some financial investigations for me. I had a feeling he'd come in handy. As for Tim, my pet geek, he'd rather be at the office than at home. I'd bought him all the tech he needed to handle even my smallest need, and anything digital or electronic, and that meant his little hidey-hole was stocked with the latest and best Silicon Valley had to offer. I paid him well and, as long as he worked when I needed him to, I didn't care if he played with the toys on his own time. I spent a few seconds telling him what I needed and then hung up.

By the time I got to my car, I'd made all the phone calls I needed to make. I'd even pulled in my personal assistant, Jacque.

As I walked to my car, I smiled. I always smiled. It was a thing of derision among the members. They all knew I could afford to drive something a little more in keeping with my status, but I didn't. Back then I drove a Maxima. It was the only one in the Club parking lot, too. Sure, it looked a little off, parked as it was amid the Jaguars, BMWs and Mercedes, but it was my baby and I loved it.

You see, I may be wealthy—my mother left me a hefty trust fund when she died many years ago—but I prefer to be practical instead of flashy, and my five-year-old black Maxima did just the trick, and then some. If you listened carefully, you'd probably notice that it had gone through several modifications over the years. It had more under the hood than its looks suggested: that sucka could do zero to sixty in less than four seconds. She's gone now, bless her... but that's another story.

My offices are in downtown Chattanooga, not far from the Courthouse. As a private investigator, it pays for me to be within walking distance of the place where most of the lawyers in the city ply their trade and have their offices, the more so since many of them were, and still are, my clients.

Downtown Chattanooga can be a bit of a ghost town on a Sunday afternoon, as it was that day, so the drive to my office took less than fifteen minutes. I used the time to mentally gather together the pieces Larry Spruce had given me about the two murdered teenagers. It was a real Romeo and Juliet story. Hunter and Samantha's story had ended in a tragedy that would have made Shakespeare proud.

By the time I pulled into my parking lot, I had a preliminary list of questions already in mind. I'd put them into three categories: stuff for Tim to handle, stuff Ronnie could look into, and the stuff that required the kind of legwork that Bob and I would need to do.

We had us a fourteen-year-old cold case, and I was under no illusions: it was likely unsolvable, even for my team. The trail had gone cold almost before I'd even become a cop... I was still in uniform and driving a cruiser when it went down, for Pete's sake! But I was going to give it the good old college try. Larry was a friend, and I owed him that much. More than that, though, by the time I walked into my office that afternoon, I felt I owed it to the kids, too. The slaughter of innocents will do that to you.

Jacque greeted me with a smile as I entered through the side entrance. "Well, look what d'cat dragged in! You take one day off and you already look like a retired old man."

I smiled at her. She'd lost her Jamaican accent many years earlier, but she always managed to find the appropriate moment to put it on for me. She's my business partner now. Has been for more than a year. Back then she was my PA, my right arm.

"Hello to you, too, Jacque. I'll be out in a minute. Tell everyone to meet me in the conference room, okay? And... if you made coffee..."

She nodded, gave me a mock salute, and I headed for my office.

My office was dark, cool, and designed to impress the clients. For me, though, it was all about comfort. The wood paneling and red carpet and the large, oak desk made it feel like a bastion of power, old money, of success. It was my home away from home, complete with a bathroom, shower, and several changes of clothes.

I went to my desk and pulled open one of the drawers to reveal a small gun safe bolted into the frame. I entered the security code, retrieved my gun and holster, clipped them onto my belt, grabbed my leather jacket from the hook in the bathroom. Glanced in the mirror and took a deep breath: I was ready for business.

I left my office and went to the conference room and almost bumped into Bob Ryan as he walked out of the breakroom, a mug of coffee in hand and a grin on his lips.

"What did I miss, boss?"

"Will you stop calling me that? You didn't miss anything. We're gathering in the conference room so I can explain it to y'all at once."

"Yes, boss," Bob said, as he ducked into the conference room.

Jacque gave me a wink and a smile.

Me? I took a deep breath, followed him in and took my seat at the head of the table.

Jacque set a cup of coffee down in front of me and took her seat at the back of the room, crossed her legs and set her iPad on her knee, ready to take notes.

4

I spent the next hour talking them through the details of the two murders as Larry Spruce had given them to me, and what little I knew of the two victims and their families.

Bob listened thoughtfully. I knew he'd be the perfect wingman for this case. He'd remember all the little details, and he was a quick thinker. He would keep track of the small stuff when I became distracted by the big picture.

He's a year older than me and, like me, an ex-cop—Chicago PD. He's also a marine—there's no such thing as an ex-marine—six feet two, two hundred and forty pounds, all of it solid muscle. He's quiet, dedicated, and not someone you want to screw around with. In other words, he's the perfect foil for my rapier, though he did have a tendency to act first and ask questions after. Still, there was no one I'd rather have at my back than Bob Ryan.

Ronnie Hall, my financial officer, spent the hour quietly taking notes. A graduate of the London School of Economics, he wasn't a field operative... He was more of a spreadsheet kind of guy, a wizard of the numbers. He knew more about banking and the manipulation of funds than anyone I've ever met... with perhaps the exception of TJ Bron, my present financial officer.

And that brings me to Tim Clarke, my resident tech genius. He's been with me since he dropped out of college when he was seventeen, just one small step ahead of the law. I found him in an Internet café hacking the IRS for the father of one of his idiot friends. Yeah, he was a hacker then and he still is today, but only when he thinks he needs to be, and he rarely asks for my permission. He knows I wouldn't give it, but he also knows I might be inclined to look the other way. He's tall, skinny, weighs less than a hundred and fifty pounds and wears glasses. He was twenty-two years old back then and looked sixteen. He speaks in tongues, binary, computer speak. If Bob was my right arm, Tim was my left, still is.

Tim had his laptop open on the conference table and was clicking away, making notes as I spoke. He raised his hand to speak. It was like we were back in school again. I wanted to break him of that habit but, truth be told, I also had to remind myself that he was still very much a kid.

I nodded for him to go ahead. He frowned, poked the bridge of his glasses, pushed them up a fraction of an inch and said, "You aren't kidding about the differences in class between the families."

"I figured as much," I told him. "You have something you want to share with the class?"

He grinned. "Oh, may I?"

"Go ahead, Tim."

He picked up a remote control from the table and turned on one of the large screens on the wall behind me. A few taps on his laptop brought up a series of photos.

The images were divided into two columns. On one side

were the Goodkinds. I already knew their faces. They were Chattanooga blue bloods, and they were loaded!

Walter Goodkind—a small label appeared beside his photo in response to Tim's click of the mouse, then disappeared again —was seated behind a large desk, wearing a fine Italian suit and no fewer than three gold rings on his fingers.

He had a full head of curly white hair though it was beginning to thin and recede at the temples. Time had been good to Walter. His face was smooth, his lips thin, his blue eyes narrowed to almost slits. He was smiling, showing his teeth... it was more snarl than smile, the look of an aging lion, feral and threatening. And I knew the old man was willing and able to back up the look.

Other members of the Goodkind family, unnamed, posed for social media profile pictures on horseback, on the golf course, or with their quarter-million-dollar cars. They were the epitome of the rich and spoiled.

On the other side of the screen were what the majority of the population in Tennessee would consider the trashiest bunch of rednecks I think I'd ever seen. These folks also posed with their vehicles—mostly pickup trucks—or were looking under the hoods of said pickup trucks. At the top of that column, also labeled by Tim, was the patriarch of the family, Steve Flagg, presumably Hunter's father. He wasn't a bad looking fella, slightly on the heavy side, but not obese. He wore a faded, Atlanta Braves baseball cap with—I kid you not—a couple of fishhooks hanging from it. He had a thin face, a broad smile and leathery skin, skin that had spent a lifetime in the sun. His face was accented by a salt and pepper Van Dyke goatee. The look reminded me of Nathan Bedford Forrest, the Confederate cavalry general, although Steve Flagg's uniform was a red and black flannel shirt, blue jeans and a belt with a silver buckle the size of a small dinner plate.

"And these," Tim said, "are Samantha Goodkind and Hunter Flagg."

The two photos that came up told us a sad story. Samantha was strikingly beautiful. Golden blond hair cascaded down around her shoulders. Her eyes were blue like jewels. Everything about her screamed beauty and wealth. Hunter, on the other hand, was a rough-looking, rugged individual, the beginnings of a goatee of his own on an otherwise smooth face. His hair was brown and cut short. Not quite a buzz cut, but almost. He looked strong in a wiry sort of way.

"Not bad, Tim," I said.

"Thanks!" The kid beamed. "It wasn't easy finding photos of them. There wasn't much in the way of social media back then, you know." Again, he self-consciously did the thing with his glasses and looked away.

Bob frowned. "Hey, yeah. If this case is fourteen years old, we're talking 1998. Man, that feels like a lifetime ago."

I knew exactly what he meant. The 2000s in 2012 felt like a twenty-year-long decade, beginning with 9-11, the rise of the smartphone, Facebook, YouTube and God only knows what else. The 90s felt like an eon ago.

I put on my business face and said, "Tim, I need everything you can find, every scrap of information publicly available about the Goodkinds, the Flaggs and the murders."

Tim looked at me, a sheepish smile on his lips and said, "Only what's publicly available?"

"Yes... for now, anyway." I knew what he meant. Tim was something of a prodigy when it came to... let's say, acquiring information that was hard to find. For legal reasons, I try not to use the word "hacking," but we all know that when you get down to it, that's exactly what it is.

"There won't be much on the murder," he said. "A lot of newspapers didn't even post their stuff online back then. Most news outlets will have their archives on microfiche. A few may have computerized them. Those, I'll be able to ha... I'll be able to find, but there won't be much... What about the PD's files? I could—"

"No! You can't," I said, interrupting him. "ADA Spruce is sending his files over in the morning. I also want to know everything there is to know about those two kids: who were their friends? Who did they hang with? Most important, I want to know if they had enemies: ex-boyfriends, girlfriends, jealous rivals, stalkers, whatever.

"Jacque! Those files. They will be your first order of the day. If they're not here by nine, call Larry and tell him you'll go fetch them. When you get your hands on them, go through them. See if anything grabs your attention. You know what to do."

I switched gears again. "Tim! Get what you can and send it to Bob and me as you get it. Oh, and send anything that looks financial to Ronnie." I looked over at Ronnie. "Can you look over that stuff for me?"

"Sure. What am I looking for?"

I shrugged. "Anything out of the ordinary, I guess. Larry seems to think Walter Goodkind killed the kids or paid someone to do it for him. If he hired a hitman, I think we might find evidence of that."

Ronnie shook his head. "I'll look, Harry, but I doubt it. Goodkind is a half-billionaire. He'll have dozens of accounts, many of them offshore and hard to trace. He can play shell games with money until the proverbial cows come home. Remember how it was with Gordon Harper? That was some kind of rat's nest... Okay, okay. I'll see what I can find."

"Thanks Ronnie. Find something and I'll give you a raise."

He smiled. "I'm the accountant, remember? You might sign the paychecks, but I write 'em."

"Okay, smartass, so find something juicy and you can give yourself a raise." We all laughed.

Bob rubbed his hands together. "And what are we doing first? Going out to see where the bodies were found?"

I thought for a minute, then looked at my watch and said, "Yes, let's do that. There won't be anything to see, but maybe we can get a feel for what happened that night."

"That second sight of yours, right?"

I shook my head. "There's no such thing, Bob. Just my gut. Tomorrow, you and I will hit the streets, early. I want to talk to Walter Goodkind while we're waiting for the files."

Bob looked puzzled. "Why d'you want to interview him first?"

"For two reasons. First, Spruce said he was certain that Goodkind committed the murders. Second, I want to look him in the eye and see for myself. Maybe we can crack this thing wide open with one conversation."

Ronnie chuckled. "You're good, Harry, but you're not that good."

Bob shrugged and said, "Sometimes he is, brother. Sometimes he is."

I ignored him, drank what was left of my coffee, then stood up and said, "Let's go take a look at Sailmaker Circle."

And we did!

5

The drive to the crime scene from the office was fairly short. I knew from the verbal directions Larry had given me roughly where to go—Sailmaker Circle is actually a gated community. If you didn't know the area, though, finding the spot might be a little confusing. The city planners had taken a quarter-mile section of Webb Road that stretched east from the community's main gate almost to Bales Road and, for reasons known only to themselves, they'd named it Sailmaker Circle. It was on that lonely section of Sailmaker that Hunter and Samantha had met their end.

Larry had told me to drive northeast, past the main gate, for two-tenths of a mile, almost to the point where Sailmaker became Webb Road once more. There I'd find a paved pull-off on the left side of the road. The bodies had been found among the trees on the opposite side of the road.

I slowed almost to a stop, drove across the oncoming lane onto the paved section, turned off the motor, and we sat and stared out at what we thought must have been the crime scene.

The pull-off was wider than it looked; *plenty of room to park and make out a little,* I thought.

It was lonely out there. We were there no more than ten minutes, but during that time I counted only five passing vehicles. Maybe it was because it was Sunday afternoon. Maybe it was always that way.

"Let's walk," I said, opening the car door.

I stepped out onto the pavement and walked around the front of the car to stand at the edge of the pull-off and looked through the sparse undergrowth, down at the river. The slope was steep. It couldn't have been more than five or six yards to the water. I turned my back to the river and looked across the road. The undergrowth was much denser over there, and the terrain rose sharply upward. I noticed what once must have been a paved path through the trees. It was a path no more, just the remnants, pieces and patches of paving that soon would be lost forever. As it was, it was still passable, just. Fourteen years earlier it would have been in much better shape.

"Why did he strip the bodies, Bob? And why carry them across the road and into the trees? Why not simply roll them down into the river? It would have been much easier... and what happened to the pickup truck? They never found it or the murder weapon."

"Your guess is as good as mine, boss. Who knows how their minds work?"

"Don't call me that," I said without thinking. "There must have been a reason. It would have been a whole lot easier just to kill 'em and leave the bodies in the truck."

I could think of no good answers to any of those questions. In my mind's eye, the scene as it must have happened played out before me.

I saw the killer, no more than a dark wraith, jerk open the passenger-side door and... I even heard the shots. Those two kids couldn't have known what had hit them. I figured the autopsy report would make for some interesting reading.

"So," Bob said quietly, breaking into my thoughts. "What d'you think?"

"I think... I think some son of a bitch is going to pay dearly for what he did that night."

"He? You think the killer was a male?"

"Could have been a female, but a forty-five is a big weapon, so it's unlikely. Well, you know that. You carry two of them."

"Not all the time, I don't. I just have the one today," he said, holding open his jacket to reveal the vintage Colt 1911.

"When are you going to get rid of that old thing, trade it in for something more modern?"

"When hell freezes over," he replied. "They belonged to my old dad. Carried them all through WWII, he did. That's good enough for... I ain't swapping 'em out, okay?"

I smiled and said, "One of these days one of them is going to jam on you, and you'll die for it."

"That's why I usually carry two of 'em, sonny!"

"Sonny? Sonny? Why I oughta... Ah, let's get the hell out of here."

6
___

L egacy Health was located near the Walnut Bridge, four blocks from my offices, catty-corner to the Tennessee Aquarium. It was a nice day that following morning, so Bob and I decided to walk and take in the fresh spring air.

"I gotta ask," Bob said as we turned north off East 5th and walked on toward the Walnut Street Bridge. "D'you really think Walter Goodkind could have killed his own daughter just because he didn't like her boyfriend?"

"I don't know. It all depends."

"Depends on what?"

I gave a half-shrug. "Well, what kind of man is Goodkind? Maybe he loved his daughter, but maybe he loves his family name even more. Or maybe Samantha Goodkind did something so rebellious, so despicable, that Walter was ready to murder her. Parents kill their kids all the time, Bob. You know that. Maybe the boyfriend was just collateral damage."

"So you don't think the class differences between the families had anything to do with it?"

I smiled. "Maybe. Maybe not. I'm not going to judge a book by its cover. You know me better than that. In fact, I feel like we haven't even seen the cover of this particular book yet."

Bob pointed. "And that's the bookshelf, right?"

There it was: the Legacy Health building.

The five-story building was built almost entirely of glass. Strange geometric patterns folded in and out along the sides of the building, putting edges and angles where there didn't need to be any.

I hoped the architect won an award for the design. If not, I hoped Walter Goodkind had paid him or her handsomely. Otherwise the crystal structure was just a glare hazard for drivers crossing the Market Street Bridge, especially when the sun was at just the right—or wrong—angle.

We entered through the main doors to be confronted by a reception desk—unattended—a building map, and a bank of elevators.

"Just as I thought," I said, looking at the building map.

"What's that?"

"Legacy Health is on the fourth and fifth floors only. The first three floors are rented out to other businesses."

"What does that matter?" Bob asked.

"Well, think about it. We're trying to get a picture of the man's psychology. He has a building constructed that's much bigger than he actually needs, so he can look more important than he actually is. It's called *Goodkind Tower,* for Pete's sake."

Bob frowned. "Okay, so he's trying to make a name for himself, sure. That's fine. These movers and shakers do that all the time... Calling it a *tower,* though. That's a bit of a stretch for five stories, don't you think?"

I nodded, mentally preparing myself for the kind of man we were about to meet. At least I hoped we were.

"I don't know, Harry. Maybe he's just business smart."

I looked at Bob. "What do you mean?"

"I mean he could have built a smaller place, or bought one or whatever, but now he's making money off the other companies that rent here. Who knows, you might have offices in this 'tower' one day!"

Bob was grinning, and he drew out the word "tower" to emphasize his sarcasm.

"Doubtful," I said as we entered the elevator and I pressed the button for the fifth floor. I could have gone to the fourth floor, but I had an idea that Goodkind's ego wouldn't allow him to have his personal office anywhere but the top of the building.

The doors opened to reveal a receptionist posted at a desk opposite the elevators, a young man in a suit that probably cost more than I paid Bob in a month. He smiled broadly.

I introduced myself and Bob and asked if we could speak to Walter Goodkind.

The young man frowned and said, "Do you have an appointment, Mr. Starke?"

I offered him my best smile. All teeth and eyes. "No, I do not. But I think Mr. Goodkind will want to speak with us. This is about his daughter."

"Ah, I see. I can call her secretary to see if—"

"His other daughter," I interrupted. "Tell Mr. Goodkind we're here to talk to him about Samantha."

Again, the young man frowned. It wasn't an angry frown. He obviously was out of his depth; didn't quite know what to do, or even who I was talking about. I figured he couldn't have been more than ten or twelve when Samantha died. Finally, after laboriously thinking it through, recognition blossomed on his face.

"Oh, I see. Uh... I think he's in a meeting. But I'll have someone take care of you while you wait. I can't promise that

Mr. Goodkind will be able to see you today, or that he'll even want to see you."

"Oh, he'll want to see us," Bob added. "Trust me on that, young man."

The receptionist tapped a button on his earpiece, turned his back on us and began talking to someone elsewhere in the building. In the meantime, I arched an eyebrow in Bob's direction.

"Young man? You're not that many years older than he is."

Bob grinned. "What can I say? After that walk over here, maybe I'm feeling my age."

I didn't believe that for a second. Bob was a year older than I was, sure, but he was in peak physical condition. He could have run from my office to that building and back again in a couple of minutes flat, several times over, and still not be winded. In fact, Bob Ryan was in better shape than I was. And I was no slouch myself.

Finally, a young woman wearing a crisp white blouse and black skirt appeared and came walking toward us, and when I say young, I mean she looked young enough to be fresh out of college. She had dazzling green eyes and highlights in her honey-brown hair.

She smiled as she offered me her hand and said, "Hi, I'm Zoe. You are Mr...?"

I took her hand. She was lovely, mesmerizing.

"Starke," I said. "Harry Starke."

She turned to Bob, offered him her hand, and said, "So you must be Mr. Ryan, then?"

He smiled broadly and shook it with a gentleness I'd never seen before.

"I'll be taking care of you gentlemen while Mr. Goodkind is in his meeting. If you'll follow me, please..."

She turned and headed back down the hallway, her high heels clicking on the tile floor.

I stared. I didn't look at Bob, but I'd have bet my Maxima that both he and the receptionist were staring, too.

"Gladly!" I heard Bob say.

Zoe took us to a plush conference room where every detail had obviously been designed to exude luxury and success. The table was solid walnut and handsomely polished, the chairs padded and covered in fine, Moroccan leather.

We each took a seat, while Zoe stood near the door.

Bob couldn't take his eyes off her. I couldn't blame him. But at least I managed a modicum of self-control.

"So, Zoe," Bob said. "How long have you been working here?"

The dazzling smile returned. "Just over a year. Why do you ask?"

I couldn't be sure, because it was fleeting, but I thought I saw a hint of fear pass through her eyes. It was quick, like a ghost, and then it was gone. But the question seemed to spook her. Why?

Bob leaned back on his chair. "Oh, I was just wondering," he said easily.

I looked at Bob in amazement. He was wearing a tan leather jacket over a fitted black, long-sleeve button-down shirt and it seemed to be getting tighter by the second.

He's flirting? Really?

Work hard, play hard was Bob's motto, which is fine, but I wasn't happy when he tried to do both at the same time. I was about to tactfully—very tactfully—remind him that we were on the job when someone walked into the conference room.

It wasn't Walter Goodkind. But it was a face I recognized from the pictures Tim had flashed on the screen the day before.

She looked to be in her late thirties, blond, with a no-

nonsense, pixie cut hairstyle. If Zoe dressed to attract attention, this woman's outfit commanded it. She wore a gray business suit, four-inch heels and minimalist silver jewelry. The look was so sharp it could cut a man in half. I stood to greet her, as did Bob.

Her eyes locked onto mine. Somehow, in about half a second, she'd sized the two of us up and decided I was the one in charge.

"I'm Jennifer Goodkind. I understand you're here to talk to my father about Samantha's murder," Jennifer said matter-of-factly. "Are you with the police?"

"No, ma'am," I replied. "We're private investigators looking into—"

"You're fishing for a job, then?" She cut me off. "You want my father to hire you so you can pick at an old wound."

"Not at all. You misunderstand," I said, smiling. "We're working for the district attorney. We simply want to ask Mr. Goodkind some questions."

Jennifer looked at me for a long moment, then turned to Zoe and said, "Escort these people out of the building, Zoe. If they give you any trouble, call security."

"Yes, Mrs. Young," Zoe said, her eyes downcast.

Mrs. Young? So Jennifer Goodkind was married? I mentally kicked myself for not knowing that. What the hell was I doing there when I hadn't done my homework?

Well, it was too late to cry over spilled milk. The fact was we were there and I wanted to talk to someone, preferably Walter Goodkind.

"Excuse me, Mrs. Young?" I said.

She'd already turned to leave the room. She'd dismissed us, and as far as she was concerned, that was all there was to it.

"Did your father tell you to kick us out?" I asked.

I was fishing, I admit, but I was following my gut. And my gut rarely led me to a dead end.

She stopped, stood for a second, her head down, then turned again, made eye contact with me, pursed her lips and said, "No, he didn't. But I will not allow you to upset him. If you have questions, you can talk to me, but I'm extremely busy so you'll have to make an appointment."

"Ah, I see."

It was then that I noticed someone else at the door whispering to Zoe.

"You see, Mrs. Young," I said, holding her attention. "I'd be happy to talk to you, when you have time, but I do need to talk to your father. When would that be possible?"

Jennifer drew herself up to her full height and, I have to admit, she was impressive. I swear I saw steam coming from her nostrils. The dragon was about to incinerate me. But alas, such things are reserved for comic books and fantasy novels.

"Uh, excuse me, Mrs. Young?" Zoe said.

"What is it, Zoe?" Jennifer snapped without taking her eyes off mine.

I held her stare. If she was trying to intimidate me, it wasn't working.

"Mr. Goodkind is ready to see the investigators now," Zoe said.

Jennifer Good... no, Young let out a long sigh. "Fine, take them in, Zoe. Thank you."

She turned to leave.

"I will be making that appointment," I called after her, smiling. "We can chat some more."

She didn't respond. The door closed behind her.

"Well," Bob said, his hand covering his mouth so that only I could hear him. "That was interesting. What do you think? Protecting Daddy or herself?"

I shrugged and said, "Too soon to tell."

I knew then that it was going to be an interesting case. I still didn't know if I'd be able to solve it or not, but I was already having fun. And I had a feeling that interviewing the rest of the family would be... entertaining.

7

W e followed Zoe out of the conference room, down a long hallway to a pair of fine hardwood doors, intricately carved with woodland scenes that turned them into works of art.

"I think maybe I should get into the insurance business," Bob said under his breath.

I smiled at him. "In a way, we are in the insurance business."

He didn't answer.

Zoe knocked on one of the doors, then opened it and motioned for us to enter.

The large corner office was bright, floor-to-ceiling windows on two of the four sides. Along one of the glass walls was maybe the largest antique desk I'd ever seen. Another multi-thousand-dollar piece of furniture, I figured.

Spread around the room were a number of pieces of ultra modern furniture: couches without arms, oddly shaped aluminum chairs and stools I couldn't imagine anyone actually putting their feet on, floor lamps that looked more like pieces of industrial sculpture than functional lighting fixtures.

The room was a clash of sensibilities. On the one hand ultramodern, light-colored, metallic, strange and uncomfortable. On the other hand was that massive, antique desk, the two Chesterfield chairs positioned in front of it. The desk had to be at least a hundred years old. Everything else looked as if it had been purchased yesterday from Ikea for millionaires.

And behind that old, dark and rustic desk sat the king himself, Walter Goodkind.

He didn't smile when we entered, but he did nod, which I figured was his version of "Welcome. Nice to meet you!"

He looked good for his age—about seventy, give or take a couple of years. He wore an expensive, dark gray suit and a white shirt with a plain, navy blue tie. His hair was white, full and curly... frizzy, almost, like a cloud of white wrapping around the back of his head, framing a tall forehead and a slightly receding hairline.

Walter Goodkind's most striking feature, though, was his face: smooth, tanned, and stern with a narrow white mustache.

"Mr. Starke, is it? And Mr. Ryan?" The old man spoke in a refined American English accent, like old money, like... Cary Grant in one of those old black and white movies.

We both nodded, and I said, "Nice to meet you, Mr. Goodkind. It's good of you to spare us a few minutes."

He nodded and said, "Please, sit down." He motioned to the two armchairs.

"You can leave us, now, Miss Mullins," Goodkind said, looking over our shoulders. "Thank you."

I looked over my shoulder to see Zoe nodding as she backed out of the room, closing the door behind her.

I glanced at Bob. He arched an eyebrow and I knew exactly

what he was thinking: "Miss," which meant maybe she was available.

I shook my head slightly, and we both turned our attention to our host.

Goodkind looked at us through narrowed eyes and said, "You're making inquiries about my late daughter, Samantha. Why?"

"My company has been hired to look into her death," I said. "It's protocol to interview the family members of both victims first."

Goodkind's eyes narrowed even further, almost to slits. "And who hired you?"

Normally I wouldn't give out that kind of information. I figure my clients are entitled to the same kind of confidentiality they expect from their attorney, doctor or confessor.

Well, I'm no doctor or lawyer, and I'm certainly not a man of the cloth, but I do like to protect my clients' privacy. And Larry Spruce was no ordinary client, and this wasn't just any case. However, I needed to know all I could about this man, this Walter Goodkind. I needed a window into his soul, so I was willing to make an exception. Besides, I'd already asked Larry back at the country club if I could use his name, and he'd given me his blessing.

"My client is the Senior Assistant District Attorney, sir," I said, watching him carefully. "I think you know him. Larry Spruce?"

The gray eyes changed ever so slightly. They widened for a split-second. What was he thinking? What were his feelings? Fear? Anxiety? There was no way to know, but I'd been at the game long enough to know there was something there, and that meant I was on the right trail.

Now I needed to poke him a little and see where the trail might lead.

"Why would the DA hire you to investigate a fourteen-year-old murder?" Goodkind's voice was level, controlled, emotionless. But that meant nothing. The man was a seasoned negotiator. He was used to playing hardball, deceiving, manipulating, and getting his own way.

"The murders of your daughter and... Hunter Flagg... were never solved." I emphasized Hunter's name, watching him for a reaction. The emotion was unmistakable: anger. Even after all these years?

I leaned back in my chair. "The murders were planned, Mr. Goodkind. Whoever killed those two kids and laid them out that night had an ax to grind. That's premeditation, capital murder. There's no statute of limitation on first-degree murder... Besides, Spruce doesn't like loose ends and"—I leaned forward to emphasize the point—"I have to tell you, Mr. Goodkind, neither do I, and I intend to catch the killer."

Goodkind stared at me for a long moment. I let that moment stretch out. Finally, he responded.

"Thank you, Mr. Starke. I'm glad you feel that way. I've heard of you. I've met your father. He's a good man, a fine attorney. Tough. I'm happy to answer your questions."

Now that, I wasn't expecting. The man's face was still expressionless, a brick wall, and I couldn't tell if he was sincere or not. One thing was for sure, though, he played a good game, but so did I.

"Okay," Bob said aggressively. "Where were you on the night of April first, 1998, the night your daughter was killed?"

That was Bob. Always ready to go for the throat.

Goodkind didn't miss a beat. "I'm sure I told the police. You'll have to check their files. But I believe I was home that night. In fact, I'm certain I was."

Goodkind's eyebrows tightened for a moment. Was it

anger? Frustration? He probably wasn't too happy to be asked that question right off.

I sat back in my chair, took out my notebook and pen, then said, "That's fine. We'll check it out. Now, if you wouldn't mind, please tell me about your daughter."

As I expected, the anger left his face to be replaced by a distant sadness.

He lowered his eyes, looked at the top of his desk, picked up an ornate fountain pen with his right hand and began to twirl it between his fingers.

"She was the light of my life, Mr. Starke. I know that sounds cliché, but it's true. She was my youngest daughter and reminded me so much of her mother, my wife, Nancy. I lost her many years ago, you see. And Samantha reminded me of her constantly. She was a good child, clever, good grades, popular, a cheerleader, you know... and she loved me. How someone could have... why someone killed her... I don't know. I miss her terribly."

He looked at me, his eyes soulful, and I swear his lower lip trembled slightly.

I nodded and said, "What about..." I was going to ask him about her relationship with Hunter Flagg, but before I could, the door flew open and Jennifer Goodkind-Young stepped inside.

"Father? You're needed on a call. It's urgent."

I turned to look at her. She stood in the open doorway, her hands on her hips, and I do believe she had a slight smirk on her lips.

"I'm sure it can wait, my dear," Goodkind said. "We must cooperate with these detectives—"

"Private detectives, Father," Jennifer corrected, interrupting him. Apparently, the distinction made a big difference to her. "And the call can't wait. It's from the legal department in Miami."

Goodkind sighed and said, "Very well. It seems we'll have to cut our conversation short, Mr. Starke, at least for now."

I got up from my chair. "It was nice talking to you, Mr. Goodkind. I hope we can speak again."

"Yes, as do I. In fact, why don't you come by my home tomorrow evening. My family's having dinner together. Come as my guests, both of you. After dinner we'll talk, and I'll answer your questions as best I can."

I smiled. "Thank you, sir, for your kind offer. We'll be pleased to accept."

"Wonderful. Seven-thirty for cocktails. Dinner at eight."

As we turned and left, I couldn't help but wish I had a camera to snap a photo of Jennifer's face. It was a picture. She really didn't want us asking questions about her sister's murder.

The question was: why?

8

As we left Goodkind's office and headed for the elevator, who should we bump into but Zoe Mullins. Whether it was by design or by accident, I don't know, but I walked on and was joined a moment later by a smiling Bob Ryan. The man had her number: sneaky dog!

I can't say I was happy about it, but, then again, maybe a night out for drinks or dinner could lead to a break in the case. And who was I to stand in the way of serendipity?

"Wipe that silly grin off your face," I said. "You're old enough to be her father." He was pushing his fortieth birthday at the time.

"Come on, Harry. You've got Kate. You got to let the single guys have a little fun. Besides, she's older than she looks."

"How d'you know?"

"I... I just know, that's all."

"Good enough, I hope. Now get your head back in the game."

I found out later that he was right. Zoe was twenty-six.

He frowned as the elevator doors opened. "Hey, my head is

in the game."

"I'm talking about a different game. Not the call of the wild."

"Give me a frickin' break, Harry. My head is in the game. Hey, did you see how pissed off Jennifer was when the old man invited us to dinner tomorrow?"

"I did," I said as we walked out of the building. "But why is she so dead set against us talking to him, much less anyone else in the family?"

"She's got a mean streak a mile long in her, that woman. Maybe she's the killer."

"Maybe. Maybe not. It's way too soon to draw conclusions. I'd hoped to see Walter Goodkind's innocence or guilt painted right there on his face. But the man's a rock. Nothing was obvious to me except..."

"Well go on. Tell me," Bob said.

"There was a lot of pent-up emotion inside the man. Conflicting emotions. He still mourns his daughter... I'm pretty sure of that, but I also think he may be hiding something."

"I saw some anger there, too," Bob said.

I smiled. "Yes. That too, but why? Who's he angry at?"

"Hunter Flagg, of course," Bob answered. "Did you see his eyes when you mentioned the boy's name? It's been a decade and a half, and still he's enraged at the mere sound of his name. Angry enough to commit murder, d'you think? Could his daughter's death have been an accident, a bullet meant for Hunter?"

I shrugged. "I'd say that's unlikely. I can't see him disrobing her and leaving her out to dry like that... No! If Goodkind's responsible for the murders, it's because he hired someone to do it. Then there's a possibility her death was an accident."

As if he could hear our conversation, which, when you're dealing with a hacker is always a possibility, I suppose, Tim pinged my phone. The email included a complete family tree for the Goodkinds and for the Flaggs, with pertinent information on each family member. I shook my head. *Why the hell didn't I bring my iPad with me?*

Trying to read reams of detail on an iPhone 4s was a trial, to say the least.

That aside, I was pleased to receive the information. It was what I'd needed from the beginning. I texted him back and asked him to lay it all out on my desk in a format I could read. It was like a chessboard, each person represented by a piece. I closed my eyes and tried to assemble it all in my head. It was all but impossible. *Where are the pieces now, and where were they fourteen years ago?* I wondered.

"Each piece has a story," I said out loud.

"What?"

I looked up. "Oh, sorry. Talking to myself. I think we need to get in touch with Hunter's family, next. You know, complete the circle."

"Sure, but can you do me a favor?"

"What's that?"

"Can we drive to the next interview? My dogs are barking."

I laughed. "Sure, as long as you promise to stop flirting with everyone you meet."

We stepped up our walking. I was on the hunt. Half an hour earlier, the trail had felt so cold. After meeting the principal Goodkinds, however, it felt fresh and new and ready to show us the goods.

Larry Spruce is a great DA; one of the best, in fact. And the CPD has always had many great men and women serving the city of Chattanooga, but they all had to play by the rules, stick strictly to the protocols and bend to the whims of internal politics. I'd left all that behind. Within reason, I could do pretty much as I pleased, and my team was the best of the best.

9

W e arrived back at the office some ten minutes later. Jacque had left to go pick up the files from the DA's office so, before we left to visit Steve Flagg, I decided to check in with Tim.

He'd already managed to work up quite a collection of newspaper articles and other documents about the murders, the investigation, and the two families involved.

"I can get more for you," Tim said, leaning back in his fancy chair. He linked his hands behind his neck and gazed up at me. "But I'll need to go through some, let's say, less-than-official channels."

I shook my head and said, "Absolutely not... Unless we have to."

"Your wish is my command, great leader, but I was just trying to save you from having to talk to Henry Finkle."

I'd already turned away and was about to walk out of the room, but at that I stopped and did a double take.

"Say what now?"

"Finkle!" Tim grinned at me. "He was the officer in charge on the Flagg-Goodkind murder case. You didn't know?"

"Uh-uh. I thought Charlie Monk was."

"Monk was the lead detective," Tim said. "But the then Captain Finkle was his boss, and his fingerprints are all over it, per several self-serving press conferences, the details of which you can read for yourself." He let his chair fall forward, picked up a sheaf of papers from his desk and waved them at me.

I let out a long breath. "Son of a bitch... Larry failed to mention that. But it makes sense, I guess."

I took the papers from him, leafed quickly through them, then handed them back. Finkle was a wrinkle—no pun intended—I wasn't expecting, nor was it one I wanted to deal with. Not then, anyway. "Hang onto it till I come back. I have another interview. I should be in later this afternoon. In the meantime, stay out of the CPD's britches. Got it?"

"Got it." He grinned at me, shoved his glasses further up the bridge of his nose, and turned again to his keyboard.

Me? I left the office in a slightly grumpier mood. Sooner or later, I'd have to go to Henry "Tiny" Finkle for help, and I wasn't exactly savoring the idea. At that moment, however, we had somewhere else to be.

I found Bob waiting by my Maxima, his eyes glued to his phone, scrolling through Tim's info.

He looked up at me, smiling. "You know where we're going next?"

"To see Steve Flagg," I said.

"Right, but you know where he is? The American Flagg!"

I frowned. "What?"

"The name of Steve Flagg's mechanic shop is American Flagg," Bob said. "Kinda cheesy, right?"

Cheesy didn't even cover it. But I had to give the man kudos. It wasn't the kind of name you could easily forget.

"Get in," I said, smiling.

It was time to talk to father number two.

10

American Flagg Auto and Diesel Repair was on Rossville Boulevard, near East 42nd Street. That stretch of road was basically dedicated to two things: fixing cars and booze. We passed several liquor stores, auto parts stores and bars, even a Taco Bell, which kind of stood out like a sore thumb.

American Flagg, with two G's, looked about as redneck and cheesy as the name sounded. Bob had been reading to me about the business as we drove, but his narrative tailed off as we approached.

"Oh yeah," he said. "I thought I knew this place! There it is. You can't miss it!"

Boy was he ever right!

American Flagg Auto and Diesel sported a—you guessed it —giant American flag on a pole sprouting like a unicorn's horn atop the building. You could see the flag from several blocks in either direction. In fact, the flag was so big, I figured it could cover a whole house, or at least a double-wide trailer.

The lot was fenced in. The blue and white building was fronted by a half-dozen vehicle bays and an office complex. There were vehicles parked everywhere: pickup trucks, over the road tractor units, dump trucks, all either waiting to be serviced or repaired or waiting for their owners to pick them up.

I eased up the gas and slowed almost to a crawl, then pulled into the lot and parked in front of the office. Barely had I turned off the motor when a mechanic appeared from inside the bay next to the office and stood there staring at us.

We exited the vehicle and were about to go to the office when...

"Howdy! Can I help y'all?" the mechanic called. He was wearing a greasy white cowboy hat and blue mechanic's coveralls—no shirt—covered with splotches of black grease. "Y'all pickin' up'r whut?"

"No," I said. "I'm looking for Steve Flagg. Is he around?"

The mechanic frowned, wiped his hands on his coveralls and looked around. "Who wants to know?"

I exchanged glances with Bob before answering. The guy seemed a little antsy, but why?

"I'm Harry Starke. I'm a private investigator. I'd like to talk to him, is all."

The mechanic turned, eyes wide, and called out in a distinctive Texas drawl. "Danny! They's another investigator here lookin' for your daddy!" And then he turned and walked back into the bay.

Bob and I stepped away from the car, but we didn't follow the mechanic. Something didn't feel quite right.

The guy who walked out from behind a huge Kenworth tractor unit in one of the center bays carried a large wrench in his right hand. Well... *carried* might not be the right word. Perhaps I should have said he wielded the wrench, which was longer than my forearm and looked about as heavy as a sledgehammer.

The man's face was twisted with anger. There was little doubt about what he intended to do with the wrench.

"You boys get the hell out of here!" he said. By then he was within fifteen feet of Bob, and I recognized him as Danny Flagg, Steve Flagg's oldest son, Hunter's older brother. "An' tell those lawyers that they ain't welcome here... an' neither are you!"

He was in his mid-thirties, with a close-cropped, scruffy beard. He was heavy, too. His coveralls were stretched tight over a burgeoning beer belly. He wore a camo baseball cap on backwards. His face was twisted into a wicked snarl. Danny Flagg was a man to watch.

As he approached, violence in his eyes, Bob and I pulled our weapons, but we didn't point them at him. We let them hang beside our thighs.

Seeing the guns brought Danny to a dead stop, but he showed no fear. "Is that how it is now? You take all our money and now you're gonna shoot us?"

The mechanic with the cowboy hat had reappeared and looked as if he was about to pee himself. His eyes were big as saucers.

"Danny Flagg," I said, my voice low but firm. "You need to put that wrench down. I don't think we're who you think we are."

He frowned, looked confused and said, "You're not from Johnson & Kern?"

"The law firm?" Bob asked, frowning.

I smiled and said, "No, we're not. We're here to talk to your father about your brother, Hunter."

The wrench slipped from his fingers and landed with a

clang on the concrete. "Hunter's dead. Long dead. More than a decade ago, he was taken from us."

I holstered my weapon, nodded for Bob to do the same. "I know that," I said. "We're investigating his murder. Now, can we just calm down and talk in a civilized manner?"

Danny's face shifted from confusion to resigned sadness. "Uh, sure. Sorry about the mix-up. Texas here said you were investigators an' I thought the worst."

"I completely understand," I said. I was lying, of course. I had no idea what the hell was going on. I knew of Johnson & Kern. I'd even done work for them in the past, but why would this man be acting violently toward anyone representing them? I was clueless.

Danny picked up the wrench, this time holding it like a tool instead of a weapon. "Okay... Well, you'd better come on in. I'll make some coffee. We can talk in my office."

Texas, the mechanic, followed us inside. He'd taken off his hat and was wiping the sweat from his brow and running his fingers through his mop of thick, brown hair. "Sorry 'bout all that, fellas. Thought y'all were somebody else."

"No problem," Bob said.

We followed Danny Flagg into a small, sparsely furnished office. An outdated computer monitor sat to one side on the gray steel desk along with a push-button phone and two overflowing, in-and-out wire baskets. Behind the desk was a steel swivel chair and a massive bookcase full of service manuals and parts catalogs. Two tall steel file cabinets with papers stacked on top stood against one wall, and a small table with a coffee maker thereon stood against the other. Danny picked up a stack of phone-book-sized manuals from one of the steel chairs in front of the desk so we could sit down.

"Can I ask you a question?" I said. "Why all the hostility toward private investigators?"

"Yeah... I'm real sorry about that," Danny said as he stood beside the table and spooned the makings into the coffee maker. "We've had some bad lawyer trouble lately. My daddy had to deal with some lawsuits. We thought you was with Johnson & Kern comin' after us again."

"Lawsuits?" Bob asked. "Lawsuits about what?"

Danny turned and sat down behind the desk. "Sexual misconduct, but it's all lies. We had a secretary that worked here. A cleaning lady, too. Now they're both accusing Daddy of, what do you call it, propositioning them."

He must have seen the look on my face.

"Now don't you take on like that. My daddy's innocent. Them ladies, if you can call 'em that, made it all up. They couldn't prove a thing in a court of law, an' it was thrown out, so they decided to bleed us dry instead."

Inwardly, I cursed myself. I should have known about the lawsuits. I was willing to bet the details were in the information Tim wanted me to look at back at the office, but there I was diving in again, conducting interviews without having all the facts at hand. Again. I promised myself that I'd read everything when I got back to the office. I didn't intend to make the same mistake again tomorrow.

"Mr. Flagg," I said, "this has nothing to do with those lawsuits. We're investigating Hunter and Samantha's murders."

I studied his face closely as I said those two names. I remembered the anger that flashed in Walter Goodkind's eyes at the mention of Hunter's name. But Danny had only sadness in his eyes, and it intensified as we talked. It seemed to me that he was sad, not only about his brother's death, but Samantha's too.

"We were hoping to talk to your father," I continued.

"He don't come around here much no more," Danny said, his expression distant. "Daddy left the business to me after this lawsuit bullsh... uh, stuff. The bad publicity was killing our business."

"Okay," Bob said, "so maybe we can talk to you for a few minutes?"

Danny leaned back, his office chair squeaking loudly. "Sure, ask away. You want some coffee?"

I looked at the array of stained mugs beside the coffee maker and decided against it.

"No, thank you. I'm already three cups in. Anymore and I'll be wired."

He looked at Bob who also declined.

"I hope you don't mind the question," I said, "but I have to ask. Where were you on the night of April first, 1998? The night of the murder."

A look of guilt flashed across his face, a fleeting display of shame. "I was... locked up, actually. I was in Arizona State Penitentiary. I got let out two days after the murder and made it back just in time for Hunter's funeral. Would've gone to Samantha's, too, but the Goodkinds made it clear we wouldn't be welcome." He looked away to the left. *He's hiding something... or he's lying.*

I leaned back, surprised. "If you don't mind me saying so, Danny, that's one heck of an alibi."

He smiled, but it was a sad smile. "Thanks, I think. Honestly, I wish I'd been here. Maybe I could have protected them. I didn't know Sam, not bein' away an' all, but I heard she was a real nice gal."

"Do you know of anyone who might have wanted Hunter and Samantha dead?" Bob asked.

"Oh, I know who wanted Hunter dead: just about anyone in the Goodkind family. Especially the dad. But who'd want to kill both of 'em? I don't know. And, trust me, I did some sniffin' around myself when I got back to Chattanooga. Didn't get nowhere, though."

I smiled and said, "So, you've no suspicions, no one comes to mind?"

Danny frowned, then said, "I mean, have y'all talked to the Goodkinds at all? They're a weird bunch, man. They think they're somethin' special, like they're some kind of royalty. They hated that Hunter and Sam were seeing each other. It was like Hunter was going to contaminate their bloodline or something."

"Really?" I asked. I had my notebook out now, jotting down what he was saying.

"Yeah. They all look down on normal folk like us. Hated that Daddy was a mechanic and that I was in jail."

"Okay," I said, making notes. "But anyone else? Friends? Ex-boyfriends? Girlfriends? Rejected boy or girlfriends? Grumpy neighbors? Remember, Danny, the wider we cast the net, the more fish we catch."

He smiled, nodded and said, "Yeah, okay... There was this one guy. Jack something was his name... Stone, maybe? Anyway, he was the varsity quarterback, you know the type. He was... like, the most popular guy at school. And Sam was a cheerleader, and, according to Hunter, the prettiest girl in school. Anyway, you can guess where this is going, right? They were a couple, this Jack and Sam. A couple of years, I think. I was two years older than Hunter, and I got locked up in Arizona when I was nineteen, so I don't know all the details."

I made note to find this Jack character.

"Oh, it was Sloan!" Danny said. "Not Stone. No! It was Jack Sloan, but see he and Sam broke up. Hunter told me on the phone once that the guy was pissed with a capital "P" when he and Sam started going out. You should talk to him, if you can find him."

"Will do, Danny," I said. "Thanks for your help."

"No problem," he said. The distant sadness was back in his eyes. "Come on back if you have any more questions. And go talk to Daddy. He was here during all of it. He'll know, and he'll want to talk to you. I'll tell him to expect you. You know where to find him?"

We did. Danny Flagg confirmed the address, anyway. We thanked him and left, and I realized as we walked out of his office that day that Danny had been so distracted that he'd never actually turned on the coffee pot. It sat empty with the "ready" light blinking.

Poor guy. Either he was too caught up in the conversation or he really needed to hire a new secretary.

As we left, crossing the parking lot, the thin mechanic, Texas, gave us an enthusiastic wave.

"Well, that was exciting," Bob said as we pulled out of the American Flagg Auto and Diesel Repair lot and onto Rossville Boulevard.

"Yeah it was. Are you ready to go talk to Steve Flagg?"

Bob smiled. "As long as he doesn't come after us with a chain saw!"

11

From Rossville Boulevard we took the I-24 on-ramp heading south to I-75. Once on 75, we took The Split and headed south into Georgia, then took the Ringgold Road Exit to Highway 41: Steve Flagg lived just over the state line on Scruggs Road.

As we drove up to the address, the first thing I noticed was the unfinished house in the middle of a large tract of land. The house was little more than a concrete pad and lumber studs. The roof and walls were covered in tarps to protect it from the rain, but the construction site looked as if it was abandoned. *How long has it been like that, I wonder?*

Not far from the house, on the edge of the property, sat an older mobile home, complete with a screened-in porch and surrounded by an assortment of vehicles, most of them pickup trucks. Some were on blocks. One was on jacks, one had its engine lifted out, dangling from a free-standing engine hoist, and several more were on their wheels. It was the home of a life-long mechanic; no doubt about it.

Three dogs—a German shepherd, a border collie, and the

inevitable Jack Russell terrier—came running out from under the porch to greet us, barking and biting at the tires of my Maxima.

Steve Flagg himself appeared at the trailer door, then came strutting down the steps, glowering at us from under the bill of a gray baseball cap emblazoned upon which was the slogan, *Shove Gun Control Up Your...* followed by the image of a mule.

I rolled the window down halfway and shouted, "Steve Flagg? Do the dogs bite?"

"Not unless I want them to," Flagg shouted back, then raised a hand to his lips and let out a powerful whistle.

All three dogs immediately ran away from the car and around the back of the trailer.

"Come on in," he said. "Danny called and told me what you're about. Wendy's already making coffee and French toast, if you want it."

I parked the car and shot Bob a puzzled look. "French toast? It's a bit late for that, isn't it?"

Bob had a childish grin on his face. "Hey, don't knock it till you try it, boss. It's just about lunchtime."

I rolled my eyes and stepped out of the car, ready to pull my gun if the dogs came back. They didn't.

We followed Flagg up the steps and into the screened-in porch, and I was impressed. The porch had been set up for outdoor living with a swing, a table and four chairs, and something I hadn't seen in many a long year, a steel glider with a half-dozen plump and colorful cushions. Several fishing rods leaned against the wall beside the door into the house. It was homey, inviting, as was the home itself. The living room was nicely though simply furnished, and the walls were covered with pictures, big and small. Many of them were of Steve or Danny, or both, holding up a big fish or standing next to a dead buck, rifles in the crooks of their arms.

"Take a seat here, at the table," Flagg said.

Wendy Flagg was at the stove. She smiled at us and nodded.

Steve Flagg was an older version of Danny. He was a little thicker around the middle, wore a plaid shirt and blue jeans and a neatly trimmed goatee. His face was thin, drawn and heavily tanned. Once again I was reminded of the images of Nathan Bedford Forrest. Steve Flagg must have been one hell of a good-looking man when he was young. He took off his hat, revealing a mostly bald head, and sat down at the table.

Wendy came around the kitchen counter with a coffee cup in one hand and two mugs hooked by one finger of the other hand. She flashed a Hollywood smile at Bob and me.

She was a handsome woman, tall, gray hair down to her shoulders, piercing blue eyes... and a figure women twenty years her junior would pay big bucks for. The makeup was a little overdone, a sure sign of an older woman trying desperately to retain the beauty of her youth.

"Y'all hungry?" she asked.

"I sure am!" Bob said. "I'll take some of that French toast, if you don't mind!"

She looked at me. "Uh, just coffee for me, thanks," I said, shooting Bob a disapproving glance. At least he wasn't hitting on the woman... yet.

"So, Danny tells me you're gonna find the piece o' shit that killed Hunter and Sam," Flagg said, pouring coffee for all three of us.

"Well, that would be the desirable outcome," I said, taking the coffee cup from him, "but it may be a lost cause. It's been a long time. We'll do our best, but the trail's cold."

I was feeling much better, comfortable even, about that interview. For one thing, I'd had Bob read more of Tim's info package out loud as I drove out there. So at least I knew Steve's wife's name. We also knew where Jack Sloan worked, but that would have to wait until later.

"Well, it's about frickin' time," Steve said. "I've waited too many years for that sick sonofabitch to get his an' be locked away for his crimes."

I raised an eyebrow. "Which sick SOB would that be, exactly?" I asked.

I sipped my coffee and inwardly sighed; I don't think, even to this day, that I've tasted better.

Flagg fixed me with a comical stare. "You're kidding, right? Walter Goodkind did it. Everyone knows that. But the police couldn't prove it. Either that or they were bought off, I don't know which. But just follow the evidence, and you'll see that Walter did it."

I took a deep breath. Wendy came back with two plates, each stacked high with French toast. She slid one in front of Bob and the other in front of her husband.

"Well, Mr. Flagg, we haven't ruled anyone out yet, and I'm trying to keep an open mind."

He snorted. "You can call me Steve... Okay. You do it how you see best. You're the detective. But, sooner or later, you'll come to the same conclusion everyone else did. When I pop the hood of a car and see the timing belt's bad, I don't go poking around the brakes. But I get it." He smiled. "You're getting paid by the hour and want to drag it out... Who's paying you, by the way?"

That one hurt, and when he looked into my eyes, he must have known it, because he looked away and forked a great chunk of French toast into his mouth and chewed.

"No, sir," I said. "That's not it at all. As to who's paying me: I'm not at liberty to say. Now let me ask *you* something. How did you feel about Hunter and Samantha's relationship?"

Steve got up and walked to a shelf at the far end of the room and then came back with a bottle of cheap whiskey.

"Hunter and Sam? They were great together, weren't they, honey?" He looked over at his wife.

Wendy Flagg was Steve's second wife, which made her Hunter and Danny's stepmom. I watched her carefully as she answered.

"Oh, Lord yes!" Wendy said enthusiastically. "They were a real Romeo and Juliet. Sam was so good for Hunter, too!"

I raised an eyebrow. "Good for Hunter? How?"

"She was a steadying influence on him, kept him in line... most of the time." She glanced at Steve, looking for support, I assumed.

Steve nodded, sat back down and added a generous measure of whiskey to his coffee. "Look, y'already talked to Danny, so I guess you know. He was in prison for two years, for hauling stolen goods across state lines. Got caught in Arizona, of all places. They tried him there and he got off easy, if you ask me. They could have locked him up a lot longer."

I nodded. "Okay."

"Well..." Steve paused and took a sip of his coffee. "We all kind of suspected that Hunter was in on it. Hunter was a smart kid. In fact, I kind of figured he'd set the whole thing up. But Danny loved his brother and kept his mouth shut. Again, this is all supposition. Put me on a stand, and I'll lie through my teeth to protect my baby boy's name, got it?"

"Got it!" Bob said.

I nodded, watching the man's face.

"I was scared for Hunter," Steve went on. He glanced over at Wendy. "We both were. He was heading down a bad path, and I didn't want both of my boys in jail. Then Sam came along and things really changed for Hunter. He started acting right. He was changing for the better, and it was all because of her."

I nodded. It was a nice story, and I hoped it was true.

"That relationship wasn't just good for Hunter," Wendy said as she came over to sit down at the table. "It was good for the whole family!"

"Wendy," Steve said, irritation in his voice.

But she kept right on, "Imagine, the Flaggs and the Good-kinds! An alliance of two powerful families. We'd get all kinds of attention being connected to that family! All the ladies at church thought so, too."

Flagg raised a hand to quiet her. "That didn't matter, honey. Not at all. I just wanted my son to be happy and stay out of trouble. Sam was doing that for him. And he made her happy, too."

The man's expression saddened, and he said, "Then it all fell apart."

"They were planning on getting married," Wendy said, wistfully. "It would have been an amazing wedding... But Sam's family didn't approve, especially her daddy."

I leaned forward. "How do you know he didn't approve?"

It was Steve who answered. "He frickin' said so. He came out here to our trailer and told me himself. Old Walter was beside himself mad about the whole thing. It was driving him crazy. Sam'd had it out with him, told him that he could go ahead and disinherit her, but she wouldn't change her mind. She and Hunter were going to start a new life together. On their own."

Wendy made a face. "Oh, Walter would have forgiven Sam, or Samantha, as he insisted on calling her. He wouldn't have cut her off from her inheritance. Our Hunter would have been rich."

"That didn't matter!" Steve said, taking another long sip of his spiked coffee. "They were in love and happy. That's what was important!"

Wendy looked at me. "Well, I think it's all important. Especially in an investigation. Don't you think so, Mr... What was your name again?"

I smiled. "Starke. Harry Starke. And you're right, Mrs. Flagg, every detail, no matter how small, could be important, ma'am."

She shot Steve a hard look. "See? The detective agrees with me. Eat your French toast, Steven. It's getting cold."

Bob pushed his now-empty plate away. "That was delicious, Mrs. Flagg!"

Wendy beamed at him and said, "If they'd gotten married, and if no one had killed them, maybe we'd have our house finished by now."

I thought about the unfinished construction project. A large, ranch-style home, abandoned. It would be beautiful, one day, if they ever finished it.

"That ain't got nothing to do with Hunter and Sam, Wendy, and you know it. We can't finish the house yet because of those lying bi... uh, gals at the shop. Damn lawyers took everything I had. It's a damn shame, too. I didn't leave the trailer park an' move out to this piece of land just to watch our dream house fall over half-finished. But that has nothing to do with Hunter or the murder."

I nodded, but inside I still wondered.

Wendy looked angry. Frustrated.

"Where were you that night, Mr. Flagg?" Bob asked.

"You son of a bitch," he snarled, shoving his chair back. "You think I could have killed my own son? I'll—"

His wife put a calming hand on his arm and said, "Easy, honey. They have to ask these questions."

He drew his arm away from her, then said, quietly, his eyes like flints, "I was at the shop working on a Peterbuilt till after midnight with one of my mechanics, Mickey Mickelson. It's in the file. The police checked. Good enough?"

I nodded, then said, "Do you know of anyone who might have had a grudge against your son?"

"No, but why would I? He didn't never come running to me about such things. He would have gone to Danny. Ask him."

I suddenly came to the conclusion that we'd gotten all we were going to from the Flaggs, so we finished our coffee, thanked them for their time, said our goodbyes and left.

"What did you think about that?" Bob asked as we drove back to town.

"I don't know, Bob. I really don't. It couldn't have been Danny Flagg. He was in jail. Alibis don't come any better than that. Steve Flagg's alibi must have checked out too. That leaves old man Goodkind, his daughter Jennifer and Jack Sloan, that we know of. I think we still have many more questions than answers."

But it was still early in the investigation and I almost always felt further away from solving a case after the first day. I had to be patient. The answers would come. I just had to figure out the right questions, and who to ask.

12

I t was around two when we arrived back at the office that first afternoon. Bob left again almost immediately to continue working on one of his cases, and I grabbed a cup of coffee and went to my office to find that Jacque had dumped a banker's box full of files on my desk. I stood for a moment and stared at it, shaking my head, knowing how much time and work it was going to take for me to go through it all. And then there was all the stuff Tim had put together. I was in for a long afternoon... and night.

I sighed, went back out to the main area and gave Jacque instructions that I was not to be disturbed.

"But, I was going to tell—"

"Not now, Jacque. I need to go through all that crap on my desk. Just hold the fort for me, okay?"

"But—" I heard her begin to say as I closed my office door.

I locked it and flopped down behind my desk, leaned back, put my feet up on the top, linked my hands behind my neck and closed my eyes. I stayed like that for several minutes, reflecting on the events of the day, hoping a light would go on and provide me with a direction. But it didn't.

Finally, I opened my eyes, sat up and opened the box. It was stuffed full. I shook my head, got up, unlocked the door and asked Jacque to join me.

"Close the door and sit down," I said grumpily.

And she did. She sat in one of the two guest chairs in front of my desk, crossed her legs, put her hands together in her lap and then sat there, demurely, looking at me, waiting for me to speak.

"I thought I asked you to go through this stuff," I said, tapping a finger on the top of the banker's box.

"Dat you did."

I waited, but she just continued to sit there, staring at me, a half-smile on her lips.

"And?" I said, a little more impatiently than I should have. "Have you looked inside it?"

"Of course I did. And I was going to tell you—but you wouldn't listen—that I didn't know what I was looking at, that it was all mumbo jumbo to me, and also that I was going to help you sort it out. But you cut me off, didn't you?"

I looked long and hard at her, and then I started to laugh, and then she joined in. *Geez, the girl knows me better than I know myself.*

"Well," she said, finally, "are you goin' to apologize to me, or not?"

I looked at her, smiling and said, "I'm sorry, Jacque. I should have known better. I should have listened to you."

"All right then. You're forgiven. Let's get started. I don't want to be here all night."

It took a lot less time than I thought it would. Most of the contents were legal stuff that I had no need of, much less understood, so we sorted through it and set it aside. There were also financial reports on everybody involved in the case at the time. Those we handed off to Ronnie.

By the time we'd finished, we'd reduced the contents of the box by two-thirds, and what was left had been sorted into stacks and spread across the desktop. It was still a lot, but at least it was manageable.

"We need help, Jacque," I said as we sat together drinking a cup of coffee. "You need help. It's been four years since I started this business. All of you have been here from day one. The business is expanding. We need more staff. You need a secretary and I need another investigator... Maybe an intern as well. What d'you think?"

"You want me to start looking?"

"I think so. You wouldn't have any ideas, by any chance?"

"I might. I had a call from Heather Stillwell on Friday. She's looking to make a change. I told her I'd talk to you when I could get your attention... And what about Kate?"

"I've asked Kate a half dozen times. She turned me down flat, probably a good thing too... but Heather... I've met her a couple of times. She was a cop in Atlanta, right? Got co-opted into the Georgia Bureau of Investigation. What's she doing now? Why does she want to make a change? Did she say?"

"No. I asked her, but she just said personal reasons. You want me to give her a call?"

"Couldn't hurt... Yes, go ahead. Let's see where it leads. Do it tomorrow. For now, I need to go through all this stuff... and the stuff Tim dumped on me. It's what time?" I looked at my watch. "Almost three-thirty. We close at five-thirty, so give me an hour then have everyone gather in the conference room—make sure Bob's there—and we'll see if we can't make some sense of all this."

She nodded, stood, went to the door, turned and said, "Would you like another cup of coffee?"

I looked at her, shook my head, and she left me to it.

The first thing I did after the door closed behind her was grab the autopsy report. It was standard stuff, succinct and to the point. The only part of it that was of interest to me was the cause and time of death.

Doc Sheddon had put the TOD at between nine and midnight on the evening of April first. He couldn't be more specific because the weather was cold that night, which meant the bodies cooled more rapidly than they would have had they been fully clothed and indoors.

Hunter Flagg had been shot once in the neck with a large caliber weapon, probably a .45. The slug had severed his right carotid artery. Hunter had bled out in a matter of seconds.

Samantha had been shot once, in the chest. The bullet, a .45 hollow point, had been recovered. It had passed through the sternum and the right atrium of the heart and lodged in the trapezius muscle of the back. She would have died instantly.

It wasn't much, but it confirmed that the weapon used was a big one and heavy and probably unusual.

There were no official police files, but there were some tapes and transcripts of Charlie Monk's interviews. The transcripts were all neatly typed and properly dated and timed. I scanned through them and laid them aside, preferring instead to listen to the tapes—cassette tapes, would you believe?—but that would have to wait for another day when I had more time.

After that, I went over the information Tim had placed on my desk and, finally, I reviewed my own notes from my interviews with Walter Goodkind and the Flagg family and jotted down a few thoughts about those. Then I closed up shop and went to join the others in the conference room. It was time to try to put together what we had so far.

Ronnie and Tim were already there, each with a small stack of papers. Tim also had his laptop, iPad, two phones and a mug of coffee. Bob arrived a few minutes later looking a little sluggish. And I wasn't surprised after the double portion of French toast he'd put away out at the Flagg residence.

"Okay, people," I said when everyone was settled. "We really jumped right into this one. Bob and I talked to several people while you two were gathering information. The case files are here from the DA's office. Jacque and I sorted them, and she gave a stack to Ronnie, but I still need to read through it all and listen to the tapes. So, let's see where we are. Who wants to begin?"

"I will," Bob said. "Let's talk about Walter Goodkind first. We didn't get a lot of time with him, but I wasn't convinced by anything he said."

I nodded. "Okay. You're right. I think he's hiding something, but what? We do know that Larry Spruce is convinced he's the killer, but they couldn't get anything to stick."

Bob frowned. "Yeah, I don't know about that, Harry. I still don't think he did it. What kind of father would kill his own daughter? I know, I know—you said it before: there are plenty of parents that do. Hell, you only have to remember Susan Smith to know that. But I don't see this guy doing it."

"I tend to agree with you. I got the impression Walter Goodkind loved Samantha. He seemed genuinely sad to me... But that doesn't mean anything either. She could have been collateral damage, an accident. That would make him genuinely sad."

Ronnie cocked his head to one side. "So you said you thought he was hiding something. What?"

I shrugged. "Maybe he's protecting someone."

"Jennifer!" Bob said. "Jennifer was angry with us from the get-go. Maybe she doesn't want us investigating the murders because she's the killer. And maybe the old man knows... or suspects it and is covering for her."

"Could be," I said. "We'll be able to poke a little deeper into that theory tomorrow when we talk to the whole family. Tim, how about you? Anything new?"

"Only what I put on your desk. Everything I could find on the Web about the murders... Everything public, that is. So no pictures. Basically, I confirmed what the DA already told you. The bodies were shot and found naked on Sailmaker on the morning of April two, and that Hunter's truck was never found."

"It wasn't at the scene?" Ronnie asked.

He shook his head.

"That's weird," I said. "Could they have been killed somewhere else and the bodies dumped out there?"

Tim just shrugged.

I nodded. "Okay. We talked to Danny Flagg. He claims he was in prison when the murders took place. Can you confirm that?"

Tim tapped away at his laptop. "Yeah, what prison?"

"Arizona State Penitentiary."

"Okay, give me a sec."

"In the meantime," Ronnie said, "I can tell you that Walter Goodkind is planning to retire by the end of the quarter. He's already started turning everything over to his daughter, Jennifer Young."

"Huh, I figured as much," I said.

"How'd you know that?" Bob asked.

"The furniture in Walter's office, Bob. Didn't you notice how it all clashed with his desk and chairs? It didn't make sense to me at first, but I think I figured it out. Jennifer has already started adding her modern tastes and influence to the company, including that massive corner office. I think the desk and armchairs will be gone the same day Walter retires."

Bob laughed. "Yeah, I guess you're right. Why didn't I

think of that? So you think the father's trying to protect his daughter?"

"Or the daughter's protecting her father." I was talking on the fly, but it made sense to me. "If Jennifer thinks Walter did it, she won't want us finding out the month before he retires. The scandal would cripple the company. Maybe never recover. Look how much damage was done when Steve Flagg was accused of harassing his female employees."

"Ah, you know about that?" Ronnie asked. "I was going to mention it, too. Steve Flagg is in some deep sewage because of those accusations. American Flagg almost went under, and it would have if Danny Flagg hadn't stepped in and saved the day. They're still struggling, but I think they'll make it. Shame really. Things were going so well for them."

"Speaking of Danny Flagg," Tim said. "I have some bad news for you, Harry."

I looked at the kid. He was peering at me over his MacBook.

"A lot of the state prisons have put their records online. Arizona State Penitentiary has already made that switch, too, but it's a work in progress. The online records only go back as far as 2000. They'll add the rest eventually, I guess, but until then..."

"Great," I said. "So you can't confirm his alibi."

"Not officially, no."

I frowned at him. "And unofficially?"

Tim grinned self-consciously, poked his glasses with the forefinger of his right hand and said, "Well, hypothetically... Okay, look. I'm sure those records are on a state server somewhere. I could poke around, if you like."

I knew that was coming. I hesitated, pursed my lips, glared at him, then nodded. "Okay. I need to know for sure. Do it. Just don't tell me how the sausage is made. Deal?"

Tim nodded.

"Oh, and I'll need everything you can get me on a Jack Sloan, too. He was in high school at the same time as the victims. Just send it to me when you get the chance... No! Get that to me first, okay?"

"You got it, Harry," Tim said.

"Okay," I said. "Where does that leave us?"

Bob smiled. "The French toast."

Ronnie cocked an eyebrow. "French toast? You had breakfast?"

"No, lunch. Well, Bob did," I said. "When we visited Steve and Wendy Flagg. And I have to say, I don't see either of them as a viable suspect. Though I can't exactly rule either of them out, either."

"What about Wendy?" Bob said. "She seemed pretty happy about the marriage plans the two lovebirds were making."

Ronnie perked up. "They were planning on getting married? Whew! Now that really would have pissed off the members of the Goodkind clan. D'you know who Jennifer married?"

"Yeah," I said, "some guy named Todd Young."

"Not just *a* Todd Young," Ronnie responded. "*The* Todd Young. He's filthy rich, from Canada. His family is old money, railroad barons, among other things. The family's as close to Canadian royalty as you can get."

"My point, exactly," Bob said. "The Goodkinds were marrying up, not down. Hunter must have been a real challenge to them, like when Lady Sybil married the chauffeur, Tom Branson in Downton Abbey... Okay so I watched it. So what? Don't look at me like that. It's good TV. *Whatever!* Wendy Flagg was excited about the prospect of Hunter marrying money and position... Oh, screw y'all," he said when he saw everyone was grinning at him.

I finally figured out where Bob was going with this. "You're thinking about what Samantha had said, that she didn't care if her father disinherited her? Do you think that Wendy heard about that and flipped out?"

Bob shrugged. "It's possible. I don't know."

I sighed. "I suppose we'll have to look into it. That's why we're brainstorming, to generate ideas, leads. But we're done for the night. I have plenty more reading to get through, thanks to Tim and the DA. Go home, everybody. I'll see you all bright and early in the morning."

"And we're going to see that Sloan kid?" Bob asked.

I nodded. "Jack Sloan, yes. We can't get too focused on the families or we might miss the real killer. Sloan may be a dead end, or he may be just the lead we need to crack this thing. We'll go see him tomorrow."

Ronnie nodded. Bob yawned, probably still fighting a carb coma from the French toast. Tim gave me a quick thumbs-up before jumping right back into tapping on his laptop.

"Hey, Harry," Jacque said, poking her head in from the other room. "You left your phone out here and Kate's on. Can you take it?"

I padded my pants pocket to find that yes, indeed, my phone was missing. "Yes, of course. We're done here."

I stepped out of the conference room and took my iPhone from Jacque.

"Kate? What's up?"

"I heard you're on a new case, Harry," Kate said over the line.

Kate Gazzara, a detective and a lieutenant in the Chattanooga Police Department, was my—for want of a better word —girlfriend.

"True. Did Larry Spruce tell you about it?"

"Not exactly, Harry. Tiny told me."

"Tiny?"

Assistant Police Chief Henry "Tiny" Finkle was, and always had been, a royal pain in my backside. I shuddered every time I heard his name.

"Yes, him, and he's worked up about it. He wants you to come down to the Police Department."

"Oh he does, does he? Then why didn't he call and ask me himself?"

"I don't know, Harry." She sounded frustrated. "You know how he is: never do anything yourself when you can get someone else to do it for you."

"Okay, fine," I said. It wasn't how I wanted to spend my evening, but he was Kate's boss, so...

"And I gotta warn you, Harry," she said. "He's stompin' mad about something, but won't say what it is until you get here."

"All right, Kate. Tell him I'm on my way."

Five minutes later I was back in my car, on my way to the Chattanooga Police Department, a sinking feeling in my gut.

13

As I drove to the police department on Amnicola Highway that evening, I couldn't help but wonder what could possibly have Tiny so wound up, especially on a Monday evening. I figured he must have heard I was taking the case, one that he'd supervised back in '98. Tiny didn't have a very high opinion of me, so it was possible.

I figured Spruce must have reached out to him, to ask him to cooperate with me and my investigation, maybe even help me. But... hell, Larry didn't get along with him any better than I did. That would have been more than enough to make him angry. The idea of working with me had to make his stomach turn, as did the idea of me working with him.

So why was he involving Kate when he could have called me directly?

I knew Tiny had long desired Kate. After I left the force, knowing that Kate and I weren't partners in crime anymore, he'd thought he had a chance with her. Of course, he didn't. She and I were still partners, just not working together. Although, Chief Johnston did, on occasion, allow her to call me in as a consultant. Unpaid, of course. And that was something else that ticked Tiny off.

The thing that set me off that evening was that I'd been kind of hoping I'd get to spend some quality time with her. And what I'd planned didn't involve Finkle.

So I sighed as I pulled into the department's visitor parking lot and exited the car to see Kate standing at the door, waiting for me.

"What's up, Kate?" I asked and pecked her on the cheek.

"I was hoping you could tell me. Tiny's mad, Harry, and he won't tell me why."

"I think I have an idea. Larry Spruce has been talking to him, probably told him to play nice with me on a case we've started working. But I can't figure out why he's gotten you mixed up in it."

We walked into the department together. Kate pointed. "Not just me. Look."

I looked and recognized the tall woman in the business suit as Lieutenant Vazquez from internal affairs.

"What the hell's IA got to do with it?" I asked.

"Beats me."

Just then, the man himself stepped out of his office and invited the three of us in, then asked Kate to secure the door.

There was a brief moment when I thought Finkle was going to try and charge me with something. But what? As far as I knew I'd done nothing wrong. So what was it all about?

Finally, Tiny sat down at his desk and decided to get on with it and not keep us all hanging in suspense.

Tiny? That was his nickname around the PD, but not to his face, of course. He's called tiny because he was. He was a little man in every sense of the word. No more than five-nine, he was slim, and weighed maybe a hundred and forty pounds wringing wet. Nobody knew exactly how old he was, but he must have been in his late forties; his brown hair had yet to show the first signs of gray. His thin face, high cheekbones, thin nose, and beady black eyes all reminded me of a rat. He was also a bigot and a misogynist. He was Kate's boss back then and had been bugging her for years. He was the archetypal "little man," mean-spirited and vindictive. Now you know why I didn't like him.

"This afternoon," he began, his arms folded and resting on the desk, "I received a call from District Attorney Lawrence Spruce. He informed me, Starke, that he's hired you to reopen the investigation into the murders of Hunter Flagg and Samantha Goodkind. Is that correct?"

I nodded. "It is."

Finkle lowered his head, thinking about what he was going to say next, then he looked up at me and said, "The District Attorney has asked me to assist you in any way I can... I have to say, Starke, I wasn't too happy about it. The case is still open and it's police business, so I think it should be left to the good men and women of the Chattanooga Police Department."

He shot me a dirty look. I shrugged it off.

"Anyway," Finkle continued, "I consulted our digital records to bring up the files..."

Finkle paused, looking at each of us in turn: Kate first, then myself, and finally Lt. Vazquez. *What the hell's going on?* I wondered. The suspense was killing me!

"What do you think I discovered?" he asked.

No one answered. We just sat there and stared at him.

"The digital files relating to the 1998 double homicide of Hunter Flagg and Samantha Goodkind no longer exist."

I frowned. I knew for a fact that all the cold case files had been digitized years ago. They should have been there.

"That's right," he continued. "I had Lt. Willis look into the matter, and he discovered that someone has deliberately deleted the files, and that the backup files have also been deleted. It was at that point that I contacted Lt. Vazquez."

He nodded in her direction and she took up the story. "We also looked into the missing files," she began, "and I can confirm that the files were deleted at two-seventeen this afternoon. We're now actively investigating the hack."

"Hack?" I exclaimed, my heart sinking. "You're telling me that someone hacked the CPD this afternoon and deleted the files?" I was stunned, couldn't believe it.

Finkle nodded. "That's what she said, Starke. I don't know if it was an inside job or not, so IA will be taking point on the investigation. And that's not all..."

He paused for effect, tilted his head to one side and stared at Kate.

I looked at Kate, too, trying hard not to roll my eyes. This man was a drama queen, loved the sound of his own voice.

"After discovering that the digital files were missing," he continued, finally, "I went down to the evidence morgue to retrieve the physical files. It turned out that they are missing, as well. My next stop was the evidence room, only to find the physical evidence is also missing. So at this point, we have nothing. There's no record that the Goodkind-Flagg murders ever took place."

My head was spinning. How could this happen? And what about the timing? Was I ever glad I'd instructed Tim to stay out of the CPD's systems. With what had happened, he would have been caught and carted off to jail.

Vazquez spoke up. "The Tennessee State Police's Cyber-crimes division has already started looking into the hack this afternoon, and I will be heading the investigation into the missing physical evidence. I believe it was an inside job, perpetrated either by a police officer or a civilian employee."

Finkle nodded. "We *will* find the culprit. And I'm well

aware that whoever tampered with the evidence is also likely to lead us to the guilty party. That being so, Starke, I will be working closely with your investigation."

I smiled and said, "It couldn't have been easy for you to say that, Henry. I appreciate your confidence," I lied. The truth was, I was filled with dread at the idea of him being involved at all. The one saving grace, so I thought, was the fact I was reporting directly to Larry Spruce and not him.

He didn't smile. He simply stared coldly at me and, without taking his eyes away from mine, said, "Lt. Gazzara, you will, without neglecting your present duties, provide whatever assistance Starke may need to further his investigation. You will work with him, but you will report directly to me. You, Starke... I know you two are an item so I hope you will choose to share everything with her. By working together, we should be able to catch whoever is behind all of this."

I looked at Kate and nodded. She reciprocated.

"You got it, Henry."

Was I really planning to share information with him through Kate? Not a chance! I'd give whatever I learned to Larry Spruce first, but Henry didn't have to know that.

Finkle dismissed us, and Kate walked me out of the department. I immediately called Tim.

"What's up?" Tim asked.

"Tim, I know you have... that other thing on your plate right now, but I need you to do something else for me?"

"Sure thing. The prison stuff might take a while anyway. I had to put feelers out on the dark web for some security keys. It's not late enough in Arizona for any hackers to be online. We're a nocturnal bunch, you know."

I glanced at Kate. She was a sworn officer of the law, so I didn't want to burden her by letting her know what I was doing.

"I'll be just a minute, Kate. I'm talking to Tim."

She rolled her eyes, but she knew what I was up to and that she needed plausible deniability.

"I'll wait by the car. You're going to get caught one of these days, Harry. You know that, don't you?"

When she was out of earshot, I said, "Tim, someone hacked the CPD systems and deleted all the Goodkind-Flagg case files."

"Oh, geez! You know it wasn't me, right? I would never—"

"I know, I know," I interrupted him. "I would never dream that you'd deliberately do anything against my wishes, much less engage in cyber terrorism."

All that was true. Tim might look into things for me from time to time. Maybe gain access to information outside of official channels. But he would never do any damage. Deleting those files was an act of terrorism. Spruce would have had a heart attack if he thought, even for a second, that we would engage in such tactics. No. It wasn't Tim's style.

"When did it happen? Do you know?" he asked.

"Sometime this afternoon, early, two-something." I heard him start typing. "Look, Tim, I need you to put the Arizona thing on the back burner and start looking into the hack. The state police are already looking into it, but I have a feeling you're more likely to get results than they are."

"Okay, you got it," Tim said. "If I can't figure out who done it, I know some people who can."

I shook my head. There was never a day went by that I didn't learn something new about my pet geek.

"Okay," I said. "But, Tim, don't get caught, you hear me? If the state cybercrimes task force finds you rummaging around in the CPD files, they may try to hang it on you. You got that?"

"Sure, but I won't get caught."

And I knew he wouldn't.

I thanked him, terminated the call and walked on over to Kate who was fixing me with a warning stare as I approached.

"What?" I asked, grinning.

"You're up to no good, Harry Starke. I can tell. You're going to have to tread carefully on this one. Finkle may be acting all sugar and spice, but he's out for blood, and there's nothing he'd love more than to nail you for... something, if he could."

"He won't nail me. That I can promise. Besides, we're all on the same team. In fact, I bet the person who murdered those two teenagers fourteen years ago just made the mistake that will get him... or her, caught."

"Okay, so now what?"

I stepped closer to her. "Well, I was thinking drinks at my place. Maybe grab dinner on the way home?"

Kate smiled. "That sounds good. I'm looking forward to working with you again. I need a vacation." She smiled at me.

"A vacation? You think you're going to get to take it easy? I don't think so, young lady. I have a ton of reading to do. Stuff Tim dug up for me... legally, and you can help."

Kate put her arms around my neck. Her scent made me dizzy. "Well, after those drinks, I might have other plans for you, big boy."

I smiled, pulled her closer to me, and said, "And what about all that reading?"

"Well, you'll just have to set the alarm and do that in the morning."

I kissed her. She was right. The reading could wait.

14

I rose early the next morning and went for a run. I was back in my condo by six to find Kate still in bed. I let her stay there. Me? I was antsy. I had a slew of work to do, but Larry's case was foremost in my thoughts. Hunter and Samantha had been waiting fourteen years for justice, and I was determined they wouldn't have to wait much longer. I showered, dressed, then made coffee while Kate snoozed on. And then I began to read what Tim had compiled the day before, most of it from the media of the day.

There wasn't a lot of new information. Most of the reporters simply repeated what little information the police had allowed them to print.

With no police files all I had was what the newspapers reported. It was a "large caliber bullet," some wag had reported. Okay. I got that, but it could mean anything. A pistol? A rifle? Was it long distance or close up? There was no mention of GSR—gunshot residue—not even in the autopsy report, probably because the clothing was missing. If I'd had to guess, though, I would have said it was done close up. And what about those missing clothes? That puzzled me. I saw two options, but neither of them totally made sense to me.

It was entirely possible the killer happened upon the love-birds while they were already naked, but the autopsy report said there was no evidence of recent sexual activity. So that wasn't likely.

Or, and to me this was more likely, the killer removed their clothes to make it look like the work of a psychopath.

There was even a third possibility: maybe the killer removed their clothes in order to remove any trace evidence, GSR included.

I was flummoxed. The loss of the police files had set my investigation back fourteen years. It would be impossible to rebuild them. I was going to have to start over, almost from scratch.

There were quotes in the articles from various family members, too. Walter Goodkind had said he was shocked and dismayed by the appalling act. Shocked and dismayed? What the heck? He was a father. He'd just lost a child. He should have been distraught with grief. But did that make him guilty? Far from it. For all I knew, the journalists shared Spruce's conviction that Walter was the murderer, and they'd allowed that bias to affect what they chose to report.

As I said, there wasn't much to be learned, but on thinking back about my own interviews I was struck by the similarities between the two fathers. Both had been successful in business; both had lost their wives early on in life, and they both lost a child. Goodkind had two other children: a daughter and a son. Steve had another son and a daughter.

Steve Flagg had remarried Wendy, who was now fifty-five, trying to look twenty-five and failing miserably.

Walter Goodkind had never married again after losing his wife, Nancy.

Christopher Goodkind, Walter's son whom I'd yet to meet, had recently graduated from Harvard Business School. I frowned at that. Wasn't he a little too old to be going to school? I looked through the printouts. Yes, Christopher was thirty-six and had graduated only a couple of years ago. What was that all about?

The Flaggs had a daughter, too. Denise was the natural daughter of Steve and Wendy, making her Danny and Hunter's half-sister. She moved to Europe right after graduating from high school and disappeared. Tim had tried to find her without any luck... so far. He'd made a note that she could have changed her name. If so, he'd need time to track that information down.

"What are you up to?" Kate said, interrupting my thoughts, as she walked into the kitchen in search of coffee. She was wearing one of my T-shirts, which hung loose on her almost to her knees, and nothing else. I couldn't help but wonder at the way, even with her hair a mess, she made that old shirt look sexy.

"Working, of course, as you should be. Sit down. I'll get you some coffee."

I handed it to her. She grabbed it with both hands as if it was some sort of lifeline which, in a way, I suppose it was, and I sat down again. She sipped and smiled as she saw how I was looking at her.

"Don't even think about it," she said. "You have a case to work, and I'm supposed to help you."

"You don't have to do that," I said, keeping my eyes glued to her.

"I know I don't. But I figure you should catch me up, at least."

"Fine. I'm meeting with Tim and Bob later, so you can sit in and get the info as I get it... If I get any," I said with a sigh.

I took her through everything I knew about the case, about

the interviews I'd conducted yesterday and, since the deed was almost certainly already done, I also told her that Tim was going to help track down the hacker.

She gave me a disapproving look, but I knew she wasn't surprised.

Half an hour later, she was all caught up, and she ran back into the bedroom to shower and dress. The thought of her alone in the shower was almost my undoing, but I kept my cool and made Belgian waffles with runny fried eggs for two.

15

By eight that morning, I was on the road driving to my downtown offices. Kate followed me in her unmarked cruiser. I'd called Bob before leaving and made sure he was on his way, as well.

As for Tim, well, I was pretty sure he'd still be there, having probably been there all night. He'd brief us and then I'd have to force him to go home and get some sleep. I often wondered if the kid wasn't a member of the undead. For sure he was a creature of the night, kept strange hours, but I didn't want him wearing himself out.

I didn't expect Jacque and Ronnie to arrive much before nine that morning, so I let us into the office through the side entrance and put on the coffee myself. Kate grabbed the first cup, and before I could grab the second for myself, Bob strode in, took it from me and went to my personal office where I'd decided to meet that day instead of the conference room. I sighed, made another cup for myself, followed them, turned one of the two guest chairs to face the two sofas and coffee table, and parked my rear on it.

Tim joined us a couple of minutes later, laptop open in the crook of his arm and a cup of coffee in his free hand. His eyes were bloodshot, red-rimmed and half-closed, but he looked excited.

"Okay, Tim," I said. "You look like shit. What did you find last night?"

"I gotta tell ya, Harry. The hack that attacked the CPD servers is good. Really good."

I sipped my coffee before answering. "Does that mean you won't be able to spot him?"

Tim smiled. "Well, I didn't say that, now did I? But I'm not there yet, not quite. I already sorta know who he is, but I don't, if you get my meaning."

"I don't get it," Bob growled. "What the hell are you talking about, Tim?"

He pushed his glasses up the bridge of his nose and leaned back on the sofa, a self-satisfied grin on his face. "This hacker left a calling card, a signature."

Now it was my turn to be confused. "You mean he left his name at the scene of the crime?"

"Well, yes and no. A lot of hackers do it. It's not actually a signature, like... a name. It's just a line of code, buried some-where in the system. It's a way of saying 'I was here.' But you have to know what to look for, or you won't see it. There's this ongoing competition between hacks to get your signature code into the most secure systems on the planet. It's also like... I dunno, part of your resume. See, if the hack is a freelancer, his tag is his, or her, proof that he did the job. You know, in case the client demands some kind of proof."

Kate was smiling. "That's pretty cool. But you're out of the CPD system now, right Tim?"

The kid raised his hands in the air defensively. "I'm

completely out, Lieutenant. Pinky swear, and I didn't leave my tag, so no one will know I was ever there."

"Good," she said. "We don't want you getting caught by the folks up in Nashville."

"Oh, they won't find me there. I doubt they'll find the hack's signature, either. It's hidden pretty well."

"So how do you find the hacker from the signature?" I asked. "I'm betting you can't just look them up in some kind of hacker's directory, right?"

Tim nodded, chuckling. "Yeah, no, that would be weird. I have to put out a search on the dark web. I have my system working on that now, but it might take a few hours. Someone who knows someone who knows someone else who knows who the hack is will send word, eventually."

"Good!" I said. "Now go home and take a shower. You're starting to get a little ripe. And then get some sleep. You can come back later. Got it?"

At the sound of the word "sleep," Tim yawned loudly. "Sure thing, Harry. Can I leave now? I emailed you the info on Jack Sloan already."

"Yeah, get out of here." Then I added, "And good work."

Tim gave me a little salute as he walked out. I turned to Bob and Kate.

"So what do we know already, even without the hacker's identity?"

Bob gave a half shrug. "Not much, boss."

"Actually, we know a lot," Kate said.

I smiled at her. "Go on."

"Well, we know approximately when the hack took place. Lt. Vazquez said it happened yesterday afternoon at two-seventeen, right?"

"Right."

"That means someone knew you were looking into the case and wanted to keep those files from you."

I nodded. "Exactly!"

Bob perked up. "So who knew that we were investigating this fourteen-year-old murder?"

I stood, grabbed a piece of paper and a pen off my desk and started writing. I was thorough. Everyone was a suspect. It sounds brutal, I know, but if you start discounting people, you'll overlook something important.

I looked up when I had the names listed. "Okay, so these are the people that could have known about the case, in chronological order: Larry Spruce, my father, Judge Strange, anyone overhearing us at the country club, members of my staff, Zoe Mullins, Jennifer Young, Walter Goodkind, anyone that they might have told after we left Legacy Health, Danny Flagg and the other mechanics at the diesel repair place, Steve and Wendy Flagg. Did I miss anyone?"

"Yeah," Bob said with a smile. "You. Everyone's a suspect, remember?"

I nodded and added my name to the top of the list.

"Happy?" I asked, handing Bob the list.

Kate got up and stepped around the sofa where he was sitting to look at it over his shoulder.

"Walter and Jennifer are our best bets, don't you think?" Kate said.

"I agree," I said. "It was still early when we talked to them, so the timing is right. And Danny Flagg's trying to save a dying business. He wouldn't have the money to hire a hacker. Neither would Steve or Wendy Flagg."

Bob cursed, then said. "One of them is covering for the other," he said. "But who's covering for whom?"

"I don't know," I said. "But let's keep an open mind. I think getting too fixated on either of them could make us miss something important."

Bob nodded. "I agree. Besides, we're joining them for dinner, right? We'll have plenty of time to drill them then."

Kate raised an eyebrow and looked at me. "A dinner invitation? You didn't mention it to me."

I grinned. "Sorry, Kate. It slipped my mind. You're welcome to come. I could use an extra set of eyes and ears. Plus I'm sure the Goodkinds eat well."

"I'm in," she said. "But, in the meantime, I still have responsibilities, and I need to keep an eye on Henry, so I'll leave you boys to your investigating and talk to you later."

And she gave me a peck on the cheek and left.

Bob looked up at me and said, "What's the plan now, boss?"

"Let's see if we can track down Jack Sloan."

16

We hadn't been on the road more than five minutes when Kate sent me a message, the gist of which was that Internal Affairs wasn't any closer to finding the person or persons responsible for the hacking or the missing hard files and physical evidence.

I'd figured as much. They'd go weeks trying to puzzle that out. But no matter, I was confident that Tim would have the identity of the hacker later that day, after he got some much-needed sleep.

In the meantime, we had another lead to follow. I doubted very much that Charlie Monk, once he'd gotten his sights set on Walter Goodkind as the murderer, had bothered to question any of Hunter and Samantha's high school classmates. But I made a mental note to interview Charlie anyway. At that particular moment, though, I had other things on my mind, namely Jack Sloan.

Sloan worked as a manager at a KFC out on the other side of the airport, on North Lee, heading out of town toward Cleveland, Tennessee.

It was Danny Flagg, you'll remember, that put us onto Jack. He and Samantha had been dating before she broke up with him and started dating Hunter. And from all accounts, Jack didn't take it too well. *We'll see!*

Star football player? Big guy with a lot of muscle? A jock? Oh yeah, I could imagine the type, and I could imagine him being embarrassed by the breakup. It would have been a huge blow to his ego and his reputation, never mind losing his girlfriend. He would have had plenty of motive: love, hate, revenge. But I was speculating. I couldn't be sure if any of it was true without talking to the guy.

It was still early, a little before ten, and the KFC wasn't open. Some of the employees, though, were already there, cleaning tables and firing up the fryers, or whatever it is that KFC employees do.

Bob grinned. "Not my usual choice for Tuesday brunch, but I can work with it."

I parked the car out front and shot Bob a look. "You don't have to eat at every stop we make, you know. I tell you what, you show a little restraint here and I'll buy you lunch, something that's not dripping in grease."

"Gee, thanks, boss."

We got out of the car and entered the restaurant through a side door and were immediately accosted by an employee, a rail-thin girl with green streaks in her hair and bloodshot eyes.

"I'm sorry, guys," she said, her voice completely flat. "We're closed. We don't open until ten. That's ten minutes."

"That's okay!" I said as cheerfully as I could. The girl was obviously hungover. Either that or she was on something. "We're investigators. I'm looking for Jack Sloan. Is he here by chance?"

The girl, probably not a day over eighteen, certainly too

young to drink, looked us over, nodded slowly, then said, "Cool, y'all packin'?"

"Sure are," Bob said, smiling.

She nodded appreciatively and said, "Jack's in back. C'mon, I'll show you."

I nodded and we followed her behind the counter and through the kitchen to a small office.

I recognized Sloan from the driver's license photo Tim had supplied, but what a surprise. He was overweight, had a double chin and a beer belly. He also sported a large mustache and thick sideburns. He wore a tie, which made him look like the manager he was, along with striped suspenders.

When he saw us, his baby face brightened and he smiled broadly.

"Gentlemen, good morning! We're not open yet, but you're free to wait inside while we get the kitchen ready."

Wow, this guy was friendly, jolly even, but the years had not been kind to Jack Sloan. Little remained of the once muscular, handsome high school jock, and it was hard to see him as a murderer, but then no one could see Ted Bundy as a killer either, so one has to be sure.

"We're not here to eat," I said and turned to Bob. "Are we?"

Bob just grinned.

"I'm afraid I don't understand," Sloan said, the beaming professional smile locked on his face. "Do you gentlemen need some directions?"

"No, Mr. Sloan," I said. "We're here to talk to you. My name is Harry Starke. I'm a private investigator. This is my associate, Bob Ryan."

The smile faded and the look turned to one of... fear? It was hard to tell, but it was only for an instant. Then the smile returned and he said, brightly, "I see. Okay. Would you like to sit down and tell me what it's all about? Let's go out into the dining room where there's more room."

He rose and we followed him back through the kitchen to a booth next to the beverages. He sat opposite us, his belly tight against the table.

"So, would you like some coffee?" He waved for one of the servers.

"No, thank you."

"Well, I do," he said. "Coffee for one, please, Alice. You know how I like it?"

"Yes, Jack. Three sugars and two creams."

He nodded, the girl left, and he said, "So, how can I help you?"

"We're looking into the murders of Hunter Flagg and Samantha Goodkind," I said. "I understand you were at school with them."

"Wow, that was a long time ago," he replied. "You guys are a few years too late, you know. Like more than a decade, man. But yeah, I knew Sam and Hunter."

"You knew Samantha quite well, isn't that right?" Bob asked, cutting right to the chase. I needed to have a talk with him about his interviewing skills.

"Uh, yeah. We went out for a couple of years in high school. We were close for a long time, even before that. She was my best friend in middle school."

Bob and I exchanged glances. This guy seemed to be pretty open. Did he have anything to hide?

"Look, Jack," I said. "Can I call you Jack?"

He nodded.

"Okay, Jack, we've been tasked with finding their killer. Your name came up because you were publicly upset when Samantha broke off her relationship with you and began dating Hunter. Would you like to tell us about that?"

His eyes widened and the smile returned, then he leaned back and said, "You're kidding, right? You think maybe I killed them? No way!"

"We're going to need more than a 'no way,'" Bob said.

"Look, was I upset when Sam left me for Hunter? Yes, I was. Sam was the hottest girl in school. It was... I don't know... expected that we'd always be together, she and I. But the relationship... it just fell apart."

I said nothing and sat there staring at him, putting on the pressure.

"You want to target someone?" he continued. "Sam's big sister, Jennifer, hated her. They fought constantly. I think it was because Sam was Daddy's favorite, and Jennifer couldn't stand it."

I didn't reply. Instead, I continued to stare at him, keeping the pressure on, and I watched his eyes as he spoke, looking for the slightest tell. There was none. As far as I could tell, he was being open and truthful.

"Oh, and Sam had a stalker, too."

Bob and I both perked up at that.

"A stalker?" Bob asked. "You have a name?"

He looked up at the ceiling as if trying to recall. "Clyde something? I don't remember. But he was very weird. Personally, I always suspected he did it. But I don't know, man. All I can say is I didn't kill anybody."

"Where were you the night of April first between nine and midnight?" I asked.

He grinned and said, "I was out, in my car, cruising."

"Can anyone corroborate that?" I asked.

He shrugged. "Maybe. I was dating Lucy Adams at the time, but..."

"But what?" Bob asked, sharply. "Where can we find her?"

"You can't. She's dead. Killed by an IED in Afghanistan last year."

I sighed. It was easy enough to check. I believed him.

"You said, maybe. What did you mean?"

"Well, we met with other folks that night. I can give you some names, but later on we... after ten, drove up to Signal Point Park and... well, you know. I remember there were a couple of other cars up there that night, but we didn't know anybody. We just kept to ourselves. Know what I mean? So I guess I don't have an alibi, right?"

"Right," I said, "and I do know what you mean. I'm sorry about Lucy. That must have been tough."

He shrugged, looked sad, said nothing.

"Okay," I said. "Thanks for your time, Jack. We'll be in touch if we have any other questions. In the meantime, if you think of anything, please give me a call." I handed him one of my business cards and we left; the thin girl with the green hair waved goodbye.

"Well, that didn't get us much," Bob said.

"I don't know, Bob." I got into the car. "We have someone else pointing the finger at Jennifer Goodkind. That's something."

"And what about this stalker guy?"

I shrugged. "Clyde something? Huh. Not much to go on, is it? But you never know. All we can do is keep it in mind and ask questions. But for now, Robert, you were a good boy back there, a little too aggressive for my taste, but a good boy nevertheless, so let's call Kate and see if she wants to meet us for an early lunch."

Bob smiled. "Shock and awe, boss. Shock and awe."

17

We met Kate for sandwiches at the Boathouse on Riverside Drive. I had Bob drive, and on the way I called Legacy Health and spoke to one of Walter Goodkind's personal assistants. Not Zoe Mullins, but a young woman who sounded about the same age. *Does Walter have a thing for the young ladies, I wonder?*

I asked her to confirm that dinner was still on at the Goodkinds, and that it would be all right for Lt. Gazzara to accompany us. She put me on hold and came back some minutes later with the confirmations. She also told me that Goodkind had requested we arrive early, at six-thirty, for drinks in Walter's personal study. Now that sounded interesting, so I confirmed and hung up.

Kate was just walking into the restaurant as we pulled into the parking lot. I tapped the horn to get her attention. She turned, waved, and waited for us at the door.

"Productive morning?" she asked as we joined her.

"You could say that," I said. "For one thing, I was able to

convince Bob to stay away from a lunch of deep-fried fast food and wait for something with substance."

Kate smiled, winking at Bob. "He offered to pay, right?"

Bob grinned. "Sure did."

It was early enough that we were able to get a table on the covered outdoor patio overlooking the river. I ordered a gingered chicken sandwich, Kate a Veggie Pannie, and Bob... a Po-Boy Catfish sandwich on French bread. We also ordered iced teas and some house-made potato chips to share.

"So," Kate said, sipping her tea through a straw, "you interviewed the ex-boyfriend. How did that go?"

"Yes, Jack Sloan," I said. "Unfortunately, his alibi died in Afghanistan last year, but I have a feeling he's on the up and up. If not, he's one of the best liars I've ever met."

"What was he doing that night?"

"According to him, cruising and making out with one Lucy Adams, but we can't corroborate it. As I said, Lucy was killed by an IED last year."

Kate nodded. "That's tough. Well, that's something. You already looked at the site where they found the bodies, right?"

"We did, on Sunday, but I'm thinking I'd like to take another look at it. Maybe even this afternoon. Why? D'you know something?"

"Yes. Finkle confirmed it. Just as the newspapers reported, Hunter Flagg's vehicle wasn't found at the scene. He thinks it was a dumpsite only, that they were killed somewhere else. The truck was never found. It's probably at the bottom of the river, somewhere."

"I can see why the police would go with that theory, but Bob and I came up with a few of our own."

Kate raised an eyebrow. "Do tell."

"Well, one theory is that Hunter and Samantha were meeting someone there, for reasons unknown. Lonely road, probably fog off the river, low visibility, it would have been a good spot to meet someone."

"Or," Bob added, "that was where they met up to, you know, get it on."

Kate smirked.

"That second theory would explain the lack of clothes," I said.

"What about the lack of a second vehicle?" Kate asked.

"Either the killer was already in the vehicle with them," I said, "or he could have walked up on the couple, killed them, dumped the bodies, and drove off with Hunter's truck."

Kate shook her head and said, "Finkle's looking through his personal files today to see if he can find the notes he made on the case."

I nodded, but I didn't have my hopes up. Police officers aren't supposed to hold onto their personal notes. All of Finkle's handwritten notes should have been in the missing evidence box. But many cops were lazy when it came to finally closing a case and compiling everything. Notebooks with scribbled thoughts and details were thrown into desk drawers and forgotten. So it was entirely possible that Finkle might have something hidden away among his voluminous collection of minutia, something that might jog his memory and give us a leg up.

"Oh, and I have an update from Vazquez," Kate said.

"Do tell," I said.

"They are treating the investigation into the missing files as two separate cases."

I frowned. "Why's that?"

"Because they've apparently confirmed that the evidence boxes went missing years ago. In fact, they aren't sure how long. They think it could have happened pre-2000."

Bob leaned back, wiped his mouth and said, "Wow. So someone's been trying to cover it up from the get-go, huh?"

Kate nodded. "We know the hack happened yesterday. And..." She paused, looking around. I knew she still didn't feel comfortable about Tim and what he did for me. "And I know Tim will probably be able to track down whoever did it, but... geez, Harry, I do so hope he doesn't get caught."

"He won't," I said. "So what about the physical evidence? Do they have any idea of how it was stolen, or by whom?"

Kate shook her head. "If it really did happen years ago, it's probably a dead end. They may never figure it out."

I could see the irony in that. We were looking into a cold case. And the evidence for that cold case was missing, and the theft itself was now a cold case. Cold trails upon cold trails.

"But Vazquez did find something," Kate said, "and she wanted you to know about it, Harry."

"What's that?"

"Walter Goodkind has been sponsoring criminal justice students for years. He set up a scholarship program almost twenty years ago, in his late wife's name. The Nancy Goodkind Fund helps Tennessee kids get into universities across the country. He sponsors law and medical students, and he sponsors cops, as well."

My eyes went wide. "You mean he pays for kids to go to the police academy?"

She nodded. "He's put probably a dozen high school graduates through college and then the academy. IA figures there are several cops, some of them higher-ranking officers, in Chattanooga and elsewhere that only got where they have because of the Nancy Goodkind Fund."

"Geez," Bob said, half under his breath.

My sentiments exactly!

"So we have all kinds of cops and lawyers in this town

that're indebted to Walter Goodkind," I said. "Any one of whom might have stolen the files from storage."

Bob shook his head. "It doesn't have to be that complicated, Harry. Walter has more money than God. He could have bribed someone, anyone, at any time to steal the evidence. IA could spend the next month questioning everyone that benefited from that fund while the real culprit could have been one of the janitors."

"Now you boys see the task IA is facing," Kate said. "The evidence is long gone. And we may never know who took it."

I took a bite of my sandwich. I knew from the beginning that it wasn't going to be an easy case.

Who was I kidding? There were never any easy cases. At least not for me. I always seemed to land the tough ones. But hey, it's why we get paid the big bucks!

"Well," I said wearily, "Walter Goodkind looks more guilty by the minute. And yet, I just don't see him killing his own daughter!"

"What about Jennifer?" Bob asked.

"The sister?" Kate said, raising her eyebrows.

"Yeah, her," Bob said. "She was aggressive toward us from the start. Right, Harry? And she tried to stop us from talking to Walter. We thought maybe she was protecting him, but maybe she's protecting herself."

I nodded, then said, "Jack Sloan said Jennifer hated Samantha and didn't like Hunter, either. She'd have the means to hire someone to steal the files, and she'd have access to the recipients of the fund."

"Sure," Kate added, "and she could have paid a hacker to delete the digital files yesterday afternoon. She could have made that phone call right after you left their offices."

I slapped my hand down on the table. "Yeah, in fact, she

could have made that call even before we left, while we were talking to her father."

Bob nodded.

"Well," I continued, "maybe we'll learn more when we get to chat with the family tonight. You still coming with us, Kate?"

She shook her head, frowning. "I wish I could, but I still have shift schedules to submit. The joys of being a lieutenant, you know."

I rolled my eyes. Of all the reasons I'd left the police force, the paperwork was front and center. Now, thank the Lord, I have people do it for me. Ronnie loves dealing with the minutia, and Jacque's more organized than I'd ever be. She keeps everything running smoothly. I don't know what I'd do without them!

"Okay. It looks like it's just you and me, then, Bob."

Bob grinned. "Looking forward to it. What could be better? An evening of wine, good food and confrontation."

"Sure," I said. "There isn't much more we can do until we meet with Walter Goodkind and ask the hard questions. Tell you what, Bob," I said, looking at my watch. "We still have several hours. How about we go take another quick look at the dumpsite, or whatever it was?"

"Really?" he asked skeptically.

"Yes, really!"

18

It was a twenty-minute drive from the Boathouse to Sailmaker Circle and, so I figured, about thirty minutes from the Goodkind residence on Lookout Mountain, all depending upon the traffic, of course.

Hunter and Samantha's bodies had been found just inside the trees on the east side of the road. That particular section of Sailmaker ran parallel to and just a few yards from the Tennessee River.

I parked once again on the paved section of the west side of the road, facing the oncoming traffic, of which there was little. Staring out through the windshield at the singularly unremarkable stretch of pavement, I thought to myself how nice it would have been to have had access to the official police files.

And nobody has access to those files right now.

The area looked secluded. The bend in the road made it perfect because there was practically no visibility in either direction along the highway... No, not a highway. More a backwater.

I opened my door and got out. I was on the edge of the hard

shoulder, the river just yards away at the bottom of a steep slope.

"Okay, Harry," Bob said as he joined me, his hands in his pockets. "What did you expect? Nothing's changed. It's just a boring piece of rural road."

"But why here?" I asked.

"What do you mean?"

"Well, it's a question you have to ask at every crime scene or dumpsite. Why here? Why not somewhere else?"

Bob looked around. "It's kinda off the beaten path. There's nobody around. That's a good reason."

I nodded. But was it reason enough?

"We're close to the river," Bob added, nodding down at the slow-moving water.

I perked up at that. "No vehicle," I said aloud. "You think the killer could have brought the bodies here in a boat? A bass boat would make it to the bank easily enough, and there's plenty of those around here."

Bob shrugged. "Could be. But we're a lot closer to the road than the river. I can't see anyone hauling two bodies up that riverbank. It's as steep as hell. And why cart them all the way over there? Why not just leave them on the riverbank? Sheesh, for that matter why not just dump 'em in the river and be done with it?"

The man made a lot of sense.

"And why strip the bodies?" I asked. "Hmm. Probably to get rid of any trace evidence," I answered my own question.

I stepped around the car, looking at the ground, studying the trees. What was I looking for? Hell if I knew. But you never know what you'll find if you just keep your eyes open long enough.

"Maybe the killer just wanted to see 'em naked," Bob said. "Maybe he was a pervert."

It was as good a theory as any, I supposed.

I cursed out loud. "This would be a lot easier if we had those frickin' police files!"

"Yeah, I think that's probably why someone paid for the files to get lost," he said sarcastically. "Hey, maybe Henry will find his notes. At least that would be something."

I nodded. "That might be a help. I don't know how good a note-taker Finkle is, but you're right. It would be better than nothing. We don't even know if there were tire tracks found, trace on the bodies, gunshot residue... nothing."

I was beginning to feel that our visit was a waste of time, that there was nothing to learn from simply staring at the road, river and trees. There sure as hell was no new evidence to be found, not after fourteen years...

Then something caught my eye, up ahead. A yellow sign along the side of the highway.

Fog warning. Use caution.

I frowned. The sign looked relatively new, maybe just a couple of years old.

I turned toward the river, then turned and looked at the trees on the far side of the road. Late at night, especially during winter, the fog would rise from the river and cover the road and fill the woods.

"You know something?" I said. "It was the first of April, still winter, in the middle of the night, and it would have been cold, which means it would have been foggy, right?"

Bob looked around, as if the bushes and trees would give him the confirmation he needed. "Sure, I guess so."

"And we are at the middle of a fairly tight bend in the road."

"Right. So?" Bob looked at me expectantly.

"So this would have been the perfect place to meet someone without being seen."

Bob nodded. "Or the perfect place to sneak up on someone."

I smiled and said, "Okay, Bob. I think we're done here. See, it was productive coming out here, after all."

Bob was frowning as he got in the car. "I don't see how. I could have told you about the fog the first time we came out here. Hell, I could have called you from the comfort of my bed."

"Ah, but that's not what it's about, Bob. It's about using the imagination. Don't you see? We have to visualize, put ourselves in the shoes of the victims... and the killer. I think we just did that."

"If you say so," Bob said grumpily, "boss."

I rolled my eyes, started the Maxima, and drove Bob back to the office to get his car. Me? It was just after four in the afternoon. I still had a couple of hours to burn. I needed to think. I knew if I went into the office, I would be inundated.

I went to the Sorbonne. Where else?

19

I f you didn't know better, from the name you'd think the Sorbonne might be a ritzy, downtown restaurant. You know, the type of place where the maître d' has a pretentious little French mustache, and the prices aren't on the menu because every item costs almost as much as your mortgage.

Well, that's not the Sorbonne, far from it. In reality, it's a bar—although Benny Hinkle, the owner, insists it's a night club —a sleazy little hole in the wall where the drinks are cheap, the music loud, and the lighting is so bad that newbies walk in and touch their faces, thinking maybe they left sunglasses on. There are no prices on the menu there either, but only because they don't have menus... You wouldn't want to try the food anyway... although I must say the ham and cheese sandwich isn't at all bad.

So, if the Sorbonne is such a sleazy place, why do I go there as often as I do? Kate often asks me the same question.

The truth is, I really don't know. I do like to keep my finger on the pulse of the dark underbelly of the city, a habit I picked up early in my career as a cop. I like to keep tabs on the movers and shakers of our little underworld: the pimps, drug dealers and mobsters. The Sorbonne is a great place to do that.

Over the years, I've gotten plenty of work from frequenting the joint. You'll recall that my first-ever case as a private investigator fell into my lap right there in the Sorbonne.

And, if I'm being honest, even though the place is loud and nasty, I do some of my best thinking there, watching the lowlifes study me out of the corner of their eyes, trying to figure out if I'm a cop or not.

So, as I walked in, out of the early afternoon sun, and allowed my eyes to adjust to the dim light and my ears to the blare of the jukebox, I couldn't help but smile to myself.

As my eyes slowly adjusted, I noticed someone smiling back at me from across the room.

Laura Davies gave me a wink and nod from a table at the far end of the bar where she was serving drinks to a couple of bikers.

"Kind of early, aren't you, Harry?" she asked as she walked past me. "Only drunks come to a bar this early." It was four-fifteen.

One of the biker types shot her an angry look.

"Present company excluded, of course," she said smoothly, smiling down at the biker.

"Just bring me my usual, Laura, and not the watered stuff, okay?"

She nodded and said, "As if." And wove her way between the tables and back behind the bar.

Me, I found an empty booth in a dark corner of the room and settled in to wait for my drink.

Laura's more than just a waitress at the Sorbonne. She's actually a part-owner of the business, along with the aforementioned Benny Hinkle, a fat slob and creature of the night. The exact details of their relationship were a mystery to me, but I knew Laura had a husband and two kids at home. She may have dressed and acted like a slutty barmaid, but that was all just an act. The blonde in the cut-off jeans, tank top and cowboy boots was all business. And customers quickly learned they could look but not touch. If they did, one of Laura's pointy-toed boots would visit the family jewels. She kept a bottle of Laphroaig behind the counter, just for me. Yup, I paid double for it, but it was my favorite poison and well worth it.

I was on the job, and driving, so I couldn't drink much. Especially when I knew Walter Goodkind would be serving drinks later that evening, but I figured one little drink couldn't hurt.

Besides, when I drink scotch, I don't throw back shots like a frat boy. I sip it, savor it. It helps me think. And that's what I was there for, to think.

You see, I was skeptical about the way Larry Spruce, Charlie Monk and Henry Finkle had all zeroed in on Walter Goodkind as the killer. Me? I was sure that someone else was guilty and that the original investigation had been all about bias and unfounded assumptions, which was why they were never able to close the case.

But someone was determined to thwart me in my quest for justice. The missing evidence? Sure, Walter could have bribed any of the people he'd sponsored to take the boxes from storage, but so could any number of people. And what about the hack? That had happened when only a few people in the universe knew I was looking into the case. I mean, Larry certainly didn't hire me to find the killer and then hire a hacker to make sure I didn't.

To nail a killer you need to be able to prove three things: motive, means and opportunity and, so far, no one we'd spoken to seemed to have any of those things. For one thing, we didn't have the means—the weapon. If we could find that...

Well, it was doubtful that we ever would. It was probably disposed of... long... ago. *And where was the most likely place to dispose of it? The river, of course.* For a moment I was quite excited, but then I thought about the fourteen years of mud and silt that must be covering it, if it was indeed there. Divers could search that stretch of the Tennessee for weeks and never find it.

Danny Flagg had a cast-iron alibi. Steve and Wendy Flagg were possibilities, but did they have motive, means and opportunity? I didn't think so. Jack Sloan? Again, I was doubtful. He talked a good game, and he didn't have an alibi, but my gut feeling was that he was telling the truth.

So, in spite of my doubts, Walter Goodkind and Jennifer, Samantha's sister, currently shared first place in the "prime suspect" competition.

Laura brought my glass of amber goodness and smiled down at me.

"You look like you have the weight of the world on your shoulders, Harry," she said.

I took the glass from her, nodding gratefully. "Have you ever refused to believe something, even when all the evidence points toward that one thing being true?" I asked. I didn't expect her to answer, but she surprised me.

She nodded and said, "When I was pregnant with my second kid. I didn't want to believe it. I was late... you know. And I had morning sickness. And let me tell you, Harry Starke... You've been hungover, right?"

I nodded. It wasn't something I was proud of, but it had happened, more than once.

"That ain't nothing compared to morning sickness," she continued, "but I didn't want to admit it, that I was pregnant."

I frowned. She wasn't helping.

"But hey," she continued. "The same happened again about

a year later. The exact same stuff. But I wasn't pregnant that time. So there you go, see?"

She turned and walked jauntily away. I had to admit, the sight of the way she filled those cut-off jeans, which barely covered the cheeks of her ass, almost made me feel better. Almost.

So, what were my options? I mulled them over as I sipped the drink, letting the warmth tickle my throat.

Either Walter Goodkind was the killer or Jennifer was. Or one of them... or both of them was covering for the real killer.

Danny Flagg was broke, so how could he pay for a master code-monkey to hack the police computers?

Only one other person knew about our investigation at the same time as Jennifer and Walter: Zoe Mullins.

I made a mental note to learn more about her. *Hmm, but she couldn't have been more than ten or twelve...*

Bob had mentioned earlier that they would be going out for drinks. *Can he be trusted to keep his head around a beauty like her?* I wondered. He was a good investigator, and he'd saved my life on more than one occasion, but I trusted him less with women than I trusted myself.

I fell into the rhythm of the place, the loud music, the people milling around, and I finished my drink.

I'd learned long ago that thinking about a mystery only did me so much good. Often times, it was when I wasn't thinking about a puzzle that the solution presented itself.

Did I receive a major revelation there in the Sorbonne? Not exactly, but I had cleared away a few of the cobwebs. I looked at my watch. It was almost five o'clock. Time to go home and ready myself for our visit to Walter Goodkind's lair on the mountain.

20

I went home to shower and change into something more suitable for the occasion. Once in the Maxima, I headed south on Broad to Scenic Highway, then on up to the top of Lookout Mountain, and from there to West Brow Road, where some of the wealthiest homes in Hamilton County were located and, believe it or not, where I live now.

It wasn't long before my GPS informed me that I'd arrived at my destination: a large mansion set back from the road with a stunning view over the Lookout Valley.

The semi-circular driveway wrapped around a small grove of trees, designed to look like a miniature forest, carefully maintained and manicured.

The house itself was two-and-a-half stories with a single-story wing on each end, one of which was a four-car garage. The structure was brick and partially covered in vines. The driveway was two-lane and paved and probably cost more by itself than most people pay for their homes.

I pulled in front of the wide flight of six stone steps that led up to a two-story porch and exited the car, just as Bob pulled up behind me. I waited for him to join me and was surprised to see that he, too, had dressed for the occasion, be it no more than a black button-down shirt, dark red tie and fresh jeans. His hair was gelled and spiked, and I could smell the cologne as he approached.

"Well, well, well," I said. "Aren't you the pretty boy? Hot date later?"

Bob smiled, looked a little embarrassed. "Yeah, that, so I hope we don't have to chase anyone down the mountain."

"Zoe Mullins?"

"Yeah, her," he replied.

I raised an eyebrow. "Bit young, don't you think?" I asked as we walked together up the steps.

He shrugged. "She's twenty-six. I asked her."

"That must have been brutal for her. You never were the shy one."

"Yeah, well, you know."

"You look good, cowboy," I said. "I only hope you can keep your head in the game while we're here."

"Oh, don't worry. I'll stay focused. For all we know, we're walking into the arms of a killer."

I nodded. From the look in Bob's eyes, he'd been puzzling over this case, just as I'd been. And, knowing the way he thinks, probably asking himself the same questions.

Just as we reached the porch at the top of the steps, we heard another vehicle enter the driveway. We paused and turned to see a sleek, royal blue Audi R8 Decennium sports car pull up behind Bob's SUV. The two figures inside could barely be seen through the tinted windows. I wanted to wait to see who they were—Jennifer and her wealthy, Canadian husband? But the front door opened and an older man in a black suit stepped forward and looked expectantly at us.

"Uh, good evening," I said. "My name is—"

"Mr. Harry Starke and Mr. Robert Ryan. Do come in. Mr. Goodkind is expecting you." And he stepped back for us to enter.

I looked back at the Audi one last time, but the occupants had yet to exit and we were ushered inside before either the driver or the passenger exited the car. Whoever it was... well, we'd have to wait and see.

We were escorted from one room to the next, each fancier than the last. Two women in—I kid you not—traditional maid's uniforms hurried past us carrying vases of flowers.

This was Walter's home, all right. Just like that old desk in his office, a symbol of old money and tradition. The house looked like it could have just appeared out of a time warp from the 1920s.

Finally, we were led to a large library. Books of ancient origin lined the walls. The sun was setting over the Lookout Valley and the room was filled with golden light that filtered in through two huge windows. I hadn't realized there was a chill in the mansion until I was welcomed by the warmth of the fire.

Sitting there in a leather armchair, in front of the fireplace, Walter Goodkind was sipping amber liquid from a crystal glass, the said liquid probably older than I was.

He looked around and smiled as we entered the room. Gone was the stern old man we'd seen in his office yesterday, replaced by a mild-mannered man resting in the lap of luxury... or perhaps a murderer fourteen years overdue for justice.

"Mr. Starke, Mr. Ryan, please join me by the fire. I thought you were to be accompanied by Lieutenant Gazzara?"

"Unfortunately, she had to work," I replied. "She sends her regrets."

He nodded and said, "Can Sawyer get you something to drink? Scotch? Whiskey? Wine?"

Bob grinned. "Do you have any beer?"

Walter's eyebrows lifted, but only for a second. Then that same peaceful smile reappeared once more.

"Sawyer?" he said.

The butler, who hadn't introduced himself, stepped forward, nodded and said, "I believe we have some in the kitchen, sir."

"And what about you, Mr. Starke? You look like a whiskey man, like myself."

I nodded. "I prefer scotch, if you don't mind. And please, call me Harry."

"Very well." The old man waved for Sawyer to go. "And you may call me Walter. I don't often have guests in this study. I'm a man with few friends, you know."

I sat in the comfy leather chair across from Walter's. Bob took a seat next to mine. "Really?" I said. "I'd imagine you have plenty of friends."

"No, no. Business partners? Yes. Acquaintances? Many. But my friends are few. I don't entertain like I used to when Nancy was alive. All I have these days is my family."

I nodded. "You care a lot about your family."

It wasn't a question, but Walter took it as one. "Yes, I suppose I do. My children are everything to me. That's why I'm happy you're looking into Samantha's death. I loved her dearly, you know."

I could tell he meant it. There was something in his eyes, in the tone of his voice. Honesty? Sincerity? Perhaps.

Sawyer returned with a glass of a dark and foamy beer and handed it to Bob. "There will be more for you at dinner, sir. I've seen to it."

"Thanks," Bob said.

Sawyer went to pour me my drink. I didn't recognize the label on the bottle, but I'd have bet that it cost a small fortune. It probably first went into a barrel during the Kennedy administration. The man poured a generous measure into an identical glass to the one Walter was holding and handed it to me. I thanked him. He nodded, turned and left the room.

"I know why you came to see me yesterday," Walter said.

"Oh?" I took a sip. *Oh yes, this is the real thing.* I closed my eyes for a second, savoring the fiery liquid.

"DA Spruce believes me to be the killer. So does Captain Finkle, as does that detective... Monk, I believe was his name."

I opened my eyes. "That would be Assistant Chief Finkle now," I said. I didn't mean to correct our host. In fact, I'm not sure why I did. Perhaps, in the moment, I was hoping to intimidate him.

But the old man simply smiled and nodded.

"Why did they suspect you?" Bob asked.

"Because I threatened to kill Hunter Flagg. Very publicly, I might add."

I almost dropped my drink. He'd said it so casually that I thought for a second he was going to confess right there and then.

"Okay," I said. "So you threatened him. Would you like to tell us about it?"

He thought for a moment, then said, "It was three days before her murder. The entire Flagg clan heard me." Walter looked into the orange glow of the fire. One of the logs crackled and flared, sending a shower of sparks up the chimney. "So I can't really blame the police for suspecting me, can I?" He turned his head to look at me. He was smiling.

"Sir," I said slowly. "You're not going to tell me you killed those two kids, are you?"

His eyes narrowed. "No, Harry, I'm not. I didn't kill them. Would you like to hear my story or not?"

I didn't say a word. I just nodded.

Walter continued. "I never liked that boy, Hunter Flagg."

He practically spat out the name. "And it wasn't for the reasons you'd think. I didn't care so much that he didn't have money. I offered the young man a job in my company. He would have had money, if he'd worked for it."

Walter shifted in his seat. "But that was the problem. The boy didn't want to work. He just wanted to ride his motorcycle with that delinquent brother of his and get up to God only knows what. He had no ambition. He was lazy, a liar... And, I'm sure, up to no good. I couldn't stomach it."

Walter paused and sipped his drink.

"So you threatened him?" Bob said.

The old man lowered his eyes. "So I threatened him," he agreed. "That particular day I realized I'd had enough. First, my son, Christopher, rebelled, and then my little Samantha? I couldn't take it. I drove to the boy's home and I yelled at him, in front of his people. I told him I'd kill him if he tried to take my daughter away. I told him that there was nowhere he could run, that I'd find him and kill him."

He looked down at his now-empty glass and smiled distantly. "Not the smartest thing I ever did, but... Well, I might have been a little drunk that day... I was upset, you see, scared I'd lose Samantha. And then she appeared, came right out of the front door while I was yelling at the boy. She came down off the porch, inserted herself between Hunter and me... and she defended him."

He paused, sat there for a long moment, so long that I leaned forward and said, "And then what happened?"

"I'm not proud of what I did, gentlemen, but I was too angry to think straight. I struck her across the face. Everyone saw me do it."

I hadn't seen that coming. Why hadn't Steve Flagg bothered to mention that Walter had threatened his son and struck his own daughter in public? I mean, no wonder he was the prime suspect.

I glanced at Bob. He seemed as stunned as I was.

"That doesn't mean I killed her, of course. I felt horrible about what I'd done. I assumed I'd get the opportunity to apologize to her, you see... But I never did."

I looked down into my drink. Walter Goodkind was a sad old man. And no wonder! He'd been carrying his regrets around with him for all those years.

"I didn't hit her out of anger," Walter added.

"You didn't?" Bob asked. "Then why the hell did you do it?"

The old man looked at him, taken aback by the anger in Bob's voice, and said, "I struck her out of fear. She made it clear that she would choose the boy over me, over her family. She was willing to reject her inheritance to be with him. It was so stupid of me. After I hit her, I was even more afraid I'd lose her. And, as it turned out, I did, but not in the way I'd thought."

Sawyer came in and offered us all refills. He also said that Todd and Jennifer would be running a little late.

"That's fine, Sawyer," Walter said. "We'll stay in here a little longer. I'm sure the detectives have a few more questions for me."

I accepted my refilled glass from Sawyer with a nod of thanks. And Walter was right. I did have more questions for him.

"Walter," I said, "the police have discovered that someone tampered with the evidence. You wouldn't know anything about that, would you?"

From the way the old man's eyes flickered, only for a fraction of a second, and then glanced to his left and then quickly back again, I knew we'd struck gold!

21

I could tell by the way Walter Goodkind looked away and slowly sipped his drink that he was trying to recover from my question, that he knew he'd reacted and was trying to control it. *Oh yes, the old man's hiding something.*

"Tampered with the evidence, you say?" Walter said carefully, slowly, finally looking at me.

"Stole it, more like," Bob added.

"A long time ago," I said, locking eyes with him. "Someone removed the files and physical evidence from storage: trace evidence, the bullet recovered from Samantha's body, fibers, photographs, everything. It's all gone, Walter." I paused, continued to stare at him, then asked the definitive question, "Did you have anything to do with that?"

The old man took a quick breath and his whole demeanor changed. Gone was the friendly, casual old man, replaced by the hardened, no-nonsense businessman. His eyes turned into two chips of ice, his face to stone, unreadable, even his body straightened a little.

It was apparent that the man had been prepared to talk

about his daughter's death, even about his slapping Samantha and threatening Hunter in front of witnesses, and he was happy to talk about all the reasons why he should be our prime suspect. But stealing evidence? No! That was something he wasn't prepared for.

"Of course not," he replied, his voice flat, toneless. "This is the first I've heard of it."

"Really?" I said. "You're the obvious suspect. You have motive... and I hear you have a lot of friends in the police department, beneficiaries of your scholarship fund, some of them in high places. So you also had the means and the opportunity. Are you sure you don't know anything about the theft?"

His eyes narrowed to slits filled with anger. "I've already told you. I know nothing about it."

I held his stare. He could put up a wall, but I wanted him to know that I knew he was lying. That stare of his might intimidate his employees, but it had no effect on me.

"Okay," I said finally, shrugging. "Fair enough. The state police have been called in. I'm sure they'll figure it out. And I don't need whatever was in that box anyway."

Walter casually sipped his drink and said in a low voice, "I'm glad to hear it."

I nodded, tilted my head a little to one side, raised an eyebrow and said, almost casually, "And, that's not all. Someone hacked the police servers yesterday afternoon and deleted all the digital files, everything. That's quite a coincidence, wouldn't you say?"

Again, Walter's eyes registered surprise, but he quickly recovered and said, "Yes, quite a coincidence, indeed."

"So now," I continued, "we have nothing. It's as if it never happened... Actually, that's not quite true. I do have the DA's files, but they are far from complete."

"It looks like someone doesn't want us looking too closely at this case," Bob said. "And what's really funny is the hack happened only five hours after we talked to you at your offices yesterday."

Walter settled into a confident smile. "I don't think that's funny, Mr. Ryan. A little disconcerting, perhaps... Another coincidence, would you say?"

The corners of Walter's mouth tightened just a bit. I knew that expression. He was angry, but with whom? Was it us? Was he mad at us for pressing him so hard? Or was he angry with someone else for botching the hack job? There was no way to tell.

You see, it was pretty dumb to go in and delete only the Goodkind-Hunter files, a big mistake, but was it Walter Goodkind's mistake? Or was it someone else's? And therein lay the kicker. Who else besides Walter had the motive, means and opportunity? I could think of only one other person: Jennifer Goodkind-Young. But was she—if indeed it was her—working alone or with her father?

I leaned forward in my seat, set my elbows on my knees, my hands locked together in front of me. It was time to follow a hunch. A hunch... hmm, maybe it was something more. Kate will tell you I have a sort of second sight. Me? I think it's just a gut feeling of a kind I can never explain.

At that particular moment, I knew with some certainty that Walter was responsible for the missing evidence and that he was protecting someone. The hack, though...

It was time to go for the throat.

"And what about Jennifer?" I asked, watching his expression carefully. "Do you think she would know anything about the hack? I only ask because she's one of the few people, at the time, who knew we'd reopened the investigation."

I'd hit a nerve. The old man's face hardened. I could see the rage in his eyes. It was as if I was watching a thunderstorm gathering on the horizon. I had a feeling it was about to turn into an F5 tornado. But Walter Goodkind was better than that. He knew better than to act out of anger. In fact, I was pretty sure that if I'd been dealing with the Walter of twenty years ago, he would have shown no emotion at all. Even so, in an instant, he regained control, relaxed and gifted me with a confident smile.

"I understand your thinking, detective," he said lightly. "And I know what you're trying to do, but it won't work. You can make all the hollow accusations you want, but you can't turn them into facts, not without proof... *evidence*. And you don't have any... do you?"

He was calm, collected, exercising impeccable self-control.

"Like a *dog*," he continued, emphasizing the word, "I know you have to dig deeply sometimes. If not, you might never find the bone? However, I can assure you that my daughter had nothing to do with that hack. Someone is playing games with you, Harry. But I don't expect you to believe me, so, when Jennifer arrives, why don't you ask her yourself?"

I leaned back again, nodded and said, "Yes, I think I'll do just that." I lifted my glass, held it up to the light and studied the amber liquid. It seemed to glow in the firelight.

Walter had me, check and mate, and he knew it. After all, at the end of the day all I had were hunches, suspicions. Without evidence all I could hope for was to push someone hard enough to make a confession, and somehow I didn't see that happening. I'd learned a lot from studying Walter's face and eyes throughout the conversation, and he knew that he'd slipped, but both he and I knew that a hunch and a fleeting expression in the firelight would not be enough to solve the case.

"By the way, this is really good," I said, still staring at the glass. "What label is it?"

The old man was completely relaxed. "Oh, I don't know. I never drink scotch myself. It's some odd label Sawyer orders for me."

Again, he looked away to the left, then brushed away the thought with the wave of his hand. He was lying again. This time to impress me. I knew my scotch, and I was certain that the whisky was extremely expensive and probably one of Walter Goodkind's guilty pleasures. He was showing off, bending the truth, challenging me to call him on it.

Kids these days would call it flexing. I call it being a cocky son of a bitch.

I had to admit, though, Walter was good. If we'd been playing poker, I doubt even Ronnie would know when to call his bluff.

We kept chatting for a few minutes more, mostly about my business. He seemed truly interested. Other than that, we were simply passing the time until dinner was called. Bob sipped his beer, stared at the fire, seeming infinitely bored. He never was one for small talk. He was a man of action and making polite conversation with rich strangers was not something he enjoyed.

And so we played the waiting game, knowing full well that, soon enough, we'd have plenty of interesting people to... interrogate? Well, perhaps that's not the best word for it. Entertain, might be a better one. We were, after all, to have dinner with the entire Goodkind family.

22

I t wasn't more than ten minutes later that Sawyer was back to inform our host that Jennifer had called again to say that, since they were only a few minutes out, we were to go ahead and get started on dinner without them.

"Very well," Walter said. "Perhaps we should gather in the lounge. Take them through, please, Sawyer."

Sawyer gave a little bow, stepped away to the door and opened it. Walter got up from his seat, his joints audibly clicking as he grunted and straightened.

"Take some advice from an old man, Harry Starke. Enjoy your youth, because old age is nothing but aches and pains. Follow Sawyer. I'll join you shortly."

Sawyer led us from the study to a much larger room, with an even larger fireplace—a faux inglenook—and a number of elegant couches and chairs laid out in a large semicircle facing it. It was obviously the family gathering place.

Two people were already in the room. One I recognized from Tim's reports: Christopher Goodkind.

Christopher was tall, and I knew him to be thirty-six years old. He was blessed with seriously good looks, a strong jaw, blue eyes and dark blond hair shaved to the tops of his ears and left long on top. He wore a button-down shirt, jeans, and a navy blazer with a white handkerchief overflowing from the breast pocket.

He'd been standing in front of the fire, his hands in his pockets, looking down into the flames, but he turned around and smiled when we entered.

His companion, I didn't recognize. She looked to be about thirty, with olive skin, large dark eyes, and black hair that fell in tight ringlets to just below her shoulders. She didn't smile. Instead, she looked confused when she saw us.

"You must be the detectives my sister told me about," Christopher said as he crossed the room and offered me his hand.

I accepted and said, "Yes, I'm Harry Starke. This is my associate, Bob Ryan." His grip was strong, firm and confident.

He shook Bob's hand and said, "It's nice to meet you, Bob."

"Likewise," Bob said. "Nice car, by the way. Audi Decennium, V10, right?" he asked, confirming what we both suspected, that the fancy car belonged to Christopher.

"Yes, that's right. Thank you. We like it, don't we, darling?" he said, turning to face the young woman, who was still sitting on one of the plush leather couches and looking at us with some consternation.

"Honey, these men are private detectives," Christopher said to her.

"You didn't tell me there was going to be visitors, Chris," she said. "I thought it was to be just the family. Why are these men here?"

To say this woman sounded nervous would be an understatement. But why? Hell if I knew. All I could see was an overly nervous girlfriend. No... not girlfriend, I realized when I saw the large diamond on her left hand. Apparently, she was Christopher's fiancé.

"They're investigating Samantha's death, honey," Christopher said calmly. "I'm sorry I didn't tell you earlier, but I know how emotional you've been these days."

It was then that I realized the woman wasn't just nervous. Her eyes were red, puffy. She'd been crying recently. But why? And why hadn't I noticed sooner?

Bob and I exchanged glances and, from the look I received, he'd noticed it too.

And she looked as if she was about to start crying again... At the mere mention of Samantha's name?

Christopher crossed the room, sat down beside her, put an arm around her shoulders and said gently, "It's all right, Stacy. I should've told you earlier. I'm really sorry I didn't."

The woman sniffed loudly. "It's okay, Chris. It's just a surprise, that's all. Did your father hire them?"

"No," I said, taking a couple of steps forward. "The district attorney hired us. Were you a friend of Samantha's, Miss...?"

"Oh, I apologize," Christopher said as he tenderly rubbed her back for comfort. "This is Stacy Hudson. She's my fiancé, but she was also Sam's best friend."

Stacy Hudson, huh? Well now, that was a new name to add to the list. I smiled at the couple on the couch.

"It's really nice to meet you both," Bob said as he sat down on one of the other couches, making himself at home.

I decided to do the same.

"Oh, I'm pleased to meet you, too," Stacy said in a soft voice. "So is that why you're here, to ask us questions?"

I nodded. "Yes, exactly. You and Samantha were close, I take it?"

She nodded, obviously trying to hold back more tears. "Oh,

yes. We were best friends. Joined at the hip, you might say. Had been for years, ever since first grade."

I looked back and forth between the two of them, and I had to wonder, how did Samantha's brother and her best friend end up together? And why now? It had been fourteen years, and they were only now engaged to be married?

"I know it must seem strange to you," Christopher said, as if he'd read my mind, "but, Stacy was married before... I guess you could say we finally made the circle back to one another, although I didn't know her that well when Sam and she were friends."

Circle indeed. I was curious, but I was kind of at a loss as to what questions to ask—not like me at all. Stacy Hudson was obviously emotionally fragile and, while I needed to get more information from both of them, I didn't want to upset anybody, especially just before dinner.

"So, Ms. Hudson, your first husband was...?" I trailed off, trying to choose my words carefully.

"In Nashville, sleeping around," Stacy said, a little more strength, conviction, present in her voice. "It's all right, Mr... Starke was it?" I nodded but didn't say anything, and Stacy continued. "I married my high school boyfriend, you see. A football player. Very handsome."

Bob jumped in. "It wasn't Jack Sloan, was it?"

I cut him a glance. I couldn't tell if he was making a joke, or what. Of course it wasn't Jack Sloan.

Stacy giggled at that. "No, of course not! Don't be silly. Jack was Samantha's beau."

I realized what Bob was doing. It was a joke, meant to lighten the mood. And it worked!

"You never really know yourself when you're young, do you?" Stacy asked. "My boyfriend as he was then, Freddie, then my husband, had always been such a nice boy. But he didn't stay nice. Everyone has a secret, I guess. And Freddie's was his drinking. After a couple of years, it wasn't a secret he was able to keep at all. He got himself fired, and after that he couldn't hold down a job."

"That man was a jerk and a bully, Stacy." Walter's voice cut in from behind me. I hadn't noticed him come in. How long had he been there, listening? I wondered. "I'm glad you were able to get away from him," he continued, "and find someone more sensible, like Christopher." He joined us, sat down on one of the leather chairs.

"I am pretty glad about that, myself," Christopher said with a smile. "Of course, Stacy would never have paid any attention to me back then. She and Sam were good girls, and I was... well, a bit of a rebel really."

I frowned as I looked at Christopher. "But you turned things around, didn't you? You recently graduated from Harvard Business School, I believe. That's quite an accomplishment!"

Christopher looked down at his hands, seemingly embarrassed. "It doesn't feel like much of an accomplishment when you're my age and graduating with a crowd of twenty-two-year-olds. But, yes, it took me a while, but I have turned my life around and now that Stacy and I have found each other"—he gazed fondly at her—"and a second chance at love. I feel as if both our lives are finally back on track."

"That's wonderful," I said. And I meant it! "I do have just a couple more questions for Stacy, if you don't mind." I looked at Stacy expectantly.

She didn't mind, and she didn't look as if she was about to cry again. In fact, she managed to produce a small smile. "I'll do my best. I'm happy to help... if I can."

"Thank you," I said. "Bob and I have been talking to anyone that knew Samantha when she was in high school. Friends, for example. So, as you can guess, we're really happy to meet you." I was trying to put her at ease, and it seemed to be working.

Stacy gifted me with a little giggle, looked down at her hands, then said, "Well, as I said. I'll do what I can." Then she frowned, as if an unsettling thought had just occurred to her. "You mentioned Jack Sloan earlier. Have you talked to him yet?"

"Yes," Bob said. "We know he and Samantha dated for a while in high school. We heard he was pretty upset when she and Hunter started going out."

I added, "Did you ever see Hunter and Jack fight over Samantha?"

Stacy shook her head. "Oh, no! You've gotten it all wrong. Jack and Hunter were the best of friends, always. They used to ride motorcycles together. In fact, I'm pretty sure that was how Samantha met Hunter in the first place. And, I know there were a lot of rumors going around school about Jack being upset with Hunter because he stole Samantha away, but he wasn't. It was all... just rumors. Stupid gossip!"

I glanced at Bob. I could tell he was thinking the same thing I was. Jack Sloan hadn't told us the whole story. Maybe we'd have to go back to the KFC and talk to the one-time star quarterback again.

"That's very helpful, Stacy," I said with an encouraging smile. "Can you think of anything else? Was there anyone you can think of who would have wanted to hurt Samantha or Hunter?"

Stacy seemed to be thinking, her eyes looking up at the ceiling as she tried to remember.

Bob jumped in with another question. "What about someone who was interested in Samantha romantically? We heard there was a stalker. A Clyde something?"

Stacy's eyes grew wide. Bob had hit a nerve. "Oh yes. I forgot about that. Not Clyde, though. Clint! His name was Clint Fykes. He was a junior, and he was so weird. He always dressed in black and kept to himself. I don't think he ever had any friends. Anyway, he began hanging around Samantha and looking at her with these weird, creepy eyes of his. He really freaked everybody out."

Stacy's eyebrows scrunched together suddenly. "You don't think he had something to do with their deaths, do you? I do remember one time Jack and Hunter were going to go and tell him to back off. I don't know if they ever did, though."

I made a mental note of the name Clint Fykes. I would have Tim do a skip search on him ASAP. Unfortunately, I couldn't call him until after dinner.

I smiled at Stacy. "Thank you, Miss Hudson. You've been very helpful and I really appreciate it." I took a business card from the inside pocket of my jacket and handed it to Christopher. "And, I know we'll be able to chat again over dinner but, if either of you, at any time, remember anything else that you think might be helpful, please don't hesitate to call me."

Christopher Goodkind smiled coolly at me as he accepted the business card.

The butler, Sawyer, came back into the room and announced, "Jennifer and Mr. Young have arrived. Dinner is ready."

Walter rose from his chair. "Thank you, Sawyer. Well, I hope this little trip down memory lane has been helpful, detectives. I suggest we continue our conversation over dinner."

We all rose from our seats. Bob was smiling broadly. He

was obviously looking forward to an outstanding meal, and I have to admit, from the smell that was wafting in through the open dining room doors, so was I.

On top of that, I was especially excited at the prospect of being able to question everyone's favorite sister, Jennifer!

23

D inner was served in an ornate dining room overlooking the gardens where we were joined by Todd and Jennifer Young, bringing our somewhat eclectic group to seven.

Todd Young looked to be in his late forties. His otherwise brown hair already streaked with gray, he sported a close-cropped beard—that Hollywood scruffy look that's still popular today. He wore an Italian suit of a dusty, almost pastel blue color that I knew, even back then, must have set him back several thousand dollars, and a white, open-neck silk shirt over a heavy gold chain. The man, obviously an ass, affected a permanent expression of disdain and clearly considered himself to be slumming. He looked down his nose at everybody around him, Bob especially. Bob, however, simply grinned broadly at him, much to the man's annoyance.

I was pretty sure the only reason Jennifer had married the man was because of his money, that and the prestige that came from her supposedly wealthy and almost royal in-laws in

Canada. Having said that, I noticed pretty early in the evening that Walter Goodkind and Todd seemed to get along very well.

"You still fighting the good fight, my boy?" Walter asked Todd when we were halfway through the first course.

"Indeed I am." Todd spoke in a refined English, Oxford accent. "Several new opportunities have opened up for me along the North and South Carolina coastlines."

It was then that Stacy Hudson took on the role of tour guide for Bob and me. "Todd works in real estate," she whispered to us from across the table. "He builds condos and resorts. Things like that."

Todd overheard her and said, "Well, I'm not exactly a real estate mogul, but I do well enough with the opportunities available to me." The pretentious smirk on his face told me that he thought he was indeed such a mogul. Everything he said reeked of false modesty.

Jennifer, on the other hand, had barely said two words to me or Bob since they'd arrived. As she ate, she made a grand show of ignoring our presence completely. It seemed to me that she was playing some sort of game. If she was, it was a game I intended to win.

I looked across the table at Todd Young and said, "I'm sure Jennifer has already told you that we are investigating the death of her sister, Samantha. Did you know her, Mr. Young?"

Todd paused and put down his fork. "Indeed I did. Jennifer and I were engaged to be married when all the drama with that Flagg boy began. I must say I was very fond of Samantha. She was a friendly girl, and I always thought she had a bright future ahead of her."

I had to smile to myself when I saw Jennifer roll her eyes and look down at her meal. I don't think anyone else saw it, but it provided a little insight into their relationship. I figured all was not sweetness and light in the Young family.

"And what was your impression of Hunter Flagg?" Bob asked.

Todd affected a prideful frown. It was as if he'd just eaten something that had left a nasty taste in his mouth. "I didn't care for the boy at all. I didn't care for the family. What kind of name is Hunter anyway? I mean, is it supposed to impart some sort of Homeric... heroic... connotation? Personally, I find it... barbaric."

I heard Bob try to stifle a laugh, and I hoped no one else picked up on it.

"Oh, I think it's a nice name," Stacy said, much to Christopher's embarrassment. "Romantic..." She shut up when he nudged her with his elbow. But she wasn't done. She leaned forward as if she were going to whisper a secret, although she spoke loud enough for everyone at the table to hear, and said, "Todd and Jennifer didn't invite Hunter to their wedding. I remember there was a lot of drama over that!"

Jennifer put down her fork with a snap. "We had to draw the line somewhere," she said. "Invite the boy and the next thing you know, Samantha would have invited the entire Flagg clan. We would have become a laughingstock."

Just in case you might have thought that Jennifer was being overly dramatic, or even joking, you can put those thoughts to bed right now. She was serious, and, judging by Todd's expression, he agreed with her completely.

Now I was the one that wanted to roll my eyes.

"Oh, come on," Christopher said from the end of the table, where he'd been quiet the entire time. "Sam was happy. She loved him. Didn't any of you care about that?"

Walter Goodkind fixed his son with a hard stare from the other end of the table and said, "That had nothing to do with it. It was bad enough that you were off drinking with your writer friends. I wasn't going to have Samantha become a rebel as well."

"It wasn't being a rebel that got Sam killed," Chris fired back. "I never could get any of you to understand that! You all say you cared about her, but you all treated her like shit. You never gave them a chance, any of you."

With that, Christopher slammed his knife and fork down on the table, stood up, kicked his chair back and stormed out of the room, slamming the door behind him.

And silence descended over the table as everyone suddenly found new interest in their food. It was funny... at least I thought it was. You could have cut the tension with a knife, but then again, on thinking about it, a chainsaw would probably have been the better choice.

Bob and I briefly exchanged glances.

Now, I know that had I been the polite guest I should have been, I would have let things be. The atmosphere was already awkward enough, and I was aware that Sunday had been the anniversary of Samantha's death. But I wasn't there to be polite, nor did I intend to let things be. I had an unsolved murder on my hands, and I intended to do everything I could to get to the bottom of it. So I went ahead and opened my fat mouth.

"Jennifer," I said, as I busily went about cutting my roast beef, "we were just speaking with your father before you arrived about an act of domestic terrorism at the Chattanooga Police Department. Did you know that the police servers were hacked yesterday afternoon and all the files relating to your sister's murder were permanently deleted?"

I stopped cutting, my knife and fork suspended over my plate, looked up and locked eyes with her. If she was going to give anything away, that would have been the moment, and I didn't want to miss it.

And, just as I'd expected, she froze. All eyes were on her,

and she had to be aware of it. She stopped chewing, lowered her knife and fork, set them down on her plate, leaned back in her chair and stared at me. Behind her stare was a cold fire that would have sent chills down your spine, and I suddenly realized that Jennifer Goodkind-Young was a truly dangerous woman.

"No, I haven't heard about that," she said quietly, her eyes still locked on mine. "But then, why would I?"

I gave a little shrug. "Oh, I don't know. I was merely making conversation," I lied. "A point of interest, no more than that... You might also be interested to learn that the state police have been called in and are actively investigating the case, along with my own staff, and that we're close to finding the hacker responsible. We already know it was a professional, by the way. And when we catch him, I'm sure he will lead us to the person who hired him. I'm pretty sure that will bring us one step closer to finding your sister's killer. It's good news, isn't it?"

Jennifer paused once again, letting the seconds tick by in excruciating silence. "Yes, I suppose it is," she said and glanced at her father, who was looking right at her.

Talk about mixed signals! I still couldn't figure out who was covering for whom. Did Jennifer hire the hacker in order to cover for her father, or was it Walter covering for his daughter?

My gut feeling was telling me they were both involved somehow, but I still couldn't see either of them as killers. To be honest, the whole thing was kind of infuriating. I felt as if I was dancing around the answer, as if it was right there under my nose. It was frustrating as hell.

I decided it was time to back off, and I did, and the rest of the meal went by without incident or any more talk of the murders. The atmosphere lifted ten points, and by the time we were finished eating, the conversation was light and enjoyable. Christopher didn't return, and nobody, not even his fiancé, seemed to miss him. In fact, Stacy Hudson filled the gaps in the conversation by talking incessantly about their wedding plans, which led me to believe that she was the only one in that dysfunctional family with nothing to hide.

Either that, or she was a stone-cold killer and a sociopath to boot and could therefore deceive even God himself.

It might've been the good food, a perfectly cooked roast and vegetables, or it might've been the delicious, and obviously expensive, wine served with dinner, but, by the end of the meal, I was pretty sure I'd be useless for the rest of the evening.

After dinner, coffee was served in the lounge, but we didn't stay for it. We excused ourselves, thanking our host for a wonderful evening, and we stepped out onto the front porch. I checked my phone. I had a text from Kate: Henry Finkle wanted to talk to me, ASAP.

Great. That was just what I needed. An imperfect end to a perfect evening. Then again, perhaps he had new information. And I needed all the information I could get. I looked at the time. It was still early, almost nine, so I texted her back and told her I was on my way.

Out in the driveway, I spotted Christopher Goodkind sitting on the hood of his Audi, drinking some kind of liquor from a small bottle. He didn't look to be in a good mood. But, then again, who in that family ever looked to be in a good mood?

I told Bob good night and could tell by the way he hurried to his car that he was in a good enough mood to make up for everybody.

Before he did, however, I asked him if he was excited to be seeing Zoe.

Bob grinned at me. "You know it, boss. And before you ask, no, I'm not asking questions about the case. This is purely a social date."

"Well, take it easy, okay. She's just a kid, remember."

"She's twenty-six," he said. "Remember?" And with that he left me standing on the porch at the top of the steps.

Christopher Goodkind eyed me as I opened my car door. "I really hope you find Sam's killer," he said, his voice a little slurred. "It's long overdue, you know."

I stood for a second, looking at him, then said, "I'll try my best."

And I meant it! But, to tell you the truth, I was just excited to get away from that massive old house.

24

I had a lot to think about that evening as I drove down Lookout Mountain.

First of all, it was obvious to me that Walter Good-kind was responsible for the missing files, and that Jennifer Goodkind was somehow responsible for the hack. But more than that, she'd been acting even stranger over dinner than she had the day before at the Legacy offices. I was pretty sure she was hiding something else... but was that something murder?

Stacy Hudson had also provided me with two hot leads, even though she probably didn't realize it. First, it was obvious that Jack Sloan hadn't told us the whole truth. He didn't mention that he was best buddies with Hunter Flagg, and that they rode motorcycles together, and that made me wonder what else Mr. Sloan was hiding. And then, of course, there was Clint Fykes. From what Stacy had said, the guy should've been the prime suspect. I mean, a bona fide weirdo and Samantha Goodkind's stalker? Oh, we definitely had to chat with Mr. Fykes.

I called Tim, put my iPhone on speaker, and waited for him to answer, which he did on the second ring.

"Hey, Harry. How are you doing?" Tim's voice was bright and chipper.

"That's the question I should be asking you, Tim. How are you feeling?"

"Well, I got some good sleep today, so I'm feeling pretty good. Why? What d'you need?"

"Good, glad to hear it. Listen, Tim, I have somebody I need you to track down for me. His name is Clint Fykes."

"Fykes? That's a weird name. Can't be too many of them. Shouldn't be a problem."

"And if my sources are correct," I said, "the person behind the name is pretty weird, too. Just find out if he still lives in Chattanooga or if he's locked away somewhere."

"Geez, Harry. You expect the guy to be in jail? You haven't even talked to him yet."

"Just find him for me, please, Tim?"

"You got it. Oh, and I have some great news. I found the hacker who stole the files."

"Wow, that was fast. Good job, Tim."

"Oh, it was no big deal. Like I said before, the computers did all the hard work while I was zonked out. I was able to find a match for the tag. Would you like me to arrange a meeting?"

"You can do that?" I asked.

"Sure thing. We just pose as a new client looking for a hacker to do some work."

I have to admit that it had been a lot easier than I'd expected, but I wasn't about to complain.

"Okay, Tim. Yes, see if you can set it up, for later tonight, if you can. In the meantime, I have a date with Henry Finkle."

"Oh dear, that doesn't sound good. Good luck with that. I'll see what I can do and let you know."

I was feeling a whole lot better after Tim had hung up. I was going to get to talk to the hacker before the police did, and I was hopeful that he would lead me to the killer.

Little did I know there were still a few nasty surprises awaiting me!

25

The sun had long since set when I pulled into the police department parking lot that evening. Once again, Kate was waiting for me outside of the building.

Now, I didn't blame her for feeling that she had to protect me whenever I visited the PD. After all, even though I had been a cop for more than eight years, I didn't exactly leave the department on the best of terms. There were a number of people still there that didn't like me, and at the very top of that list was Henry "Tiny" Finkle. To say the man hated my guts is probably an understatement. Add to that the fact that he had long desired to hook up with Kate who was, at that point in my life, still very much my girl, and it was little wonder that Finkle and I didn't get along.

I was thinking about that as I walked up to Kate, and she must've noticed the smile on my face.

"You want to share the joke?" she asked, one eyebrow raised.

"I was just thinking how you're always waiting out here for me, as if you have to protect me from the Big Bad Wolf inside."

"Wolves, Harry. Plural. You're pretty good at making friends, I know, but you're even better at making enemies, and you sure as hell left a few behind in this building."

As we walked in together, I laughed and said, "Nah! Really? In the police department? I don't believe it."

"Believe it. This time, though, you're not in trouble. Go figure."

"I already figured," I said dryly.

Henry Finkle was waiting for us in his office, hunched over an old and dusty notebook, the pages yellowed with time. It was one of those narrow notebooks that flip open from the top and are small enough to fit in your pocket. The kind that cops and reporters used to love to use. Now they use miniature recorders and smartphones. Me? At the time I still used one. Not anymore, though.

He looked up as we stepped inside, a distant look in his eyes.

"Looks like you have some information for me," I said.

Finkle wasn't exactly in a good mood, but he wasn't angry at me either, which was a rare thing. He motioned to the chairs. "Starke, Gazzara, please have a seat."

And we did.

"It's a minor miracle," he began, "but I did find some of my old notes from the Flagg-Goodkind case. Well, just some of the messy, handwritten stuff that didn't make it into the evidence box."

I smiled and nodded. This, for me, was an entirely new experience: Henry Finkle, helpful instead of disruptive. I never thought I'd see the day.

"Let me walk you through some of the basics," he said, "and

then maybe I'll be able to answer your questions, now that my memory's been suitably jogged."

"Sounds good," I said.

"You already know about the murders themselves, so I won't bore you by repeating the details. The weapon, as you know... You did get the ME's report from DA Spruce, correct?"

I nodded.

"Then you know that the weapon was a 45. Probably a revolver, which is backed up by the fact that we never found casings at the scene. The gun was never found."

I took out my notebook and started scribbling. I didn't expect Finkle to hand over his personal notebook, especially since, right now, it was the only evidence that remained.

I looked up from my notes and said, "What about the bodies? Did you ever figure out if they were dumped or killed on site?" I know, I know. Finkle had said I could ask questions *after* he was done, of which he reminded me with a hard stare.

"No, and that's something you couldn't have gotten from the newspapers because we intentionally left it out of the press releases. We were certain they were killed on location, inside Hunter Flagg's truck. We found blood spatter on fragments of the driver's side window glass, on the pavement and on the grass. DNA determined the blood belonged to Hunter Flagg. The truck was never found."

I frowned as I chewed on that information.

"So the killer drove away with the truck?" I asked.

"Quite obviously," Finkle said dryly.

"Speaking of the truck," he continued. "We found a single tire track, just a couple of feet long, just off the pavement. It looked, according to Detective Monk, like the killer left in a hurry and ran off the paved section. Just a couple of feet, or so, but enough... They were the only tire tracks found, so we figured the killer either rode with them or approached on foot after they parked. Monk even looked into the possibility of an accomplice. Someone that might've parked a second vehicle some distance away, and then followed the killer when he drove off. If there was a second vehicle—and we don't know that there was—and it stayed on the road, there wouldn't have been any tracks."

I wrote down the details of what Finkle was saying. Bob and I had considered several possibilities both times we visited the site, but I hadn't thought about the possibility of an accomplice and a second vehicle. That possibility brought up a whole new list of questions, and would change the way I would have to look at the various suspects. It was something I'd have to chew on later, because Finkle continued with his debriefing.

"The fact that the victims were found disrobed, and there was no evidence of sexual abuse, were also details we didn't release to the press. We're also pretty sure that they were killed with their clothes on based on the lack of GSR around the wounds."

I looked up at Finkle, trying to piece together what it all meant. It made sense. If they had been shot while they were naked, blood would've seeped out of the gunshot wounds and stained the skin in a very specific way. But if they'd been wearing clothes when they were shot, the material would've soaked up the blood. The skin would still have been stained, underneath the clothing, but in a different way.

I nodded, and Finkle smiled, knowing that I was right with him, thinking on the same wavelength. What a scary thought! Me thinking like Henry Finkle? Just the idea of it was enough to drive me to drink.

"Those are the main points I can remember and decipher from my notes right now," Finkle said. "Now, do you have any questions for me, Starke, Catherine?"

I scanned up to the large note I had put in my notebook.

"Yeah, actually. How about the bullet that would've gone into the trees? Did you ever find it?"

Finkle looked up at the ceiling, as if trying to recall. But he also looked a little confused. Maybe I needed to give him more information.

"Well, you said there was broken glass on the pavement. So I'm just thinking, if a bullet exited the vehicle, where did it go? Surely you guys thought about that."

Finkle scowled. "Of course we thought about it. CSI spent days searching the trees on the riverbank. D'you have any idea of the odds against finding it? There weren't that many trees on that side of the road. So, no, we never found that bullet..."

He had a sudden thought. "You don't suppose it could have made it across the river, do you? No, not a chance," he said, answering his own question. "We were, however, able to run ballistics on the other bullet, but it was too badly damaged, inconclusive. Other than it was a .45, Willis wasn't able to determine the type or the make of the weapon."

I marked out the question from my notebook, a little disappointed. If that bullet had been found, it might've told us something about the angle of the shot, and maybe even the height of the shooter. Why might that be important? There was enough of a difference in height between Walter Goodkind and his daughter Jennifer, for example, to provide us with a hint as to who might have fired the fatal shots.

"One more thing," Finkle added. "Both kids were shot at a very close range. With such a large weapon being used, we were lucky that any of the bullets stayed in their bodies. But, we were pretty sure the killer stood right at the open passenger-side door. Unfortunately, there were no footprints, which means either the killer got lucky, or he knows how to cover his tracks."

Kate raised her eyebrows. "You're not saying you think it was a professional hit, are you? An assassin?"

Under normal circumstances, that would've been a pretty dumb question to ask. But, in this case we were dealing with extremely wealthy suspects, so the possibility of a hitman wasn't all that far-fetched.

I felt my phone vibrating in my pocket. I ignored it.

"We didn't think so at the time," Finkle said, shaking his head. "But I suppose it's a possibility. That's your problem now, Starke."

I smiled and nodded. "It sure is, but thanks for the information... Look, Henry, I need to talk to Charlie Monk. Can you set that up for me?"

"I can, but it won't do you any good. He's in the final stages of Alzheimer's. He doesn't recognize anyone, not even his wife. I went to see him a couple of weeks ago. He's in a nursing home, you know. Didn't recognize me. Just sat there staring out of the window. Sad, very sad... I'll talk to his wife, if you like. I'm sure she wouldn't mind you dropping in to see him."

I was surprised. I didn't think Finkle had a sympathetic bone in his body, but he sounded genuinely sorry for the man.

"Let me think on it, Henry. I've seen it before. If he's that far gone... well... Are we done?"

"Not quite," Kate said. "I have a few things I'd like to share, as well. Internal Affairs reached out to me to see how the case is proceeding. It appears Lieutenant Vasquez is interested to know if you're any closer to finding the hacker, Harry."

I rubbed the back of my neck with my hand. "Well, my team's on it, as you know, and Tim's making some progress, but I don't think we're exactly closing in on a suspect just yet. I'll keep you posted."

Kate looked hard at me, her eyes narrowed. Finkle was also giving me the evil eye. If I'd still been a cop, they would've ordered me to spill my guts right there. But I didn't work for Henry Finkle or Lieutenant Vasquez, or for Kate. So, as an independent third party, I could keep things a little closer to the vest, as they say, even though I knew it vexed the Chattanooga Police Department greatly. *When they start signing my paychecks again, maybe I'll start playing by the rules. But I'll need a pretty damn thick jacket because hell will have frozen over.*

"Anyway, Lieutenant Vasquez gave me a couple of updates," Kate continued. "It's still too early to officially call it, but she thinks it's unlikely that we'll ever know who took the missing files and evidence box. Exactly when they were taken is unknown. It could've happened years ago, and anyone could've paid off some low-level cop. After the case was shelved in 1999, nothing was ever signed out. The investigation was, for all intents and purposes, closed. They viewed it as a dead end."

I nodded. It was what I'd been expecting.

My damn phone was vibrating again. I put my hand in my pocket and turned it off.

"And I wish I could say that the Tennessee state police Cybercrimes unit has high hopes about finding the hacker, but so far they've found nothing. They intend to keep digging, of course. I would imagine it's a point of personal pride for them."

Kate and I exchanged knowing glances. I hadn't told Kate yet what Tim had said, but she already knew he was on the case and, since Kate is a pretty smart woman, she knew that if anyone could find the hacker, he could. She just didn't know that he already had.

The Tennessee state police are professionals of the first order, and I have great respect for them, but they don't have anyone that can match Tim's abilities. He truly is one in a million.

Finkle rapped the desk with his knuckles. "Well, I suppose that's all, for now. Please keep us posted, Harry... Look, I know you're one to keep things to yourself. That's always been your MO, but when you feel the temptation to do that, just remember that I shared what I had with you."

I grinned. "Don't worry, Henry. I won't forget it."

Finkle nodded and, with a wave of his hand, dismissed us. Kate walked with me out to the parking lot.

"Now that we're out of earshot, I know you have Tim working on it," Kate said. "And while I understand your reluctance to share anything with Finkle, you'd damn well better share *everything* with me, Harry. Has the kid found the hacker?"

I looked at her, my face serious, expressionless, then I couldn't help myself. I smiled and said, "He didn't just find the hacker, Kate. He's arranging a meeting." My phone vibrated again. I took it from my pocket, looking at the screen, opened the message, read it and smiled.

Kate's mouth actually fell open. "A meeting? With the hacker? You're kidding, right?"

"Not at all." I turned the phone so she could see the message. "In half an hour, it turns out. You want to come?"

I needed a partner to go with me, and Bob wasn't available.

"You bet your a... Yes, of course. Where is..." Up to that point, Kate had been smiling, but the smile disappeared when she read the rest of Tim's message.

"Oh come on, Harry! Anywhere but there."

I smiled, opened the car door for her and said, "In you get, my love. We're going to the Sorbonne!"

26

I couldn't help but smile as we drove downtown and found a parking spot on Prospect Street behind the Sorbonne. Kate, I could tell, was already dreading the experience she was about to be put through. But what can I say? Criminals of all caliber like to use the Sorbonne as their meeting place. And, sleazy as it is, Benny and Laura run a tight ship and can be relied upon to keep their mouths shut... most of the time. Benny can be a little susceptible to pressure. All that considered, where else would our hacker want to meet?

As we walked into the establishment through the rear door, Kate shot me a disapproving look and whispered, "You don't have to enjoy this, you know. Just because *you* love to patronize a place that's dirty and loud and smells like a public restroom doesn't mean I have to enjoy it."

I put up my hands in defense. "Hey, I didn't arrange this meeting. The hacker did. Or... perhaps Tim did."

"Yes, him, I bet. Tim knows you better than you think, and I'm sure he assumed you'd want to meet the hacker in Satan's kitchen."

I didn't have anything to say to that. Hell, she was probably right.

We were in the corridor, by the restrooms, when she put a hand on my arm and stopped me. "Look," she said. "The least you can do is catch me up on what I need to know before we get in there and won't be able to hear each other think. Listen to it, for God's sake."

I nodded, took out my phone, and reviewed the few details Tim had included in the text message.

"The hacker goes by the name Iron Crusader. Tim doesn't know much more about him, except that he's an up-and-coming freelance hacker with an already impressive reputation. That's it. That's all there is."

"Oh-kay," Kate said. She drew the word out. She was skeptical, I could tell. "And how are we supposed to recognize this... Iron Crusader?"

I shrugged. "Tim said he would recognize us. We're a couple of minutes early, so I guess we'll just have to see what happens when he walks in. You know these hacker types, Kate. Who the hell knows what to expect?"

Kate gave me a sarcastic look, then took the lead, continued along the corridor, pushed open the barroom door and swept inside like an avenging angel.

The music was indeed loud, but I'd known it louder. It wasn't anything I enjoyed, just that rapper crap the kids like to listen to.

We found a booth at the far end of the bar with a view of both doors and settled in to wait.

To my surprise, Benny Hinkle was walking the tables, chatting with his customers. "Well, would you look at that?" I muttered, more to myself than to Kate.

"Look at what?" Kate asked, leaning in close to me to avoid shouting over the music.

"Benny. That's what. It's still early. He never comes out of his office until after midnight," I said. "Must be a full moon or something."

Benny looked around the room, smiling, made eye contact with me, lost the smile, turned quickly and then retreated back to whence he'd come. Other than losing the smile, he gave no indication that he'd recognized me, which told me he was probably doing something illegal.

But, hey! I wasn't a cop anymore, so as long as it didn't involve me or the case I was working on, I really didn't care. Besides, he never got involved in anything too heavy and, every once in a while, I was able to squeeze him for information. So, you see, he was much more useful to me sitting on his fat butt in his office and working his little deals than he ever could be behind bars.

Laura came out from behind the bar, exchanged some small talk with Kate—now Kate, for some reason she's never explained, did like Laura—and she took our order for drinks. I had a beer and Kate a Sprite with a lemon wedge on the side, and we continued to wait for our hacker. Fortunately, we didn't have to wait long for the Iron Crusader.

Just knowing the handle this hacker used, you probably have a specific image in mind of what he looked like. I certainly did. But whatever image you have, let me assure you, you're dead wrong.

First of all, the person who approached our table that night wasn't a guy at all. It was a girl, and she looked barely old enough to be in the place. I had an eerie feeling I was looking at a female version of Tim. She was wearing what looked an awful lot like a schoolgirl's outfit, complete with a short plaid skirt, a navy cardigan over a white blouse and... yes, frickin' pigtails. As she wove her way across the room, she had to pass by a number of men. Many of them were big guys, bikers with criminal records, who gave her hungry, even threatening looks. But this girl's "get the hell away from me" stare was so ferocious that many of them suddenly seemed to find something else to look at. But it wasn't just her look that put them off; she was also wearing a pair of leather bracelets on her wrists, each with multiple, three-inch-long steel spikes protruding from the back of her wrists. This girl was dangerous. One back-hand swipe and she could spoil a man's looks for life.

She also had a black backpack slung over one shoulder and when she arrived at the booth, she plonked it onto the table and sat down facing us.

"And you are...?" Kate asked.

"Okay, so I don't normally meet in person," she said, "but I was told the job would be worth it. So what d'you need me to do, and how much are you willing to pay? I'll let you know if your offer is reasonable or not."

Kate and I exchanged glances.

"You're Iron Crusader?" I asked. I was trying to hide my surprise.

The girl ignored the question, unzipped her backpack and took out a silver laptop which was—and I swear I'm telling you the truth—covered with Hello Kitty stickers.

"I may not look the part, but I can get the job done. So what do you need? Information? Identity theft? What?"

I don't know about Kate, but I almost broke out laughing. I didn't know how long the girl had been in the hacking business, but she'd all but confessed to multiple cybercrimes, and in front of a cop. She had a lot to learn.

"I think maybe you have the wrong idea," I said, speaking slowly. "We're not here to hire you. We're looking for information."

"Okay. That's it. I'm outta here."

"Wait," I said sharply. "Just sit still for a minute and listen. All we want is information about a job you did yesterday."

The girl looked at me and then at Kate, then at me again. The hard exterior she had worn from the moment she entered the place faltered a little. She was nervous. I could see it in her eyes.

"Who the hell are you guys?"

"My name is Harry Starke. I'm a private investigator. And this is Lieutenant Kate Gazzara."

The girl's eyes got suddenly very wide and she said, "*Lieutenant?* You're a cop. Oh man, I'm so outta here." And she half stood up, but Kate raised a hand, and she paused, both hands on the table as if she was about to leap over it.

"Look, yes, I am a cop, but I'm not here to arrest you. I couldn't if I wanted to. The way we found you isn't exactly aboveboard. So, please, sit down and listen to what Harry has to say."

And she did, slowly, cautiously, like a wary cat.

I nodded at Kate, silently thanking her. She was right. She couldn't take the girl in, not without getting Tim, and me, in a lot of trouble.

I leaned forward on my elbows and said, "Look, she's telling you the truth. We're not trying to get you into trouble, Miss... I can't call you Iron Crusader."

"You don't have to call me anything. Just talk, okay? I'll listen, but that's all."

"Okay, fine," I said. "All we're interested in is the job you did yesterday. Someone hired you to delete some files from the Chattanooga Police Department system. You don't have to confirm that you did it, but you should know that the person who hired you is a murderer. We need to know who that person is."

The girl tapped her fingertips on her laptop and audibly gulped. "A murderer? You mean my client killed somebody?"

"Two somebodies," Kate said.

"Yes," I said. "So who hired you? Give us the name and you'll never see us again, I promise."

The girl looked back and forth from me to Kate several times, seemingly weighing her options. She knew we had her. Her career as a freelance hacker was over, at least in Chattanooga, but would she help us catch a killer?

Finally, she shook her head, sighed and said, "I wish I could help you guys. Really, I do. Whew, it's really bad for business to break a client's confidence... but murder? I don't want anything to do with that."

I smiled. Was she really about to tell us?

"But, to tell you the truth," she continued, bringing me down with a thud, "I don't know who hired me. That's not how things are set up in the forums where I get my work. Someone posts a job, you do the job, and they pay you. It's all set up so nobody knows anything about anybody."

Damn it! Another dead end.

"I can tell you this, though," the girl continued. "I was offered ten thousand dollars to do the job, fifteen if I could do the job immediately, which I did, and I was paid in full, in cash, at a dead drop. It was the biggest job I've done so far!"

For a moment, she looked proud of herself, like a kid who'd just gotten an A in math.

"Fifteen thousand, huh?" I looked at her through narrowed eyes.

She shrugged and said, "Yep, sorry!"

I continued to stare at her. I was screwed.

"Look, I need to go," she said. "I have a lot of work to do, and since you're not offering me a job, I really need to get going."

The girl wasn't asking for permission, and before I had time to respond, she was up and away, weaving her way to the front door, attracting a lot of attention along the way.

I leaned back in my seat. I have to admit I was more than a little disappointed.

"Cheer up, Harry," Kate said. "It's not all bad... At least we have a number. Can Tim work with that?"

I sighed and said, "I guess so."

I finished my beer and was just about to suggest we leave and go somewhere a little bit nicer, my condo, in fact, when Ronnie walked in. He saw us right away and joined us. He sat down on the bench so recently vacated by the Iron Crusader.

"Hey, Ronnie," I said. "You here to play some poker?"

"I am. As you know, there's nothing I like better than relieving the mugs of their hard-earned money. What are you guys doing here?"

Kate answered for me. "We just interviewed the hacker who deleted the case files from the PD's system. We were hoping to get a name, but she didn't have one."

Ronnie glanced at the door and said, "You mean the school-girl with the black backpack that just walked out of here? She's the hacker?"

"That's right," I said. "And a good one, so it seems. Unfortunately, all she could tell us was how much she was paid for the job. Fifteen thousand, in cash."

"Well, that's something," Ronnie said. "It helps us to narrow things down a bit."

I raised an eyebrow. "How d'you mean?"

"Well, not all of the people involved in this case would be able to afford that kind of money, especially in cash, and especially on short notice."

"Walter Goodkind could afford it," Kate said.

I nodded. "Yeah, so could Jennifer Young."

"Danny Flagg could afford it too," Ronnie said, stroking his chin. "He's only been in charge of that diesel repair business for a few months, and he's already turning a pretty good profit. I think that's partially because he started repairing motorcycles at the shop in addition to diesel engines. He's working night and day."

I thought about that for a few seconds. I hadn't realized Danny Flagg would have that much cash lying around. And my mind immediately turned to motive. He couldn't have been the killer because he was in jail. I shook my head. Those were thoughts for another time.

I looked at Ronnie, smiled, and said, "Thanks, Ronnie."

Ronnie waved the idea away. "Don't mention it, boss. I'm glad to help. Why don't you have Tim look at the bank records of the prime suspects, see if there's been any big cash withdrawals? I'd do it myself, but I'm not a hacker. Gotta go, boss. My fingers are itching."

And he did. And Kate and I decided to head out too.

We were in the car, about to join Highway 27, when Tim called. I put him on speaker and drove up the on-ramp heading south.

"Hey, Harry. You'll never believe what I found out about Clint Fykes."

"That was fast. Lay it on me, Tim."

"The guy has a record. And not just any record. We're talking about big stuff. He's been involved in armed robberies and drug smuggling. He's always managed to slip through the net, though, without doing any serious hard time, but the guy is no stranger to a jail cell."

"That's good news. We need to talk to him. Where can we find him?"

"I thought you might ask that, so I'm sending you his last known address."

That was perfect. "Okay, that'll give me something to do in the morning."

"I guess your meeting with Iron Crusader didn't go so well, right?"

I frowned. "How did you know that?"

"Well, he just burned his handle on the dark web. He doesn't exist anymore, Harry. He's a ghost."

Wow, that was fast! "Actually, Tim, he is a she, and she isn't even as old as you. But how could she just fold her business so quickly? She said she had more work to do tonight."

"Harry, these people have multiple handles. If they have to burn one, they slip right on into another. It's kind of like the avatar version of using shell companies to hide your cash. And talking about cash. Did she by any chance tell you how much she got paid?"

"She said fifteen thousand."

"That's a nice round number. You want me to do a little digging... and see what I can come up with?"

"Yeah, okay, but stay out of trouble. I'll talk to you later. Thanks for the information, Tim."

"So maybe the dead end is not so dead after all," Kate said as I hit the gas and the car surged forward from twenty to seventy in the blink of an eye.

"Maybe not," I said. "We'll see."

"So what's next? We visit this Clint Fykes guy tomorrow morning?"

"That's the plan. You coming with me? If not, I'll take Bob."

Kate smiled as we drove down the street. "Of course I am. Wouldn't miss it for the world."

"I know one thing, Kate."

"What's that, Harry?" She put a hand on my leg.

"I know that we need a break, get our minds off of the case and on to something a little more exciting."

"Something more exciting? Like what?" She slid her hand along my thigh.

I didn't have to answer, of course.

27

As usual, I rose early the next morning. I made coffee and stepped out onto the patio to drink it. It was still dark, but the sky was clear, the air was cool and the river was covered in a blanket of fog. Dressed only in boxers, I shivered and went back inside and sat down to watch the news. Kate joined me a few minutes later, and we spent a few quiet moments together before I made breakfast and she made ready to leave.

She always kept a change of clothes at my condo, so she didn't have to run home before going to work. She did, however, need to go to the PD to check in with Henry, so I sent her off with a cup of coffee and a promise that I'd pick her up at nine-thirty. She hadn't been gone long, though, when she called and said that something had come up, something unrelated and that I was to go on without her. So I called Bob and told him I'd pick him up in an hour. Then I set about sorting through the stuff Tim had sent me concerning Clint Fykes.

There was a lot to process. Fykes, as Tim had said, had been arrested more than a dozen times on various charges. He'd been in prison a couple of times, but he'd never gotten into anything deep enough to get locked up for long. Was that about to change? I wondered.

I drove to my offices to pick up Bob, but I didn't go in. I didn't want to get caught up in the daily, early morning minutia, so I called him from the parking lot and told him I was outside. He came out through the side door moments later with a huge smile on his face.

"I take it all went well last night?" I said as he climbed into my Maxima.

"Not like you think. We had drinks and talked. That's all. It was kinda nice."

I fixed him with a stare, raised my eyebrows. "Really? You just talked?" I said as I pulled out onto Georgia.

"What can I say? She's a nice girl. We really hit it off, though, Harry."

"Okay," I said, not really interested in hearing about his exploits.

"I'll tell you one thing," he said. "She's ambitious. She said her family never had a lot when she was growing up, and that she always wanted more, you know? So, after she graduated high school, she lit out on her own, worked her way through college and earned a bachelor's degree in business administration. She's going places, Harry."

"And now she's a secretary at Legacy Health," I said. "Doesn't seem like much of a step up, does it?"

"Geez, Harry, give the girl a break. She studies on weekends. Says she's going to be a bankruptcy lawyer. Maybe we'll be working for her one of these days."

"Hey, if she can afford us, I'll be glad to help!"

Bob tapped his hands on his knees, humming a song at the same time, then stopped and said, "Say, Harry, what's with this stalker kid anyway? Aren't we pretty sure it was either Walter or Jennifer? I mean, I read your messages last night about the hacker, and look at how they behaved at dinner last night. It all makes sense, doesn't it?"

"Sure, it does," I said. "But we're looking for the truth, Bob, not just a story that makes sense."

"I don't follow."

"Okay, what if that's why the case went unsolved in the first place? Henry Finkle and Monk were sure Walter was the murderer, right? So what if they overlooked the basics, and other important details, because of their bias? I don't want to make the same mistake."

Bob seemed to chew on that. "But what about the hack? Do you think this Fykes guy somehow got wind of the investigation on Monday and hired the hacker?"

"Of course I don't. Fykes had nothing to do with the hack."

"Then how can he be the killer?"

"Geez, Bob." I sounded irritated, but, to tell the truth, he was asking legitimate questions. "First of all, Goodkind and his daughter don't know about Fykes. Second, we don't know if Fykes is the killer, but we're sure as hell going to cover all our bases."

He thought about that for a minute, then said, "Right... but I'm not sure I'm following you."

"Think about it. The person that paid for the hack doesn't have to be the same person that murdered Hunter and Samantha."

Bob frowned. "I don't follow."

"Okay, what do we know about Jennifer Young and Walter Goodkind?"

"That they're covering for each other?" he asked.

"Right," I said. "So let's say Jennifer's covering for her father. She suspects her dad killed her sister. She knows we're investigating the murders so she's afraid Walter will be convicted."

"Okay, I'm following you."

"So, Jennifer hires a hacker to delete those files, on an impulse. But what if Walter didn't do it? Jennifer thinks he did, but maybe it was Fykes.

"Now," I continued, "suppose Walter is thinking exactly the same thing Jennifer is, that she's the killer. Talk about the blind leading the blind."

Bob was nodding. "Okay, I see what you're saying. It's still one hell of a stretch, though, Harry."

Boy did I ever know it! It seemed to me to be pretty likely that someone in the two families was guilty, and all I could think of was that it had to be either Walter or Jennifer, but we had to be thorough.

Fykes could have been the key to the whole case, for all I knew. And then there was Jack Sloan, who'd apparently lied about how well he knew Hunter Flagg.

So, Fykes first, then Sloan.

Little did we know that first house call would almost cost us our lives!

28

Clint Fykes lived in a trailer off Igou Gap Road surrounded by old-growth trees, many of which were in desperate need of trimming. The trailer was old. The siding, once dark brown, had peeled and faded, and there must have been a ton of dead and rotting leaves on the roof. The wooden steps that led to the tiny deck in front of the door had a decided tilt to the left.

I stopped the car in front of the trailer. We looked at each other.

"You sure you want to do this?" Bob asked. "That place stinks."

"How would you know that?" I asked. "The windows are up and you haven't left the car yet."

"Come on, Harry. I can tell just by looking at it."

I smiled. He was right, of course, but we had to go knock anyway.

"Let's go," I said. Then, I felt a tingle on the back of my neck. My instincts were kicking in again.

"Let's do this," I said, opening my door. "And, Bob, be ready for anything. I have a bad feeling about this."

Bob was wearing a light jacket, perfect for the cool spring morning. He patted the spot where he kept his gun, in an under-arm holster, much like mine.

"I'm always ready, boss."

I nodded.

We got out of the car and my first thought was that Bob had been right. The trailer smelled of rot and wet dog.

As we walked toward the steps, I had that same tingling feeling, this time in the pit of my stomach. It was so strong I almost changed my mind and told Bob to get back in the car.

But I didn't. Instead, we walked right on up those rickety steps, Bob leading the way, and onto the small deck. He seemed in a hurry to get the interview over with... as was I.

We stood on the deck for a second or two before knocking. I could smell something strange, a noxious chemical smell, almost like nail polish remover.

I should have put it together right away, but I didn't. Blame it on lack of sleep. Or maybe I'd made the coffee too weak that morning. Or maybe I was just too distracted, but, as Bob pounded on the door, sounding an awful lot like a cop, I suddenly realized what it was. You don't work as a cop for eight years and not be able to recognize the stink of a meth lab.

I looked at Bob. He looked back at me and nodded; he'd figured it out, too.

That's when we heard a sharp click on the other side of the door.

"Watch out!" I yelled. Bob was already jumping and ducking to the side, even as I leaped to the other.

The thunderous boom filled my ears, and a round hole appeared in the door and pieces of it exploded outward.

I was on my knees, my gun in my hand. Bob the same, in

sync with me. We each fired two shots through the door. Then we heard running and shouting inside the trailer.

"Let's get the hell out of here!" someone shouted.

A door slammed around the back.

I looked at Bob and said, "Front or back?"

He smiled. "Back."

I nodded. In a flash, he turned and jumped over the deck rail, then ran around the end of the trailer. An engine roared. Someone was about to leave in a hurry.

I looked at the front door, took a deep breath and, gun in hand... that's when I heard another sharp click inside the trailer.

I raised my gun and fired!

29

The rules of engagement for a police officer are strict, and they vary from state to state and jurisdiction to jurisdiction. But that didn't matter to me. I was no longer a cop. I could fire back in self-defense, and I know today that if I'd pulled the trigger a split-second later, I'd have been shot.

Instead, I fired first. I heard someone yelp and then a shotgun blast. Because the shooter had apparently been hit, however, the blast blew a hole in the top right corner of the door, the pellets and shards of wood hammering into the roof overhead, missing me by a good three feet.

I didn't wait for the shooter to fire again. I charged the door with my shoulder. The flimsy panel, already in tatters, shattered inward as I ran through it, slamming into a figure on the other side.

The guy let out a screech as I smacked him upside the head with the barrel of my gun. I slammed the gun down on his arm, forcing him to squeal and drop the shotgun. I kicked it away and stuck the muzzle of my weapon hard under his chin. Only then did I see the guy's face.

Hello, Clint Fykes!

Outside, I heard an engine thundering around the back of the trailer, and then a flurry of gunshots, and I recognized the boom of Bob's .45. Suddenly, there was a loud crash and the truck's engine died.

I grabbed Fykes by the collar and hauled him to his feet. Not a difficult task since he'd had all the fight knocked out of him.

He was a wild-looking individual with a mop of greasy, black curly hair, so slick that a single spark could have set it on fire. On his pale, gaunt face he had the beginnings of a wispy black mustache. He was thin, scrawny, with a confederate flag tattooed on his right bicep, if you could call it a bicep; the man was seriously undernourished. The meth-head look was completed by a pair of filthy jeans and a worn-out leather vest over a bare and boney chest.

"You're hurting me!" he whined as I twisted his arm up his back and shoved the muzzle of my S&W into his ear, then hauled him through the destroyed front door and out onto the deck. "Cops ain't allowed to do that!"

"Good thing I'm not a cop, then, huh?" I said. "So, sit the hell down!"

I kicked the back of his knee, forcing him down onto the steps. I looked him over. Had I shot him? Nope. It turned out that my bullet had hit the wall beside him and some of the wood paneling had splintered in his face. Lucky shot, I guess.

I looked around for Bob. The pickup truck had collided with the trunk of one of the old trees, hitting it hard enough for a long-dead limb to fall off and smash through the windshield. Bob had two guys sitting on the grass beside the truck with their hands up. He grinned at me.

"I think I need some range time, Harry," he shouted. "Took me three shots to blow one of the tires. What you got there?" He took a step forward, looked at Fykes and said, "Hey, is that our guy?" and then he stepped back again, his 1911 waving threateningly in the faces of the two heroes.

"Sure is," I said with a nod. "Ain't he something, though? He thinks he's being abused."

Bob grinned up at me and said, "You want to trade places? I'll give him something to whine about."

The two rednecks on the grass looked at Clint accusingly. Clint's eyes widened.

"You came for me?" he asked in feigned disbelief. "Why? I didn't do nothin'."

I frowned down at him. "Really? You frickin' shot at me, you crazy son of a bitch. Twice! That's going to put you away for a long time, Clint."

I looked around again. Neighbors were standing out in their front yards or on their porches, watching.

"Did anyone call the police before coming out to gawk?" I shouted.

An old man standing in front of the house next door raised a white wireless phone with a telescopic antenna. I hadn't seen one like it in more than twenty years.

"I did, sir. You bet your ass I did. About time we got those punks out of there!"

I nodded at the old man and turned back to Clint, then sat down on the top step beside him.

"Mr. Fykes, I have some questions for you."

Clint's shoulders slumped comically.

He knew he was done for. But were we going to add a fourteen-year-old double murder to his growing rap sheet?

That's what I aimed to find out!

30

I watched all three rednecks while Bob quickly cleared the inside of the trailer and its perimeter to make sure no one else was hiding from us. The last thing I needed was another surprise shotgun blast. It turned out, however, that the three lugheads were alone in the trailer. Bob returned a few minutes later to keep an eye on the two from the truck, while I had a little heart-to-heart with Doc Holiday.

Fykes was shaking violently. Whether that was from nerves or from some kind of drug addiction, I couldn't be sure. Either way, he was definitely uncomfortable, and the police sirens screaming in the distance didn't improve his mood at all.

"I just don't get it, man," he said, almost as if he was talking to himself. "Why would you come looking for me? I ain't done nothing. I'm clean as a whistle!"

I decided not to bring up the fact again that he'd just shot at us twice and was actively operating a meth lab. Instead, I took out my iPhone and sent Kate a text message.

"Clint," I said. "It's unfortunate for you that I found you cooking meth, and it's even more unfortunate that you shot at my partner and me. Suppose, just for a minute, that I'd been a little Girl Scout selling cookies. You'd be going down for life without parole... The sad thing is that if you'd just been a reasonable, greasy little shit and answered my questions, we would've left you alone in your kitchen. As it is, my friend, you're looking at five-to-ten, maybe more."

Fykes' eyes were wide, and he kept looking over his shoulder at his two buddies. I'd made sure they couldn't hear what I was saying to him. I figured if it looked like he was snitching, he might be a little more inclined to talk. After all, they already knew just how much trouble they were in, and all because of Clint's itchy trigger finger. That being so... well, let's just say that Mr. Fykes was going to need friends in prison much more than he needed enemies.

"Questions? What kind of questions?" Clint's eyes slanted, and I could almost see the wheels turning beneath that mop of greasy hair. They were rusty wheels, mind you, but they were turning, nonetheless. "Say, maybe we can make a deal?" he said. "How about I answer your questions and you forget all about me trying to shoot you? What do you say about that, huh?"

"Now you listen to me real carefully, Clint," I said quietly. "You think you have a bargaining chip, but you don't. I'll tell you what, though. You answer my questions truthfully, and I won't press charges. How does that sound?"

He nodded slowly, then craned his neck to look at Bob. "What about him? You think he'll drop the charges too?"

"I can't force him to do anything. But I might be able to persuade him. He had a hot date last night, so he's in a good mood. Let's just say that might play in your favor."

Clint nodded vigorously. "Okay. So what are your questions all about?"

"Samantha Goodkind and Hunter Flagg. You remember them?"

Clint's eyes narrowed. For a minute I thought he didn't know what the hell I was talking about. Then he got it. His face lit up and he actually smiled. "You mean those kids that was killed back in high school? Yeah, I remember, but why do you want to ask me..."

His eyes suddenly widened. I fixed him with a narrow stare and he started shaking his head.

"Oh no. No, no, NO! Don't you even think you can hang that on me. Look, I might have done some bad shit over the years, and my daddy sure as hell slapped me around for it, an' the prison therapist said that he was the start of a lot of my troubles, but I never killed nobody. Hell, even if I'd clipped you with my shotgun, you wouldn't have died. It's just a little birdshot, and most of it was stopped by the door!"

I wasn't about to argue the technicalities of ballistics with this knucklehead, especially as the police sirens were getting closer. Even if Kate had managed to get hold of the officers in those cruisers, I couldn't be sure they'd let me finish my conversation with him before they arrested all three of them. So I decided to cut right to the chase.

"Clint, I have a dozen witnesses that say you were stalking Samantha Goodkind. What do you have to say about that?"

Again, Clint shook his head enthusiastically. "It was never like that, I promise. Look, I was just a kid. I was younger than her, see? And, I mean... well look at me! It's not like I ever got a lot of girls. And Samantha was real pretty, like. So, I guess I had kind of a crush on her or something. But I never stalked her. I can promise you that! I had some friends in her neighborhood and would sometimes walk by her house, is all."

"Clint, you and I both know you never had any friends up on Lookout Mountain. Now, you want me to press charges on you or not? You've got about forty-five seconds to tell me the truth. Once the police get here, it'll be out of my hands."

"Okay, okay! I didn't have no friends up on the mountain. So sometimes when I was walking around up there... I'd just look through the window or something, you know. It was just horny teenager stuff. Weren't you ever a teenager? Didn't you never do stuff that weren't exactly correct because of hormones and whatnot?"

The man was scared, and, even though it surprised me that he even knew the word hormone, I believed what he was saying. Clint Fykes just didn't seem like the killer type to me. I stared long and hard at him, hoping to intimidate him and force the truth out of him, but I was beginning to think it was a lost cause—we'd been shot at for nothing—and then:

"Besides," he said, starting to stammer as the first of the police cruisers came screeching to a halt behind my Maxima, "I'd never mess with Samantha; her boyfriend would've killed me dead, and he would've done it with a lot more than some frickin' birdshot!"

I frowned. "Are you talking about Jack Sloan or Hunter Flagg?"

"Hunter, o' course. He was bad news, man. Everybody knew it. He and his brother used to pull these jobs, see? Stealing stuff and then selling it off. And the word around town was that Hunter had gotten his brother in big trouble. He messed up bad and Danny Flagg went to prison for it."

He was talking faster and faster, as Bob started a conversation with the police officers who were now out of their cruiser, weapons drawn.

"After Danny went away," he continued, "that's when Jack and Hunter started hanging out together. I was sure Jack Sloan was helpin' Hunter pull another job, but they kept it really hush-hush."

"Mr. Starke," one of the officers said as he walked to the bottom of the steps. "Lieutenant Gazzara contacted us and told us to tell you you'll have an opportunity to continue speaking with these three gentlemen when we have 'em in holding. In the meantime, sir, we need statements from you and Mr. Ryan."

I turned to the police officer, a young guy with a black goatee. I recognized his face, but I couldn't remember his name.

"Officer, I appreciate that you have a job to do, but I need just a few more seconds with this guy before you take him. Just one more minute, I promise."

The officer seemed to consider it, then finally said, "Okay, I guess that's fair. We'll go take a look inside the trailer. You have one minute."

I nodded my thanks and turned back to Fykes. "You mean to tell me that Jack Sloan was involved in criminal activities with Hunter Flagg? That's the story you want me to believe?"

Clint nodded. "It's the truth. I swear. Would I lie to you?"

I could think of plenty of reasons why he would, but I didn't think he was lying. As I said, Clint Fykes did not strike me as a cold-blooded killer. That's what my gut feeling was, and I usually go with my gut, unless the evidence says otherwise, of course.

Finally, I reached over and patted him on the shoulder. "Okay. I believe you. But if you're lying, I'll find out, and you'll regret it. You hear me?"

Clint nodded, his eyes wide. "I told you the truth, man. I swear it!"

I watched as he was cuffed and a second police unit took him and his companions away, then we stayed for a few minutes more and gave the officers our statements.

We were just about to leave when Kate arrived in her unmarked cruiser.

Her eyes were wide as she exited the vehicle and joined me.

"*They shot at you?*" she asked, incredulously. "Geez, Harry. Are you okay? That will put him away for a long time."

"As much as I'd like that, Kate... It's not going to happen, at least not for shooting at me. I promised him I wouldn't press charges. As far as putting him away for a long time, your officers will find plenty of evidence inside the trailer to do that."

Bob, who'd just finished giving his statement, caught the tail end of what I'd said.

"You're not pressing charges?" he asked, not at all pleased by the idea. "But the guy shot at us... Twice! With a shotgun, for God's sake. Through a door."

Kate looked incredulous, as did Bob.

I turned on Bob, but I had a smile on my face. "And where did you get hit, my ornery friend? Are you bleeding somewhere I can't see?"

"Well, no, but..."

"Then I don't see the problem. I promised him I wouldn't press charges if he answered my questions, and he did. And the answers he gave me were better than good, if they're true, that is, and I think they are. But you can do what you want. I told him I wouldn't force you."

Bob seemed to consider it for a moment, then shrugged and said, "Well, I guess you're right. They're going away no matter what. I'll keep the faith. I won't press charges either."

I turned back to Kate. "See? It's settled then. Let's get outta here." And I turned to go to my car.

"Hey, whoa," Kate said. "Not so fast. You said he gave you some answers. So talk to me."

And I did. I gave Kate and Bob the short version of what Fykes had told me, including his story about Hunter getting Danny Flagg into trouble and Jack Sloan's possible involvement in Hunter's criminal activities. I also told her I intended to talk to both Sloan and Danny Flagg again.

Kate, unfortunately, couldn't go with us. She had to deal with Clint Fykes and the mess he and his friends had made at the trailer.

I didn't envy her. She had to take statements and assess the situation before she could hand the three stooges off to Narcotics. We, however, were done. We'd given our statements and were free to go... Or, so I thought.

"Harry. Wait!" Kate called as we were about to get into my car. *Here we go,* I thought. I knew exactly what was coming, and so did Bob.

I turned and smiled at her. She looked at me expectantly.

"Yes, Kate? Did you need something?" I asked, innocently.

I was playing coy, and she knew it. She stepped closer to me and held out her hand, palm up.

"You fired your weapons. That means they're mine, at least for now. Hand 'em over."

Bob and I exchanged glances, then sighed in unison. It was standard procedure. And the good Lord knows that my M&P9 had been in police custody almost as much as it had been in mine. And so, reluctantly, we handed over our weapons, knowing that we would see them again, sooner or later. We hadn't killed anyone, or even wounded anyone, so that would expedite things, I hoped.

31

As I drove away along Igou Gap Road that morning, I have to admit I felt quite... naked, and so did Bob, because he said, "You want to head back to the office to get our backups?"

I thought about it but decided against it. I wasn't in any particular hurry, but I knew that a visit to the office would involve more than just grabbing my backup and leaving again, and I just wasn't in the mood for dealing with the inevitable phone calls and messages. So I shook my head and said, "There's a revolver in the glovebox. It will have to do for now. I don't want to waste time at the office."

"Good thinking, boss," he said as he took the weapon from the glovebox, checked the load, and then slipped it into his jacket pocket.

"You really think Jack Sloan was involved in stealing stuff with Hunter Flagg?" he asked.

"Wouldn't surprise me. Nothing about this case is as it seems. Everyone seems to have something to hide, don't they? At this point, I really don't know what I believe. Sloan doesn't exactly look like the criminal type, though, does he? But then, who does? It's possible, I suppose."

"You're right. Anything's possible... but no, I don't think it's very likely, either."

I remembered the way Jack Sloan looked yesterday morning when we talked to him: clean, well-dressed and businesslike. Bob was right. He was no "wild thing." He certainly didn't look the type that would ride with a known redneck criminal. But looks are often deceiving, and people and things can change over fourteen odd years.

And what exactly did it really mean anyway, if Sloan was Hunter's motorcycle buddy back in the day? Not necessarily a damn thing, even if he was consorting with criminals.

"I didn't get breakfast this morning, Harry, and I'm hungry, so I'm gonna eat some chicken, greasy or not, so don't try and stop me, okay?"

I smiled. To tell you the truth, fried chicken sounded pretty good to me too.

"Okay, Bob. You got it. I might even join you."

"Does that mean you're buying?"

I laughed and shook my head. "Not this time, cowboy. It's your turn to buy today."

32

Jack Sloan was working behind the counter when we walked into the KFC that morning, and I couldn't help but wonder what had happened to the one-time high school jock, the most popular kid in school, the quarterback. Based on his rotund appearance, those days were long gone, replaced by the overfed, beer-drinking, overachiever behind the counter of a fast-food restaurant. Was he the franchisee, I wondered? If so, where had he gotten the money to buy his way into that lucrative career? I was about to find out, I hoped.

His eyes opened wide when he saw us, and he didn't seem the least bit pleased.

Bob and I got in line and ordered. I motioned for Sloan to join us at a table in the corner, away from the other customers.

"Look, detectives," he said as he sat down, the chair creaking beneath his considerable weight, "I don't have time to chat with y'all today. We're about to get really busy, and I have to be behind the counter... to make sure everything runs as it should."

I could smell the almost intoxicating aroma wafting up from the plate in front of me. I smiled at Sloan and said, "And it would appear that you do a fine job of running things, Mr. Sloan. Are you the franchisee, by the way?"

"Hah, don't I wish. No, I'm just the manager. One day though... Well, that's my dream. D'you have any idea what a KFC franchise costs?"

I didn't, but I could have guessed.

"More than one and a half million," he continued. "Where the hell would I get that kind of money? Look, I really am busy, so can we hurry it up? What can I do for you?"

"We have a couple of questions," I said. "It won't take long, no more than five minutes. We are, after all, paying customers."

He rolled his eyes, then nodded, and said, "Okay, but please make it quick."

"Thank you," I said, leaning forward so I wouldn't be over-heard. "Who do you think we talked to this morning?"

Sloan shook his head slowly, as if he wasn't interested in playing guessing games, but that was okay. Truth be told, neither was I.

"Clint Fykes," I said. "Do you remember him?"

Sloan slapped the table. "That's him! That's the stalker. I never could remember his name. Damn. How'd you find him? Did he kill Hunter and Samantha?"

"Probably not, Jack."

He nodded, and I continued.

"He did have something interesting to say about you, though, which is why we're here. I thought maybe you'd like to revise the story you told us yesterday morning, or at least add to it a little bit."

Sloan frowned, narrowed his eyes in confusion and said, "What are you talking about?"

"He told us that you and Hunter Flagg were pretty close,

that you used to ride motorcycles together. He claims that you two were best buds. Now don't tell me you forgot about that, Jack."

He opened his mouth to speak, but I held up my hand to stop him and continued, "He also said there was a rumor going around that you and Hunter were planning some kind of heist together." Again he opened his mouth, and again I stopped him. "You see, Jack, he told us that Hunter screwed up, and because of that, Danny Flagg went to prison in Arizona, and that you stepped into the breach to help him do another job. Now, what do you have to say about that? Go ahead. You can speak now."

The color had drained from his face. He was as white as a sheet. I thought for a moment that he was going to pass out, but somehow he managed to keep it together.

"I... I never did anything like that with Hunter Flagg! I swear it."

"But you did hang out with him," I pressed. "You don't deny that, do you?"

"We have multiple witnesses that will confirm it," Bob said.

He looked back and forth between us, then said, "Yeah, Hunter and I... we hung out sometimes. In fact, that's how he met Samantha in the first place. They started going out after it became clear that things weren't working out between Sam and me."

I nodded, trying to encourage him to continue talking. But I was becoming a little confused. First, the story was that Jack was jealous because Samantha and Hunter were dating. And now Jack was telling us that he was practically their matchmaker. What was that about?

"And, yeah," he continued, "after Danny went to prison, we did talk about doing a job together. Hunter had it all set up, and I went along with it, at first, but the truth is... well, I chickened out. I guess I never would've made a very good criminal." He smiled ruefully.

"So you never did anything illegal with Hunter Flagg?" I asked.

"No. As I said, we talked about it... but talking about doing it isn't illegal, not if you don't go through with it, is it? We were kids... just... kids. Anyway, that was a long time ago."

"So were the murders," Bob said. "And, as you probably know, there's no statute of limitations on first-degree murder."

Jack's eyes went wide again, filled with nervous fear.

"What my associate is trying to say," I said, "is if you have anything else to tell us, you better say it now."

"Look, I told you," he said. "We did talk about pulling a job. It was all Hunter's idea. He was kind of the brains of the operation, but he was stuck without his brother. Hunter would set up the deal, and Danny would follow through on it. Hunter had some kind of contact that would tell him when and where they could pull off a theft. Danny would figure out where they could sell the stuff, usually out of state, since it would be harder to trace the stolen goods back to them."

I raised an eyebrow. "Do you know who the contact was?"

Jack shook his head. "I never knew who it was, I swear! And, since I never went through with it, I never gave it a second thought. Like I said, I never was cut out to be a criminal, and I think Hunter and Sam knew that."

Bob frowned and said, "Are you telling us that Samantha knew about the Flagg boys' criminal activities?"

"Knew about it?" Jack laughed. "She encouraged it. They needed money so they could run away together. She'd already told her father that if he wasn't willing to support her and Hunter, he could shove her inheritance. And he smacked her in the mouth for it, in front of the entire Flagg family. He was pissed. Believe me."

Bob and I looked at each other. He shook his head, confused, and so was I. The case was beginning to smell and come apart like an onion. There were layers upon layers, and I was beginning to get the idea that right there in the middle of that onion was a firecracker just waiting to explode.

I looked again at Sloan and said, "So you're saying that you weren't jealous of Hunter Flagg, that you weren't angry because they were going out together?"

"That's right," he replied.

"So why did everybody think that you were?"

He sighed and shook his head, then looked me right in the eyes and said, "Look, the 90s were a different time, right? See, I was a jock back then. You know, the starting quarterback and all, and I was tough... I really was," he said, a little wistfully. "I had a reputation to maintain. You know how it is... was. Everyone expects you to go out with the cheerleader, right? Except, I wasn't too interested in dating a cheerleader... or any girl, for that matter... if you get my drift. What I was interested in wasn't exactly kosher back then." He continued to look at me, cocked his head to the left, and he smiled, ruefully.

Bob frowned and narrowed his eyes. But, as I looked at Sloan's neatly trimmed beard, the well-groomed eyebrows, and the color-coordinated tie and suspenders, it all began to fall into place. He wasn't exactly the cliché homosexual, but upon closer inspection, the signs were there.

"You're gay, Jack?" I asked, smiling at him.

He smiled back at me, nodded and said, "That's right. I think it was dating Sam that finally made me realize it. She was a beauty, a total babe, but she did nothing for me. Oh, I was fond of her, you understand, but... And, even then, it would be years before I felt comfortable about coming out. So, when Sam and Hunter started dating, me and Hunter... we fabricated this story about me wanting to beat him up. You know, the classic jealous boyfriend thing."

I shook my head. "Why didn't you tell us this yesterday, Jack? It's 2012, and you obviously don't mind talking about it now."

Sloan shrugged. "I don't know. I guess remembering my time back in school made me hesitant to bring it up. Plus, thinking about Sam and Hunter makes me remember what I almost did, the person I almost became. I'm not exactly living the dream working here at KFC, but my life is a heck of a lot better than it would have been if I'd gone to prison, don't you think?"

I nodded. "That's fine, Jack... Well, I think that's all the questions we have right now. And, just in case you're wondering, no, you're not going to get into trouble for thinking about stealing something fourteen years ago. That said, if there's anything else you've been hiding, you better come clean, now."

Jack shook his head. "I wish I knew who Hunter's contact was. If I did, I'd tell you, I promise. I remember one time Hunter telling me he was having some trouble with this other guy. In fact, I think this mystery contact was putting serious pressure on Hunter to find another partner. But it never happened. In fact, it wasn't too long after I gave up on the idea of turning to a life of crime that Hunter and Sam were murdered. Thinking about it now, I guess it all could be connected, but I just didn't see things that way back then. Besides, what was I going to tell the police? That we were planning a robbery and that's why Hunter was killed?"

"Thanks for your help, Jack," I said, leaning back in my seat. "I'm not quite sure what it all means, but I'll figure it out, eventually." I handed him one of my business cards and said, "Call me anytime, okay?"

He nodded and rose to his feet.

Bob held up a half-eaten drumstick. "You cook a mean chicken, brother."

Sloan smiled at him, then left us to finish our lunch.

Me? I spent the next fifteen minutes or so trying to process what we'd learned. By the time we were through eating, I was beginning to feel that we were on the edge of a breakthrough but were still missing some vital information. I also had a feeling that Danny Flagg could help us clear things up. That being so, we decided to head on over to American Flagg and have another chat with him.

We finished our lunch and headed out to my car. And, I don't know why, on a whim, I suppose, I called Tim.

"Tim," I began. "I know you've been busy doing other stuff, but were you able to find anything new on Danny Flagg? We're heading over to talk to him right now."

Boy, had he ever, and I sure as hell wasn't prepared for what he told me.

"Harry! I was just about to call you. You're not going to believe what I found." He sounded excited.

"Okay, so spit it out, Tim. What *did* you find?"

"I was finally able to, umm, access his prison records. I was real careful, Harry, so you don't have to worry about me getting caught or anything. You ready for this?"

There was a pause.

"Oh, for Pete's sake, Tim, get on with it," I said grumpily, but he didn't seem to notice.

"I found out that Danny Flagg..." He paused, "...lied about when he got out of prison!"

I was about three steps from the Maxima's driver's side door. I stopped walking, stared at the ground, my hand in the air to signal Bob not to speak, in case I might miss something. I was frickin' stunned.

"What did you say?"

"Danny Flagg told you that he was released three days after Hunter Flagg was murdered, right?" Tim asked.

I nodded, even though I knew he couldn't see me.

"That's right," I said.

"Well, he wasn't. He was released three days *before* the murders. It's right here in the official records. He was released on March 28, 1998."

I didn't know what to say, so I simply thanked him, hung up and put my phone back in my pocket.

Bob was looking at me expectantly, but I shook my head. To tell the truth, I was lost for words. After all, between our conversation with Jack Sloan and my phone call with Tim, we'd just discovered that Danny Flagg had both motive and opportunity, and all in the span of about thirty minutes.

"Get in the car, Bob," I said. "I'll explain on the way. I think we've found our killer."

33

A merican Flagg Auto and Diesel Repair wasn't that long of a drive from the KFC where Jack Sloan worked. On a good day, maybe twenty minutes, but on that particular day there was a bad accident at The Split on I-75 where 75 and I-24 meet, thus it took us a little over an hour.

In my mind, things were beginning to snap into place, especially while I explained them to Bob as we waited in the stalled traffic that day. Mostly it was speculation. But be that as it may, I was excited at the prospect of grilling Danny Flagg. I felt like a coon hound with his nose to the ground, hot on the trail.

I told Bob how Flagg had lied to us about his release date and so had no alibi. To me, that alone made him look as guilty as sin. Not the fact that he didn't have an alibi, but that he'd lied about it.

"Ronnie told us last night that Danny Flagg probably has enough money to pay for a hacker," I said, "and he had the opportunity. He was one of the few people that knew about our investigation early enough on Monday morning to do something about it. We met with him at just after ten-thirty, remember?"

Bob nodded thoughtfully, but he allowed me to continue.

"On top of that, we have what Jack Sloan just told us about Hunter and Danny. If Hunter really did mess up all those years ago, and Danny took the rap and spent two years in Arizona State Prison, then I'm guessing he would have been pretty damn pissed at Hunter when he got out."

"Mad enough to kill his own brother? I don't know, Harry." Bob tilted his head and tapped his hands on his knees in a rhythmic pattern. "Yes, I suppose it could happen. Like you said, people have murdered family for less."

"My thoughts exactly," I replied. "Now, add to that the fact he has no alibi, and you have to wonder what the hell he was doing the night Hunter and Samantha were murdered. And why didn't he bother to show up at the funeral?"

"I gotta say," Bob said skeptically, "you make a pretty persuasive argument, but there's just one small problem."

"Oh yeah? And what's that?"

"We don't have our firearms."

I nodded grimly. That was indeed a problem. If we were going to confront a double murderer, I would have liked to have had a little more firepower than just the backup revolver Bob had taken from the glovebox.

But, just like that coon hound, I was hot on the scent, and I wasn't about to run back to the office, not after sitting in traffic for almost an hour.

It was just after one o'clock that afternoon when we pulled into the parking lot at American Flagg Auto and Diesel Repair.

The place was indeed busy. Maybe Ronnie was right. If so...

There were several mechanics on the property, all working hard on various trucks ranging from pickups to massive tractor units. The skinny guy with the cowboy hat was also present, and he grinned at us and waved as we exited the Maxima.

Danny Flagg appeared at the edge of the first bay, wiping grease from his hands on a blue commercial wipe. He was wearing a Coors Light baseball cap and a broad smile on his scruffy, unshaven face.

"Well, if it isn't Sherlock Holmes and his assistant Watson!" he said as we joined him. "Y'all got some more questions for me? Are you any closer to finding out who killed Hunter and Sam?"

I fixed Danny with a hard stare and said, "Danny, I don't think I've ever been any closer to your brother's killer than I am right now. Perhaps we should step into your office."

His eyes widened, the smile disappeared and, with a shaky voice, he invited us in.

All was calm and casual as we made our way to his office. But when we went inside and he invited us to sit down, I was... motivated. After all, I wasn't just sniffing out my raccoon. I had him treed. The hunt was just about over.

Or so I thought!

34

Danny Flagg looked nervous as he sat down behind his desk, the chair squeaking in protest. The office was just as messy as it had been a couple of days ago, with the exception of a half-dozen Styrofoam coffee cups from a local gas station scattered all over the desk.

"I'd offer you guys some coffee, but the coffee maker's broke. I knew something wasn't right, then the frickin' thing just quit on me. I'm not going to buy a new one until we get another full-time assistant in here, someone to tidy the place and make coffee that doesn't taste like sludge."

He tried to force a smile, but I could tell he was nervous.

Bob and I were seated on the two chairs in front of the desk.

"So?" I said. Then we both stared at him without speaking. The silence was deafening.

Finally, Danny broke and said, "So you said you had some more questions for me?"

I was about to speak, but Bob beat me to it. "Does the name Iron Crusader mean anything to you?"

Now, I have to admit, that wasn't the question I would've

begun with. But in truth, it was a good strategy. Bob wanted to see this guy's reaction. If Flagg had paid for a hacker on Monday afternoon, his eyes would have given him away.

Flagg frowned, looked confused and said, "Is that like a hockey team or something?"

Bob glanced at me, and I tried a different tack. "Danny, do you want us to find your brother's killer?"

Danny's frown deepened, as did his look of confusion. "Well, of course I do. Whoever killed my brother and Sam should get what's coming to them, even after all these years."

"Then I would like to know," I continued, "why you lied to us. I'd like to know why you've lied to everyone all these years."

The tic in his left eye, and the way he glanced quickly down and to the left, was practically an admission of guilt, but he quickly recovered his composure, sort of, and said, "Is this about Arizona?"

"If by Arizona you mean that you got out of prison three days before your brother's murder and then lied about it," Bob said harshly, "then, yes, this is about Arizona."

"Danny," I said. "You lied to your friends and family about when you got out of prison. You lied to the police. And you lied to us when we interviewed you on Monday."

Danny was slowly shaking his head. He looked like a man whose world was falling apart.

"And then, today," I continued, "I discovered it was Hunter who screwed up and you went to prison for it." I leaned forward in my chair. "Do you know what I call that, Danny? I call that a motive for murder. And do you know what I call lying about your alibi? I call that an admission of guilt. So you tell me, Danny Flagg. Did you kill Samantha Goodkind and your brother?"

I let the question hang in the air, watching to see how he would react. I could see out of the corner of my eye that Bob was also leaning forward and scowling at the mechanic. With that much pressure on the man, I was sure he'd break.

And he did!

Finally, he let out a long, shaky breath and said, "Look, I know I lied, and I know it was wrong, and I know I broke the law when I lied to the police fourteen years ago, and that you could lock me up for that. But I was scared, see? For a long time I was scared that someone would know that I lied about my release date, and I knew I could get in big trouble for... What do they call it? Obstructing an investigation, or something like that, I think. You hear that on TV sometimes, right?"

I nodded slowly, but Danny was still talking, and I didn't want to interrupt him. So I said nothing and waited for him to continue.

"So, yeah," he said finally. "I got out March 28th, three days before Hunter and Sam were killed. That's true. But that doesn't make me the murderer, and I'm pretty sure you guys know that. You should know two things," he continued. "First, I didn't return to Chattanooga until April 3rd. After my release, I took a bus to Memphis—they confiscated my truck when I was arrested—and I stayed in a motel. If you don't believe me, you can check it out. I'm sure it's still on the motel computer, right? You'll find I'm telling the truth."

As Danny spoke, I studied his face carefully. And, as far as I could tell, he was telling the truth. Did it make any sense? Hell no. But did it look like he killed his brother? No, not exactly.

There was a pause while I considered my options, then I said, "And what's the second thing?"

For a moment, he seemed confused, but he quickly recovered and said, "Oh, yeah, and the second thing you need to know is I didn't invent the lie about when I got out of prison. That was Hunter's idea. He told everybody that I was supposed to get out on April 3rd. In fact, he arranged for me to stay in Memphis. He was going to drive over and meet me there."

Bob frowned, narrowed his eyes and said, "Why would Hunter do that?"

"Because... see, he and Sam were planning on running away together. They were going to meet me in Memphis and give me some money."

I cocked my head to one side. "Money? Where were they going to get money?"

"Look, I don't know. Hunter was the brains of the operation. He would set it up. We'd steal the stuff and sell it out of state. That way it would be difficult to trace. He had these contacts, see? He knew people that gave him tips on deliveries and timetables, stuff like that. We'd grab the stuff and Hunter would pay 'em a share. He always arranged everything. I was just the muscle."

Danny pulled a rag out of his pocket and wiped his forehead with it.

"I talked to Hunter all the time while I was in prison," he continued, "and he told me that he was going to come into a bunch of money. I figured he was going to pull another job, something like that, that he had it all planned out. He told me he and Sam were going to run away together, to California, and I was to meet them in Memphis. It's on the way, see? And he was going to give me some of the money. That way, I could either go back to Chattanooga or not. Either way, I was going to be okay." He took a deep breath, looked at Bob, then at me, then continued.

"Meanwhile, Hunter and Sam would have an opportunity to start a life together somewhere else," he said, "away from all the crap and drama. I was all for the idea, and Hunter said if we met in Memphis while I was supposed to still be in prison, no one would ever suspect that he had passed some of the money off to me. For some reason, Hunter thought that was important. Like I said, he was the smart one, so I didn't question it."

I leaned back in my chair, trying to put it all together. "So you get out of prison early," I said, "or at least earlier than anyone thinks, and you go to Memphis and you book into a motel, then what?"

A distant sadness settled into Danny's face. "I waited and waited for Hunter to come. He'd booked us into this motel on the east side. So I checked in and waited for him... but he didn't never come."

Tears welled up in the mechanic's eyes.

"I didn't know what to do! I didn't have much money, so I called him, but he didn't answer. So I called Sam. She didn't answer either. So then I called Daddy, and he told me what had happened."

Danny cleared his throat and swallowed. "I was frickin' devastated. I didn't know what to do. I had just enough money to get the bus to Chattanooga, and, because I didn't know exactly what had happened to my brother, I didn't tell anybody about his plans to meet me in Memphis. And, just to make things clear, I didn't lie about my release date nearly as much as you think I did. By the time the police had gotten around to questioning me, they were already fixated on Walter Goodkind, so they didn't ask me much about my time in prison or even mention my release date. They'd already been told when I was supposed to get out by my daddy, and others."

I sighed. I believed him. I also believed that Henry Finkle and Charlie Monk had been so focused on proving that Walter was the murderer that they hadn't bothered to check Danny Flagg's story.

"Okay, Danny," I said finally. "I appreciate your honesty,

even if it did come a little late, but I have a few more questions for you."

Danny looked distraught, deflated. He wiped his face again and said, "Shoot. Ask away."

"Do you have any idea who Hunter's contact was?"

"No. He never let me in on that kind of stuff."

"Not even a suspicion?" I asked. "It would give us something to go on."

Danny nodded. "Yeah, I get what you're saying. But I really don't know. Hunter kept that stuff to himself. And by the time I got back to Chattanooga, I wasn't interested in stealing no more, or continuing whatever it was that Hunter had planned. I know he spent time with that guy Sloan while I was locked up, and I know he was doing business with someone else, but he never told me who it was."

Bob frowned and shook his head. "I'm sorry, but that doesn't make much sense to me. Your brother had a contact, and he never bothered to tell you who it was? Were you okay with that?"

A sad smile appeared on Danny Flagg's lips. "You guys don't understand, do you? Whoever told you that Hunter had messed up and landed me in prison was either wrong or they was lying. It was me that messed up, not him. See, I was carrying a load of stolen medical equipment, about ten grand's worth, an' I'd been driving almost three days and was bored stiff, so I pulled over and had me a steak and a few beers. It was stupid and I knew it. And then? Well whadda you know? I get pulled over by an Arizona state trooper, an' then one thing leads to another, and I ended up getting two years for hauling stolen property. You see, detectives, Hunter didn't have nothing to do with it. It was all my fault. Like I said earlier, he was the brains of the operation. I trusted him completely."

I looked down at my hands, feeling like we had come so

close to cracking the case and yet were still so far away. That was it, then. If Danny was telling the truth, and I was pretty sure that he was, he wasn't the killer.

"But why Memphis, Danny?" Bob asked. "Why meet so far away?"

Danny shrugged. "I never really understood that myself, except that it was on the way both ways. I-40 is the best and quickest route to LA, and from Arizona to Chattanooga. It was all Hunter and Sam's idea. I've always thought they would've told me more when they met me in Memphis. But they never made it that far."

The mechanic suddenly frowned. "And what was that you said earlier about Iron Man? Or something like that?"

I waved the question away. "Don't worry about it, Danny. We'll let you know if we have any more questions." And we left him sitting there, staring after us, like a wounded possum.

We climbed into the Maxima and I turned on the motor, then I took my foot off the gas and leaned back against the headrest and closed my eyes. To tell the truth, I was more than a little bummed out. One minute I had myself a killer, the next I didn't. I was frustrated as hell and needed a moment to gather my thoughts.

Bob, however, had other ideas. "So, boss. What do we do now?"

"Well, we've managed to eliminate all the suspects: Clint Fykes, Jack Sloan, and now Danny Flagg. It would seem that all roads lead back to Walter Goodkind and his daughter. Maybe Henry and Larry were right all along. I think it's time to talk to them again. What do you think?"

Bob nodded, and I pulled out of the parking lot.

Jennifer Young, here we come!

35

"I can't believe it, Harry," Bob said as I drove onto Highway 27. "I thought we were really onto something, but Danny had all the right answers, didn't he? Do you really think he was telling the truth?"

"I do," I said. And I did. I can usually tell when someone is lying to me, although I do sometimes get it wrong, but not that time. I was pretty sure Danny Flagg had been telling the truth. In fact, as we left his office, it seemed to me that he was relieved to have finally gotten the heavy weight off of his shoulders. *The problem now is where do we go from there?*

"Before we became distracted by Clint Fykes," I said as I took the 4th street exit off 27, "and then Jack Sloan, and Danny Flagg, we were pretty sure that the killer was either Jennifer or Walter Goodkind, right?"

"Right," Bob agreed. "If Danny didn't know anything about the hack, and it sure seemed like he didn't, then one of those two must have been behind it, right? I mean, they're the only ones with money that also knew about the investigation early enough to find a hacker on Monday afternoon."

"Either that or the someone already knew the hacker," I said. "We already know Walter's responsible for the missing evidence. He's either protecting himself or his daughter."

We found a parking spot next to a meter less than a block away from Legacy Health.

"But I didn't want to fall into the same trap that Finkle and Larry Spruce did," I said as we exited the car and closed the doors. "They were so convinced that Walter Goodkind was behind the murders they didn't bother to look elsewhere. They could have missed something important. As it is now, I'm beginning to wonder if they weren't right all along."

Bob shrugged as we walked and said, "Hey, I hear you. But you know, if we hadn't been thorough, we never would've been shot at this morning. So there's that!"

I looked at him. He was grinning broadly.

"You're something else, Bob. You really are."

It was the middle of the afternoon, and I wondered if Jennifer Young would even be there. If she was the typical daughter of a CEO, I figured she would have taken off early to go play tennis or drink martinis with her friends. But somehow I didn't think she was like that. She was ambitious, and she was looking forward to taking over the entire company, and in just a matter of weeks. *Oh, yes. She'll be there.*

We entered the building, took the elevator to the top floor, and were greeted by the same friendly receptionist. He recognized us immediately.

"We'd like to talk to Mrs. Young, please," I said.

"Yes," he replied. "She said you might drop by. If you'll just take a seat, I'll confirm that she's not in a meeting." He picked up the phone.

Now that is a surprise!

I nodded my thanks and turned to see Bob looking around, and by his expression I knew exactly who he was looking for.

I rolled my eyes and said, "Come on, Bob. Do you have to make it so obvious? Why don't you just ask the young man if you can say hello to her?"

I'd said it loud enough for the receptionist to hear, and Bob glared at me, embarrassed.

The young man behind the counter smiled at him, the phone still to his ear, and said, "I'm sorry Miss Mullins is not here today, sir. I believe she's in Atlanta, on company business."

"No matter," Bob said. "I just thought I might say hello, is all."

On the one hand, I was glad Bob was enjoying his time with the young woman. She sure was a looker! And yet, on the other hand, I wished he'd act a little more professionally while we were on the job. Besides, when you're conducting an investigation everyone is a suspect, so it's not a good idea to become involved romantically with anyone related to a case.

But then, who was I to talk? I've broken that rule myself, on several occasions, as Kate would be only too happy to tell you, so I couldn't blame him too much.

The young man replaced the phone in its cradle and said, "Mrs. Young is ready for you. If you'll follow me, please..." and he escorted us down the hall and into an office that was almost as big as Walter Goodkind's. It was tastefully decorated, though I found it too sleek, too modern for my taste. The furniture, the walls, even her desk were either stark white or white accented in black. The only color in the room was the group of three abstract paintings on the wall behind the desk.

Jennifer Young was seated at her desk, and she smiled as she looked up at us and said, "Ah, detectives. I had a feeling I'd see you today. My first thought was to refuse to see you. After all, you have no official standing, do you? But my father said I should humor you, so, please, won't you sit down?"

And we did. We sat down in front of her desk on what can

only be described as a pair of modern sculptures, designed more for visual impact than for comfort.

"So, Mr. Starke, Mr. Ryan," Jennifer said with a fake smile that any good politician would have been proud of, "what can I do for you?"

"Perhaps I should begin by correcting you," I said. "My company was hired by the DA's office, so we do, in fact, have official standing."

I paused and watched as her eyebrows lifted expectantly. Part of my strategy was to unnerve her, to cut through the aloof, unshakable businesswoman's shield and perhaps get her to show a little emotion. Hell, I wanted to make the woman angry. If I could, maybe she'd let something slip.

Her expression hardened, just a little, and she said, "Is that so? Then you'd better continue, Mr. Starke."

"Thank you. I understand you didn't like your sister very much. In fact, we have several witnesses that will testify that you were jealous of your sister. Isn't it true that she was your father's favorite?"

The expression hardened further, but the serene smile never left her lips. Inwardly, I smiled. The storm clouds were gathering.

"No, it isn't," she said. "Everyone in my family loved Samantha, especially me. I think my father loved her as much as he did because she reminded him of our mother, who died many years ago."

I nodded along with her answer, knowing she was telling me exactly what she thought I wanted to hear. I was ready to dig deeper.

"I'm sure you're right, and I'm sure you care very much for your family, isn't that also true?"

"Of course, Mr. Starke. I love my family. Don't you love yours?" she snapped.

"Well, yes, of course, but I think you love what your family represents, Mrs. Young. You care about your family's reputation, and about the company, which you are soon to inherit, isn't that right?"

Jennifer's smile was beginning to falter. Her eyebrows flattened. She was showing the first hints of the anger she was trying to keep under control. Before she could answer, however, I kept right on going.

"Would it be safe to say, do you think, that as someone who cares so much about your family's reputation, you were upset with Samantha because she was dating an individual you considered... shall we say someone of a lower class... like Hunter Flagg? I have to wonder just how upset you were, knowing that your sister's choice of partner might well affect your business. Did it upset you enough to kill her and Hunter, I wonder?"

I studied Jennifer carefully as I spoke. I knew I was being provocative, but I also knew that the woman, much like her father, was well able to hide her feelings. My goal was to break through that polished exterior and get to the real Jennifer Young, and it worked. When she spoke, it was with a tone of icy indignation.

"Now you listen to me, Mr. Starke. You listen very carefully. I do not appreciate you coming into my office to accuse me of murdering my own sister. Yes, I was upset when she dated that boy, just as my father was, just as everyone else in the family was. She was too good for him, and not just because of the money. He was a criminal, and we all knew it. We all knew he'd been working with his brother. So, yes, I was upset. But, no, I did not murder my sister, and if you dare to accuse me or anyone in my family of something like that, well I'll just have to—"

The door behind us opened, and Jennifer stopped talking. Bob and I turned to see who it was.

Christopher Goodkind, Jennifer's older brother, was standing in the open doorway.

"Oh, I'm sorry to interrupt, Jen," he said. "I was going to ask you if you wanted to go grab a late lunch or something. Your assistant said you hadn't eaten, and I was in the area so..."

"No, Chris. I can't go anywhere right now," Jennifer replied. Her voice was cold, her answer abrupt, impatient. "I'm rather busy at the moment, as you can see, and I'm also waiting for an important call."

Christopher looked uncomfortable, but instead of leaving he took a step further into the office and closed the door.

"I understand," he said, staring at me. "It was just an idea. As I said, I was in the area..."

He paused for a second, then said, "Mr. Starke..." He looked at me and glanced quickly at Bob. "I... I'm glad I bumped into you. I'd like to apologize for my attitude yesterday evening. I'd had a little too much to drink, you see, and all that talk about Sam's murder... well, it just drives me crazy."

"There's no need to apologize," I said. "I completely understand."

"Yeah, me too," Bob said. "I think this investigation is getting to everyone." He glanced at Jennifer. His meaning was clear.

"Right," Christopher said. He looked awkward, uncomfortable. "Well, I understand you have a job to do, but I don't think I can be of much help to you. You see, I was living in Pittsburgh when Sam and Hunter were killed."

I already knew that, of course. All the same, I cocked an eyebrow and looked at him, surprised.

Why would he volunteer that information now, while we're obviously interviewing his sister?

"Yes, I know," I replied. "I was wondering about that. What were you doing in Pittsburgh?" I took the opportunity to get up out of that awful chair and turned to face him.

"I was hanging out with some writer friends, you know? As my father was quick to point out last night, I was going through a somewhat rebellious stage in my life. My twenties were not an easy time for me, Mr. Starke."

"Chris thought he was going to be a novelist," Jennifer said, the sarcasm palpable. Apparently, she didn't approve. "So he stole some of Father's money and started a little commune for writers in Pittsburgh. It didn't last long, though."

Christopher shrugged. "Yes, well, I eventually learned my lesson." He sighed. "It wasn't to be... It wasn't all bad, though, and I did ride down every other week, to visit the family. That kept father happy and eventually, when I figured out I wasn't going to be the next William Faulkner, I gave up the apartment and moved back down here. To be honest, my decision to go to business school was one of the best I ever made."

I nodded and smiled at him. "Yes, I'm sure it was," I said. "So, you weren't in town at the time when your sister was murdered?"

Christopher shook his head, but it was Jennifer who answered the question.

"No, he wasn't. And you would know that if you talked to the police officer who conducted the investigation in the first place. He went over all that with Chris back then."

I raised my hands in defense. "Okay, okay. I was just being thorough. Well, look, we've taken up enough of your time, Mrs. Young. I did have more questions, but..." I looked at her, expectantly. She didn't bite.

"Thank you for coming," she snapped. "I'll have Steven show you out."

"Oh, don't bother. We know the way. Thank you for your time, Mrs. Young. Another day, perhaps?"

"I doubt it," she muttered, and I couldn't help but smile.

I was still smiling as we walked toward the door. Christopher stepped back and grasped the doorknob. I thought he was going to open it for us, but he didn't. Instead he put his free hand on my arm and said, "I am really glad that you're investigating Sam's murder. Really, I am. And I meant what I said last night. It's about time someone did something. That was the first thing I thought when Jen called me the other day and told me you were reopening the investigation. I thought to myself, maybe it will finally happen. Maybe Sam will finally have some justice."

"I agree," I said. "Say, you weren't much older than Samantha, were you? What, about four years, would it be? I was wondering, did you know any of her friends? Or any of Hunter's friends? We've talked to her ex-boyfriend, Jack Sloan, and he's been quite helpful. Is there anyone else you can think of?"

He seemed to ponder the question, then shook his head and said, "No, I don't think so. Four years is quite a gap, you know, when you're young. Sam and I didn't have much in common."

"Well, okay. It was worth a shot. How about you, Mrs. Young. Did you know any of her girlfriends?"

"I did not."

I nodded. I'd expected as much, so we said our goodbyes and left.

To be honest, I didn't feel that we'd accomplished much at all. So far, we'd spent almost the entire day chasing down leads that turned out to be dead ends. Clint Fykes didn't seem to be the murdering type, even though he'd almost blown our heads off. Jack Sloan had indeed been hiding something, but it wasn't something that would make him a prime suspect. I'd been certain that Danny Flagg was the guilty party, until we talked to him. If his alibi checked out, he was out of it. And all I'd managed to do at Legacy Health was piss off Jennifer Young. And when I mentioned I might want to talk to her again... I couldn't see it happening, not unless I could get Finkle to have her picked up, and I couldn't see that happening either.

No, the day was a total bust. I felt as if I was no nearer solving the case than I had been that day at the country club when Larry asked me to take it on.

Bob must have noticed how sour I felt, because as we stepped out of the elevator he said, "Things aren't working out for us today, are they, boss?"

"Geez, Bob. I really do wish you'd stop calling me that. But, no. Things are not working out for us. To tell you the truth, I'm frickin' tired. I feel like we've been chasing our tails for three frickin' days and we're still no nearer the truth.

"You know what?" he said. "I think you need to take a few hours off. Recharge your batteries."

"Maybe you're right." I looked at my watch. "It's just after three-thirty. Why don't I drop you off at the office and go home. You do the same, and I'll see you in the morning, bright and early."

And that's exactly what we did... Well, not quite.

36

T he idea that I should take a little time out to relax was appealing. After all, as many people will tell you, it's often when you're not thinking about a problem that you find the solution to it. And we'd been working flat-out for three days straight. Even so, when it came right down to it, I always had a tough time relaxing. I just couldn't get my mind off of whatever case I was working on at the time.

When we arrived back at the office, Bob headed for home. Me? I wasn't ready to do that, not yet. So instead, I gave Jacque strict instructions that I was not to be disturbed, grabbed an oversized mug of Dark Italian roast, went to my private office, retrieved my backup M&P9 from the safe, slipped it into my holster, and sat down at my desk to think.

I couldn't shake the feeling that I already had everything I needed to solve the case. My instincts were insisting that, at some point that day, I'd heard it, the detail I needed to catch a killer, but what that detail might be, I had no idea.

As dependable as my gut often is, it's not yet learned to

speak to me in plain English. And that means I'm often left in the dark as to what it's trying to tell me.

Along the back wall of my office, behind my desk, I have a small minibar. I swiveled my chair, looked at it, hesitated, then stood, grabbed a bottle of spiced rum and poured a generous measure into my coffee, then settled down again to think.

As I sipped the rich and oh so tasty concoction of amber liquids, I closed my eyes and reviewed the various conversations we'd had that day.

Had Clint Fykes told me something important as we waited for the officers to arrive? I hadn't thought so at the time, but, then again, I'd just been shot at. You think I was cool with that? I can assure you I wasn't, birdshot or no, the muzzle blast from a twelve-gauge shotgun is enough to kill all by itself. The truth is, any time you're in a firefight, the adrenaline interferes with your ability to think. And that's true clear across the board. Don't let any cop or soldier tell you that getting shot at isn't a problem; it is. So no, I was more than a little shaken by the incident.

And yet, I couldn't remember anything that Fykes had said that would've made a difference.

As I continued to review the day, I thought about Jack Sloan being friends with Hunter Flagg, about Danny Flagg lying about when he was released from prison, and about Jennifer Young losing her cool in her office. I thought about what Christopher Goodkind had told me, and... A great big *nothing!*

Maybe Bob was right. Maybe I was too close to the facts. One thing I did know: sooner or later, when I was least expecting it, things would fall into place. They always did.

I sighed, finished my coffee, rose from behind my desk and stepped over to one of the two couches in front of the fireplace, stretched out and closed my eyes. It seemed like only a few minutes later that my iPhone rang, pulling me from a deeper sleep than I'd anticipated. I looked at the time. I'd been out for more than an hour!

I looked at the lock screen. I didn't recognize the number. I almost didn't answer it, thinking that maybe it was some phone room warrior trying to sell me an extended warranty for my Maxima. But I did answer it, and I was glad I did!

"Mr. Starke. This is Walter Goodkind. I understand you were in my building this afternoon. I have to say, I'm a little disappointed you didn't stop by my office and provide me with an update."

I sat upright on the couch and said, "No, sir, I didn't. That would have been premature. I simply wanted to ask your daughter some questions." And then I shut up and waited. The first one to speak loses, right?

Walter didn't speak again for a good half a minute, then he said, "Yes, Jennifer told me, and I don't appreciate you upsetting her like that."

"I didn't realize I'd upset her," I lied. "If I did, I sincerely apologize," I said, again not meaning it. I'd intended to piss her off as much as possible, and I knew I'd succeeded. The trouble was, of course, it hadn't gained me a damn thing.

"I can only ask you to trust me, Mr. Goodkind," I continued. "Sometimes, to get at the truth, I have to ask tough questions. It's all part of the job."

"Yes, yes. I suppose that's true enough," he said, sounding somewhat mollified. "And, please, call me Walter."

"Thank you. Look, Walter, I needed to be sure that your daughter's not capable of murder... and you, too, for that matter."

I'd worded the statement in such a way that it indicated I was indeed sure she wasn't capable of murder, then listened carefully to the way he responded. I needed to know if he was relieved that I'd cleared his daughter—which I hadn't—or if he was worried that, if I didn't suspect Jennifer, I might suspect him.

"I'm glad to hear that, Harry. I know my daughter. She loved her sister. She couldn't have killed her. She would have protected her."

Wow! Goodkind was in full businessman mode. There was no hint of emotion in his voice. *Okay, time to try something else.*

"Can I ask you a personal question, Walter?"

"Of course, this is a personal matter, after all." Again, a perfectly neutral response.

"Was Hunter's poverty the real reason you opposed the relationship? Was it because he came from a... Why don't we call it what it is, a somewhat redneck family? Or was it because you suspected that he was a career criminal?"

I was shooting blind. Swinging desperately at shadows, hoping to connect. But then, as I thought back to my short but heated conversation with Jennifer Young, I realized that she knew Hunter was a criminal. *What exactly does she know?* I wondered. *And what does Walter know?* I didn't have to wonder for long.

"I'm ashamed to admit that you're right, detective. In part, at least. Yes, I admit I wasn't happy about the Flaggs being... you know, the kind of family they were, but, my issues with the boy ran much deeper than that. It was widely known that his brother Danny had been arrested for transporting stolen goods across state lines, and Samantha herself had told me there were rumors that his younger brother was involved in the crime. I was devastated that she was mixed up with him, and I told her so, on many occasions, but she wouldn't listen. She was in love with him and was convinced that he'd left those ways behind."

That's not what Danny Flagg told me. He said she was up to her neck in it.

"I appreciate your honesty, Walter. And I'll be sure to call if I have an update... or any more questions."

I ended the call, dropped the phone on the table and leaned back. The back of my neck tingling like hell.

I went to my desk and opened my laptop, a piece of technology I rarely used since I had Tim to do that kind of work for me. But I needed to do a quick Google search. I could handle that!

You see, I already knew Danny Flagg had gone to prison for transporting stolen medical supplies; Danny Flagg himself had confirmed it earlier that afternoon. But I had an idea, so I searched for articles about the arrest and got lucky. I found two, both in Arizona newspapers.

I scanned through them and eventually found what I was looking for. The stolen equipment had been taken from a warehouse, here in Chattanooga, owned by a medical supply company called Viveron.

Next, I opened a new tab in the browser and brought up the official website for Legacy Health. The website was well designed, and it didn't take me long to find what I was looking for. Among the list of companies Legacy Health worked with was none other than Viveron!

I sat back in my chair and thought about it. Viveron was a medical supply company local to Chattanooga, and with a connection to Legacy Health. Would they have been working together back in 1998? It seemed likely to me.

I thought about Walter Goodkind playing golf with the CEO of Viveron, listening to him complain about goods being stolen from one of his warehouses right here in town. Then, Walter goes home to find out that the boy his youngest daughter was dating was the perpetrator of said crime.

That would have put Walter in an untenable situation. No

wonder he was so upset, but would he have been upset enough to murder both of them?

I needed to do a little more snooping, but I'd have to go it alone. Bob was already at home, probably stretched out on the couch with the TV on and a beer in his hand, so I didn't want to drag him back out.

However, just as I got up from my desk, my iPhone rang again. This time, it was Kate.

"What's up, Kate?"

"Harry, I'm at the KFC on North Lee. You'd better get over here. Jack Sloan's dead. He committed suicide less than twenty minutes ago."

The hell he did!

37

It was just after six-thirty when I drove out to the KFC on North Lee that evening. The sun was setting in a blaze of orange and red, but I wasn't aware of it. My mind was in a whirl. How could it be? Bob and I had talked to Jack Sloan earlier that day. Commit suicide, and at work? Not likely!

Even before I arrived at the scene, I was certain he'd been murdered, and I desperately hoped that whoever was working the crime scene realized it, too. If not... well, it didn't bear thinking about. What I was thinking was that if Jack Sloan hadn't killed himself, who would have wanted him dead? It had to be the same person who killed Hunter and Samantha. Of that, I was sure. But what could be the motive?

It was barely ten minutes after I received Kate's call that I arrived to find the KFC parking lot taped off, so I had to leave my car out on the street.

I got out of my car and went to the officer controlling the scene. I recognized him immediately. Sergeant Lonnie Guest and I go back a long way, all the way to the Police Academy, in fact, and we didn't get along.

"Kate says you knew this guy, Harry," he said. "I'm pretty sure that makes you a suspect."

I ducked under the tapes and walked right on past him. I didn't have time to stop and chitchat.

"Wait!" Lonnie called behind me. "I'm serious, Harry. You really are a suspect."

I stopped and turned on my heel, glaring at him and said, "You've got to be kidding me, Lonnie! I'm working for the DA and this is connected to my investigation. Besides, how could I be a suspect? This is supposed to be a suicide."

"Yeah, well. Maybe it ain't a suicide... Okay, so maybe you're not exactly a suspect, but you're definitely a person of interest."

I rolled my eyes and continued toward the back of the building where everything seemed to be happening: the county medical examiner's SUV was parked next to an ambulance, and the PD's CSI van was parked next to that. *What the hell? This isn't a suicide. It's a crime scene.*

"Harry. Stop! I mean it. I can't let you go back there."

I stopped and turned again to face Lonnie and said, "You were serious, right? Sloan didn't commit suicide after all?"

"Look, Harry, I can't comment on that. You're a person of interest. And anyway, you ain't a cop anymore."

I let out a long breath. I wasn't in any mood to argue with the guy.

"I'm well aware I'm not on the force anymore. And I guess you're just following procedure, but I don't have time for your bullshit, Lonnie. I need to look at the crime scene, if that's what it is. We're all on the same team... Look, if I let you babysit me, would you kindly allow me to do my job? I need to talk to Doc Sheddon before he loads the body into his van and leaves."

Lonnie Guest did not deserve the pleasantries, but I needed to get him off my back.

"Well... Okay, I suppose, but you just watch it, and you don't get out of my sight, not even for one second, you hear me?"

"That's fine, Lonnie, but just try to keep up, will you?" I turned and continued on around the rear of the building.

Jack Sloan's body was lying in a pool of blood beside the dumpster. His arms and legs were sprawled out at awkward angles. In his open right hand was what looked to me like an old, military issue model 1917 Colt revolver with scuffed wooden grips. The gun was over a hundred years old, and it was definitely .45 caliber. *I'll bet everything I have, including my soul, that that's the weapon that killed Hunter and Samantha.*

Just by looking at the gun and its position, I knew something was off. It looked staged to me.

Nothing about this supposed suicide made any sense to me. First, when we left him only a few hours ago, he seemed to be in a perfectly relaxed state of mind, happy. And rightly so. We'd cleared him of any involvement in the murders. So why would he suddenly decide to kill himself?

Second, the position of the body didn't work for me either. The Colt 1917 is a physically big weapon. It has a five-and-a-half-inch barrel and, when fully loaded, it weighs in at more than two and a half pounds. The kick from that thing is worse than that of a mule. He would have had to use two hands to do what he supposedly did. There was no way he would have shot himself under the chin using just his right hand, and even if he had, the recoil would have thrown it from his already dead fingers, but there it was, lying in his open palm. *Bullshit!*

And there was something about the entry and exit wounds that didn't look right either.

Let's say for a second that he did shoot himself. He would either have been standing upright or he would have been sitting down with his back against the dumpster. He would have grasped the huge weapon in both hands, put the muzzle to his chin and pulled the trigger, right? Yes, that's exactly right. But if you act it out, you'll see what happens. Even without a gun in your hands you can see the weapon would have been at an angle, pointing upward, toward the back of his head, which is where the exit wound should have been, but it wasn't. The bullet had tracked upward from under his chin, through the roof of his mouth, and exited at the hairline on the top of his head, which led me to believe that the killer had shoved the muzzle under his chin and then pushed hard, forcing his head back. *No, this isn't suicide. It's angry, vicious murder.*

I stood for a moment, looking down at all that was left of Jack Sloan. He lay there, twisted like a pretzel, staring up at the darkening sky through sightless eyes. *At least the poor bastard died instantly.*

"Hey, Harry. How's it hanging?" Doc Sheddon said, startling me out of my reverie. "Kate said she was going to call you. Nasty business, this. Not at all what you'd think."

I stepped to my left, so he could step forward and stand beside me, and said, "Hi, Doc. Yes, nasty is the word... I think what we have here is a homicide. You're thinking the same, aren't you?"

Sheddon nodded. "I don't think it was a suicide. It looks staged to me. What do you know about this man?"

"I've interviewed him a couple times. He was a suspect in a homicide investigation I'm conducting for the DA's office, which is why Kate called me. But I cleared him earlier today. It doesn't make any sense that he'd kill himself now... And look at the way he's holding the gun!"

"I noticed that, too. It's highly unlikely the gun would still be in his hand. The entry wound is another dead giveaway," he continued, confirming my own conclusions. "His head must have been tilted back as far as it would go; also unlikely, I think."

I knelt down on one knee beside the body to get a closer look. Jack Sloan was a heavyset guy, but even in death, I could see there was still muscle underneath the flab, a relic from his football days in high school, I supposed.

His beard was well groomed, his shirt crisp and nicely pressed, same with the khaki pants, shoes shined... No, this guy didn't shoot himself... And the Colt... *Someone's trying to set him up.*

I slowly shook my head. I was pissed. Whoever did this was one cold son of a bitch, and I swore I was going to make him pay for what he'd done. I never could understand how someone could deprive someone else of their life. Me? I couldn't even think about it, except in self-defense of course.

"CSI has already taken samples from his hand," Doc continued, "but I'm guessing they won't find any gunshot residue. That old gun would have sprayed it around like a garden sprinkler. I'd be willing to bet the cylinder leaks like a colander. His hand should be plastered with it."

I stood up and said, "No doubt about that, Doc... Time of death?"

"Not more than an hour ago."

I nodded. "Is Mike Willis here?" I figured the CSI supervisor would have made an appearance. He always did when there was a homicide.

Doc nodded. "He got here just before I did. He's probably in the van."

"Thanks, Doc. I'll go and have a word with him. Talk to you soon."

I found Willis in his van, just as Doc said I would. The door was open and I could see he was talking with one of his techs.

"Hey, Mike. You find anything?" I asked.

Willis turned around, but before he could answer, Lonnie arrived, wheezing, at my side again.

"Harry, you can't go around asking law enforcement personnel about an ongoing investigation! If we let you do that, we might as well let all the reporters in the city into the crime scene."

I didn't turn away from Mike Willis. "Ignore him," I said. "Lieutenant Gazzara knows I'm here, and so does Henry Finkle. So what d'you have, Mike. Anything?"

Willis looked back and forth from me to Lonnie, then shrugged. "We're pretty sure the guy didn't shoot himself," he said, confirming what Doc and I thought. "We'll process the weapon and his clothing, of course, and we've taken samples from both hands. If GSR's present, I'll have Kate let you know."

"Good luck with that," I said. "Anything else?"

He hesitated, then said, "There is something, Harry, but it might not mean anything. Someone left in a hurry. Whoever it was peeled out of the parking lot on a motorcycle. We can't be sure if it has anything to do with what happened back there, but the tire marks are fresh, really fresh. Couldn't have happened more than thirty minutes ago, which puts it—"

"Right around the time Sloan was shot," I finished for him. "Where exactly are they, Mike?"

"Come on," he said and descended the steps. "I'll show you." And he took me to a spot on the parking lot surrounded by orange and white cones.

"See?" he said, looking down at the long, single black rubber stripe on the pavement.

I nodded, looked around to get my bearings. The KFC was on North Lee Highway. The tire mark, thick and dark at the one end, stretched for maybe a dozen yards, fading as the bike picked up speed. It seemed to be headed north toward Bonny Oaks Drive and... Interstate 75.

What were the odds of it being made by the killer? I wondered. Not great, but not impossible either.

"Well, it's a long shot," I said. "What kind of bike are we talking about?"

Mike looked down at the black mark. "The print's quite clean toward the far end," he said. "We should be able to match it through the database. We'll know the brand of the tire for sure. Other than that, all I can tell you is that it was a fairly heavy motorcycle... Possibly a Harley."

I frowned at that. A Motorcycle? A Harley? Who did I know that drove a motorcycle? Only one name came to mind. I pursed my lips and closed my eyes, already angry with myself. Even so, I wasn't about to jump to any conclusions.

A new voice spoke from behind us. "Lieutenant Gazzara wants to see you inside."

We all turned to look at the uniformed officer, a young guy.

Lonnie grunted and said, "Okay, kid. I'll be in there in a sec."

"Not you, Sergeant." the officer said. "Mr. Starke."

I grinned at Lonnie. "Don't worry, Lonnie. You can tag along if you want."

As I strode quickly across the parking lot, around the end of the building and into the restaurant, I could hear Lonnie huffing along behind me, trying to keep up. *He'd get a lot more done in life if he'd just lose a few pounds,* I thought.

The KFC had been closed after the shooting, of course, and nobody was being allowed inside or out. There must have been a dozen or so customers and several employees sitting at the tables or in booths, waiting for the officers to take their statements.

Kate was leaning against the counter, her legs crossed at the ankles, her elbow on the countertop, supervising the officers, of which there were three.

"Don't look at me like that, Harry," she said as I joined her. "Keep your head in the game. We have work to do, remember?"

"I'm allowed to admire," I said. "You look amazing... Okay, I get it. And my head is very much in the game. What did you want?"

Kate sighed, looked at Lonnie and said, "It's okay, Lonnie. You can leave. I need to talk to Harry... Alone!"

I grinned at him. He opened his mouth to speak, caught the look Kate gave him, and changed his mind. He turned and left without saying a word.

"I thought you'd like to know that there's a problem with the security cameras," Kate said, still with her back against the counter. "Those on the east side of the building—there are only two—aren't working. Haven't been for months, so she said." She pointed to one of the cooks. "And the ones on the west side are all pointed in the wrong direction. The rear, the east side of the lot and Lee Highway are not covered. We do, however, have a wonderful view of the Dollar General and the trees to the west. We're taking what footage we do have to the PD. Maybe we'll get lucky, but I wouldn't get my hopes up. How about you? Anything?"

I shook my head. "Not yet... I'm pretty sure Sloan didn't kill himself, though. I hate that this happened to him. I kind of liked him. He was a nice guy. I think it's connected to the Flagg-Goodkind case. You?"

"I think so too," she replied, "but I don't see how, much less who."

I nodded and said, "Whoever it was screwed up, made a big mistake. I think what happened here may be the break we need to solve the case."

"I hope you're right," she said. "Based on the shoddy way

the killer staged Sloan's suicide, I'd say he probably made other mistakes, as well."

"What about eyewitnesses, Kate? Did anyone in here see a guy dressed for a motorbike?"

Kate shook her head. "Nope. Mike Willis mentioned the tire marks. Whoever made them didn't come inside. A whole bunch of customers skedaddled before the officers arrived. So what you see"—she waved a hand in the direction of the dining room—"is what you get, and none of them were outside at the time of the shooting."

She walked over to one of the windows and looked out. They were covered with huge paper ads announcing new special combos and cheap deals.

"There's no clear line of sight from any of the windows, either," she said. "Not that you can see much out of them anyway, not with all this junk on the glass."

"It's advertising," I said, "but I see what you mean."

"A couple of the employees ran away when they heard the shot. Most were too scared to go out. Some of the customers even ducked down under the tables. I'd say almost half of them ran to their vehicles and disappeared. Can't say I blame them."

I could imagine that happening. That Colt would've sounded like a damn cannon, even from inside the restaurant.

"So nobody saw much of anything," Kate continued. "But we do have two witnesses that say they heard a motorcycle speeding away just after the crowd had hit the street. Maybe it was our killer making a quick getaway."

I nodded. "Those tire marks are headed north toward the Interstate. Mike Willis thinks it might have been a Harley."

Kate's eyebrows shot up. "That's how one of the witnesses described it."

In that moment, something bubbled up inside of me. I was angry... And the more I thought about it, the angrier I became.

A frickin' motorbike. It was a recurring theme throughout the investigation.

Who knows I talked to Jack Sloan today? I could think of only two people and one of them lay dead at the north end of the KFC parking lot. *Who rides a motorcycle? Who lied to me?* And then I knew.

"I'll catch you later, Kate," I said. "I need to go talk to someone."

I turned and strode out of the KFC, anger burning deep in my chest.

"Harry! Don't do anything stupid, you hear?" Kate's voice echoed after me, but I was too angry to pay any heed.

Danny Flagg rode a motorcycle. He even fixed them for a living. And he knew that Sloan had been talking to me. And now he'd killed him and tried to set him up as the fall guy for his brother's murder.

I was convinced of it.

38

I headed south on I-75 toward The Split, pushing the speed limit all the way. It was getting late, already almost eight o'clock, but I figured Danny Flagg would still be at his place of business, probably cleaning his frickin' bike and destroying evidence.

Fortunately, traffic was light and the road was clear. I made it to Rossville Boulevard in less than thirteen minutes.

I thought about calling Bob and having him meet me. After all, there was a possibility that I'd need backup. But I decided not to. I was armed, thankfully, and time was running out and I didn't have any to waste waiting for him. I wanted to catch Danny Flagg while the iron, or maybe I should say motorcycle, was still hot.

Besides, the bone that I had to pick with Danny Flagg was personal. He'd lied to me, twice, and he'd gotten away with it, twice. And, as I prided myself on my ability to figure out when someone is lying, I didn't like it, not one bit. Everything he'd told me could have easily been a lie...

Danny had said that he'd gotten himself in trouble, that

Hunter had nothing to do with it, but what if he lied? What if Hunter was indeed responsible for Danny being locked up? How did I know if Hunter had planned to meet Danny in Memphis or not? I had only his word for it. The only one that could have corroborated that story was Hunter himself, and he was long dead.

Besides, I realized as I neared the mechanic's shop, Danny didn't know that all the evidence in the case had been stolen, both physically and digitally. If he used the same gun to kill Hunter, Samantha, and now Jack Sloan, he wouldn't have known that we had no way to match the ballistics. *Yeah, it all began to make sense. Kill Sloan and plant the murder weapon on him. In the words of Long John Silver, smart as paint, so he is... or so he thinks he is.*

My face and hands were hot as I pulled into Flagg's parking lot that evening. The gate was still open, but most of the lights were off, all but those in the bay at the far end of the building.

I parked the Maxima just inside the gate, turned off the motor, got out and walked slowly toward the lights. As I approached, Danny Flagg, smiling and frowning at the same time, walked out to meet me.

That last bay had been converted into a motorcycle shop, and Danny had been inside working on a bike, an old, but beautifully maintained, Harley Knucklehead. *The same one he used when he killed Jack Sloan?* I wondered.

"Detective!" Danny said, wiping his hands on his pants. "This is a surprise. You're lucky you caught me. I was just about to close up shop. I had to stay late to work on a bike. You have more questions for me, I take it?"

"Indeed I do, you sorry piece of shit."

I was angry, but not angry enough to lay a hand on him. To do so could have screwed up the entire investigation.

That said, he had no doubt I was ready to do him serious damage if I had to.

His eyes widened. He raised his hands in defense and took several steps back.

"Hey, hey," he said, raising his voice. "Back off, will you? What the hell are you so upset about? Whatever it is, I didn't do it."

"Oh, yeah. You're a lying sack o' shit, Danny!" My hands were balled into fists, albeit they were at my sides. "Where were you from six this evening until now? And don't tell me here, because I know you weren't."

"But I was here. I've been here since just after three this afternoon."

"Alone, I suppose you're going to tell me next?"

He backed away again, into the shop, his hands still raised, palms out. He was beginning to look really scared. "Well yeah... but only since the guys went home at five-thirty. Look, I need to go. I'm supposed to meet someone, and if I don't show up, they'll start asking questions."

"Calm down, Danny. I'm not planning to hurt you. Can anyone confirm that you've been here all evening?"

I walked right past him into the bay where the Knuckle-head was parked on its stand.

"Nice ride," I said. "Is it yours or does it belong to a customer?"

I bent over and touched one of the rocker covers. It was warm.

"It's mine," he said. "Not that it's any of your damn business."

"Oh, it's my business all right. The engine's warm, Danny. You must have ridden it recently."

I straightened up, turned to face him, took my phone from my pocket and said, "You have twenty seconds to come clean, or I'm going to call the police and have you arrested on suspicion of murder. So think carefully before you decide to lie to me again. Did you kill Jack Sloan?"

I know, looking back on it, I could have been a little more subtle, but I had to see how the guy reacted. I had to hit him hard, not literally, of course. If he was going to lie to me again, I'd know it.

The man's eyes bulged. He shook his head, almost violently. He looked like I'd hit him with a hammer.

"No frickin' way, man. You... *What?* No! I didn't kill nobody. Jack Sloan's dead?"

It wasn't the reaction I was expecting. I'd expected him to deny it. There was no way he was going to admit that he killed Sloan, but I didn't expect him to deny it so vehemently. But, at that point I was swimming against the current, and I wasn't sure if I could fully trust my instincts anymore.

"Then why is this engine hot?"

"Frickin' hell! Because I was just running it, for God's sake. You have to do that, you know, when you're working on a motor, but I haven't taken it out. In fact, it hasn't left the shop since I brought it in here a week ago. I'm telling you the truth, man."

I studied his face. I shook my head. I figured I must be losing it. If he was telling the truth, and I was beginning to think that he was, then I was screwed, yet again. But I also knew the man was a bald-faced liar. He'd already proved that, and I'd believed him, and now Jack Sloan was dead.

I was beginning to seriously doubt myself. Why was I even there? I mean, what did I expect? That I'd catch Danny red-handed? Stupid of me, right?

"Yes," I said. "Sloan's dead. He was killed not more than ninety minutes ago. The killer escaped on a motorcycle, probably a Harley."

Danny smiled nervously, glanced instinctively at the Knucklehead, then said, "So you immediately thought it was me? Frickin' hell, detective. I had you figured better than that. D'you have any idea how many folks have motorcycles these days, especially Harleys? Hell, I fix motorcycles for rich guys and rednecks, men, women, black, white... All kinds of folks."

I knew that, but I wasn't looking for just anyone. I was looking for someone connected to his brother's murder, and at that moment he was the only person, who wasn't dead, that I could think of.

"Hey," he said. "Come with me. I want to show you something."

He walked over to a small desk in the corner of the bay, opened the top drawer and took out what at first looked like a small, folded piece of paper. It was old and yellow and stained. He smiled as he handed it to me. "That work for you, detective?" he asked.

I opened it, looked at it, shook my head and swore to myself. *F... me!*

It was a Greyhound bus ticket dated April 2, 1998, from Memphis to Chattanooga.

I looked up, locked eyes with him. He didn't flinch.

"You saved this all these years? Why?"

He shrugged. "I'd just gotten out of prison, right? I figured the police would learn that I'd been released from prison earlier than I told them and try to fit me up for Hunter's murder. So I filed it away. It was my insurance policy, like, just in case. And I was right, wasn't I? After you and your buddy came and talked to me this afternoon, I ran straight home to get it. I was back here by three-thirty, like I said, and I never left."

After a long pause, I sighed, nodded and said, "Good enough, Danny. It's hard to argue with this." I looked again at the ticket. "Hmm, April second... Your brother died on April first. You couldn't have made it back to Memphis and..." *Could he?* I looked at the Harley, then inwardly shook my head. *No, he's not that smart. Drop it, Harry.*

I looked at him. He had a hurt expression on his face.

"I wish I hadn't had to show it to you at all," he said. "I'd hoped you'd believe me, but you didn't. Now you come back here blaming me, not just for my brother's murder, but Sloan's as well."

I shrugged and said, "You should be damn pleased with yourself that you were smart enough to keep it. If you hadn't, I'd have had your ass in custody by now," I said.

With that, I turned and headed back toward my car.

"Hey, detective," he called after me.

"What now, Danny," I said as I turned again to face him.

"I hope you find him, the son of a bitch who killed my brother. I want justice for Hunter and Sam... and the quarterback, too. I just hope you're up to it, that's all."

"Oh, I'm up to it. You can take that to the bank."

I turned again, slid into the Maxima, closed my eyes and laid my head back against the headrest. To tell the truth, I wasn't at all sure I was up to it. In fact, I was feeling more than a little deflated.

And yet, there was that familiar tingle at the back of my neck. Once again, my gut was trying to tell me something. I must have sat there thinking for several minutes. It must've been something Danny Flagg had said, something important, something my subconscious had picked up on.

But what?

39

I was already out of the Flagg parking lot and on Rossville Boulevard when my phone rang. I tapped the screen, it was Kate. I answered it and put it on speaker.

"I hope you didn't shoot anyone," she said.

"Hello to you, too," I replied. "No, I didn't, but I did think about it. I am capable of making the right decision every now and then, you know."

"You are? Sometimes I wonder. So where did you go? Who—"

"It doesn't matter," I said, interrupting her. "I was wrong. It was a wasted trip. Is that all you wanted? If so, I'm tired and headed home."

"Pretty much. My you're grumpy. What happened?"

"I told you. I made a mistake. What d'you want, Kate?"

There was a moment of silence, then I heard her sigh and she said, "Okay. Look, we've finished up here. Doc Sheddon has already taken Sloan's body to the forensic center. He said he'll do the autopsy first thing in the morning. I'm going to attend. You want to join me? If you're not out playing cowboy, that is."

I thought about it, smiled to myself, and said, "Sure. Yeah, count me in... and I wasn't out playing cowboy."

"Really. That's not the impression I had. I know that look, Harry. When you left the KFC, you were out for blood!"

There was a pause. I could hear her giving someone instructions. Finally, she came back to me and said, "Do you want to get together later for some dinner?"

Boy, did I ever, but I needed to think, and I knew all Kate would want to do was distract me.

"As much as I'd like to, no. I better take a rain check." I could hear the disappointment in my voice. "I need to think things through. I feel like I have all the pieces to the puzzle, and I just need to put them together in the right order. You know what I mean?"

There was another pause. Finally, she said, "I understand. If you're sure there's nothing I can do to help... Okay, good luck with it and... I'll see you tomorrow morning, at nine?"

"Yes, of course. Sounds good."

"And, Harry. Promise me you won't stay up late drinking at the Sorbonne?"

I laughed. "What is it with you, Kate? That's not the plan. I'm going to do my thinking at home. I promise."

"Good. Pour yourself a stiff drink of that scotch you like so much and try to relax."

And that's exactly what I did!

40

I t was after nine-thirty when I finally arrived home that evening, and the first thing I did was build myself a thick ham and cheese sandwich. The second was pour myself three fingers of Laphroaig, just as Kate had suggested. Then I took both into my living room and settled down in my most comfortable chair, with a stunning view out of the floor-to-ceiling windows.

It was a moonless night, dark. The great river was quiet, lit only by the lights on the Thrasher bridge, long fingers of gold on black. It was that view that had persuaded me to buy the condo in the first place. It was just what I needed to center myself, to concentrate.

I finished my sandwich, set the plate aside, picked up the drink, sipped the fiery liquid and stared out into the night, reflecting on the previous four days. It was all there. I could feel it. All I had to do was sort it out.

Come on, Harry, concentrate. What do you know so far?

I started with Walter Goodkind. Everyone had assumed he

was guilty right from the start. I was certain he was responsible for the missing files, but the hack? I didn't think so. He was acting cagey at dinner that night, and I was sure he was hiding something. Did he have a motive to kill Hunter Flagg? Absolutely he did. As far as he was concerned, Hunter was a lowlife and a criminal. And the boy was stealing from one of his associates not to mention planning to marry his daughter, who'd turned against him. Plenty of motive there. But was it enough for him to kill her along with Hunter? I just didn't see it. That old man loved his kids, and Samantha most of all. For me, that was a deal-breaker. But there was more. The location.

Why would Walter choose Sailmaker Circle? It made no sense. Sure, Walter could have paid someone to kill the couple. Nope, not that either.

And that brought me to the murder of Jack Sloan. Not for the life of me could I imagine Walter on a Harley. I actually chuckled trying to picture it. Sure, he could have paid someone to kill Sloan, but why would he? He was smarter than that.

And that brought me to...? His other daughter, of course, Jennifer.

Okay, so what about Jennifer Young? She and her husband, Todd, hated Hunter and his family. That much was certain. And my feeling was that she would do just about anything to protect the family name, keep it from being dragged through the mud. And, from her perspective, the Flaggs were pretty muddy, especially the younger brother. Everything I could say about Walter, I could say about Jennifer, especially as she was less than a month away from inheriting the entire kit and caboodle. But did she have it in her to kill? I thought she did. I thought she might easily have killed Hunter, but not her sister. And, for much the same reasons I didn't think Walter had killed them, or Sloan, I didn't think she did either. So, mentally, I took her off the list, too.

What about Christopher Goodkind? Apparently, he was something of a rebel back in 1998. But he didn't even live in Chattanooga when the murders took place, and, as far as I could tell, he didn't seem to harbor any bad feelings toward Hunter or his family. More than that, he said he wanted justice for his sister, and I believed him. Neither did he have the means, motive or opportunity.

And neither did Steve and Wendy Flagg. In fact, they were tickled to death about the relationship between their son and Samantha. They supported it, and for all the same reasons the Goodkinds were against it. A marriage between the two would have brought the Flaggs the prestige Wendy so desperately desired. No... No motive, no murder.

And then there was Danny Flagg. He was a liar. He rode a Harley. But the bus ticket provided him an alibi. He couldn't have killed his brother and Samantha. Sloan, though? Maybe, but why would he? Nothing Sloan could have said would put him in Chattanooga the night of the murders. And Hunter and Sam were killed late on the evening of April first. The bus ticket was dated the second. I could not for the life of me see how he could have gotten from Memphis to Chattanooga and back again in the space of twelve hours, or so. *It's three-hundred and sixty miles each way, for God's sake.* No! It was impossible. That being so, he had no motive to kill Sloan.

I must have sat there, staring out of the window, thinking for at least a couple of hours before I finally quit for the night. I knew I was close to an answer, but I just couldn't put it together. Something was missing.

I gave it up, but before I did, I sent Tim a text message. I had questions and several things I needed him to look into. And then I went to bed, hoping to get a good night's rest, but you know how that goes when you have a head full of unanswered questions.

It wasn't until I slid between the sheets that I realized I should have taken Kate up on her offer. My mind was in a whirl. I needed a distraction.

That night I was visited once again by the monster that lived in the dark corners of my bedroom.

41

I didn't sleep too well that night. In fact, I woke up almost an hour before my alarm went off, and with a headache.

I stumbled out of bed and into the kitchen, popped a couple of Tylenol and turned on the coffee maker. With that, and with that wonderful early morning aroma wafting through my condo, I began to feel a little better.

I'd hoped that a good night's rest would've cleared my head, that maybe the pieces would have fallen into place, but that didn't happen.

And yet, as I sat at the breakfast bar and drank the first cup of the day, I could feel the tickle at the back of my neck. My subconscious was trying to tell me something.

It was around eight that morning when Kate messaged me to remind me I was to meet her at the county medical examiner's office at nine. I messaged back, told her I'd be there, and then I hit the shower.

As I stood under the almost scalding hot spray, my brain once again swirled as seemingly random details popped in and out of my mind, like smoke signals, reflections of the past several days that seemed to mean nothing at all.

Hunter's mystery contact, for example. Who the hell was it?

Danny Flagg lying about when he was released from prison.

Hunter wanting to meet him in Memphis. Why?

Jack Sloan almost joining Hunter on the job to steal medical supplies.

Jennifer Young's desire to protect her family.

The Nancy Goodkind scholarship program.

And so on, and so on, ad infinitum. I came out of that shower with what seemed like a head full of concrete, and it wasn't any better when I drove into the parking lot at the medical examiner's office.

Needless to say, I wasn't in the best of moods when I strode into the reception area where Kate was waiting for me.

"Oh my, Harry," she said, looking me up and down. "You look rough. I take it you didn't sleep well last night. You should have taken me up on my offer."

"And good morning to you, too," I replied, rubbing the back of my neck. "No, I didn't. I didn't get much sleep at all. I couldn't get my mind off the case. You're right in one sense, though, but wrong in another."

"Oh, how's that?"

"You're right that I should have taken you up on your offer. If I had though, there would have been two of us that didn't get any sleep."

"Hah, so you say. I would have worn you out, big boy. You would have slept like a baby."

And that, for the first time in days, brought a genuine smile to my lips.

"See?" she said. "I always know what you need. Now, to

business. I don't know if our meeting with Doc Sheddon this morning will get us any closer to an answer. I have the feeling that we're not going to find anything world-changing here."

"At this point, Kate, I'll take whatever I can get. Where is he, I wonder?"

As if on cue, Doc Sheddon appeared behind the counter. It was only then that I noticed, not for the first time, that the room was sans a receptionist.

"Good morning, Doc," I said. "You run off the help again?"

"Like a good woman, Harry," he replied, "good help is hard to find."

"Especially help that will put up with you and your tantrums," Kate said, laughing.

"True," he replied. "So true. That being said, I'm sorry I kept you waiting, so come on back. Let's take a look at the poor chap, shall we?"

We followed him through to one of the three examination rooms—more like chop shops, if you ask me—where the earthly remains of Jack Sloan lay on a metal table, covered only by a white sheet.

"You've already done the autopsy?" Kate asked. "How come?"

"Well, Mrs. Sheddon is away visiting her sister, so there was no reason for me to go home. So, instead of wasting the evening watching TV, I decided to enlist Carol's help and get a head start... no pun intended, you understand," he said as he lifted the sheet and looked down at the top of Sloan's head.

Carol Owens was, and still is, Doc's forensic anthropologist and sometime assistant.

"Well, there are a few interesting details here," Doc continued. "The cause of death was exactly what you would expect." He pulled back the sheet, fully exposing the head. "A single gunshot to the head, entering slightly to the rear of the mandible and tracking upward through the zygomatic bone, exiting the skull through the pre-frontal cortex. As you can see, that .45 caliber bullet and the exploding gasses did quite a number on the top of his skull. The track, I think you'll agree, is a little unusual."

I leaned over and inspected Jack Sloan's head. It had been cleaned up, but it still looked gruesome.

At least he didn't suffer, I thought. *He would've died instantly, wouldn't have felt a thing. The slug would've destroyed the pain center as it passed through.*

"There were some fibers and whatnot on the clothing and on the soles of his shoes," Doc continued. "I sent it all to the lab, but I don't think we can expect them to reveal anything."

"What about under his fingernails?" I asked, as I lifted a section of the sheet to reveal one of his hands. "I noticed them during our first conversation with him; his nails were well-manicured, clean and perfectly trimmed."

"Very good, Harry," Doc said, smiling broadly. "You'll make a fine detective, one day."

I grinned at the old man. "Up yours, Doc."

"So crude," he said, as he flipped through the pages on his clipboard. "To answer your question, no, we did not find anything under his fingernails."

I frowned. "Any evidence of defensive wounds?"

Sheddon shook his head. "None, which I find to be significant."

"Yes, that is interesting," Kate said. "He must have just stood there and let someone walk up to him, shove the gun up under his chin and pull the trigger. I don't see that at all."

"Neither do I," I said. "I guess we'll have to wait for the tox screen, but I assume there were no drugs in his system. So, yeah, it is kind of interesting."

Doc nodded and said, "And, just in case you're curious, his last meal was a Number One Combo from Burger King."

"Oh. How can you know that?" Kate asked skeptically.

"I can't," he admitted, "but he did consume a large burger, with pickles, and fries. The last meal of a happy man."

"Okay, so let me get this straight," I said. "Kate, face me for a sec."

She did. She stood in front of me, eye to eye, looking into my eyes, smiling. *My, she's a formidable girl. Hang onto your britches, Harry m'boy.*

"So, let's say you're Jack Sloan," I said. "I walk up to you and start talking. I'm upset. Maybe you see the .45 in my hand. You're scared; frozen." I made my thumb and forefinger into a gun and lifted it so that it pointed at Kate. "I point the gun at you. What do you do?"

Kate looked at my finger and smiled. "Well, if it was me, I'd take the damn gun away from you, like this." She grabbed my finger and twisted it, then burst out laughing. "But, I'm not me. I'm Jack Sloan, so I wouldn't know what the hell to do... I'd probably just stand there, paralyzed."

"Right. Okay. So then I press the gun under your chin, like this." I put the tip of my finger beneath her chin. "And you, being paralyzed with fear, let me do it."

"I wouldn't have much choice, would I?"

"Right," I said, "but that's not how it was done. If I pulled the trigger now, you'd lose most of the back of your head. No, I'm angry, so I push, like this," and I did, and sure enough, back went her head.

Doc, on the other side of the table, began to clap, slowly.

"Bravo, you two. You should take your act on Broadway."

"Oh, cut it out, Doc," I said. "I'm being serious, here."

"What if the person was a stranger who came onto him," Doc asked, "a femme fatale."

"Well, it could've happened that way," I said. "Except, he was gay, so it would have been a guy doing the seducing."

Doc shrugged. "So, whatever the male version of a femme fatale is, then. What do you think?"

"It's as likely as anything else," Kate said.

"Yes, Doc," I added. "And if ever you get tired of working for the county, you can come work for me. I could always use another investigator... You, too, Kate."

"Shucks, Harry. Now I feel all warm and fuzzy inside," Doc said.

And Kate launched into her usual little speech about how she wouldn't be caught dead working as a private investigator in general and for me in particular, and I sighed. I'd heard it so many times before I could have repeated it word for word.

It was as she was making her speech that I felt my phone vibrate. It was an email from Tim. I had the answers to the questions I'd sent to him the night before.

I skimmed quickly through the information, and I couldn't help but smile.

I didn't notice exactly when Kate stopped talking, but the silence caused me to look up and see that both she and Doc were staring at me quizzically.

"What's with the smile, Harry?" Doc asked. "You just find out you've won the lottery... or what?"

"Better than that. I think I just solved the case."

Kate's mouth opened in surprise. "Then you must've gotten a message from Tim. We all know he's the real brains behind your operation."

"On any other occasion, I would take offense at that, Kate. Except this time I happen to agree with you."

"Well?" Kate said. "Are you planning to share with the rest of the class?"

I put my phone in my pocket. "Not just yet. I want to

review some of the details, make sure my duckies are all in a neat little row. If my gut's telling me what I think it is, I know who killed Hunter and Samantha. But, in the meantime, I gotta run. Bye, y'all."

When I walked out of the county medical examiner's office that morning, smiling to myself, I felt like a million bucks.

42

As soon as I got on the road, I began making phone calls. First, I called Bob and told him I'd meet him at the office later. Then, I called Danny Flagg and asked him to meet me at the Goodkind residence later that afternoon, and bring Steve and Wendy with him. I told him I'd call him later with the exact time. He was skeptical, of course, and pushed me for answers, but I told him I'd explain later when I met him at the Goodkinds. He reluctantly agreed.

I smiled to myself. My plan was coming together.

Next, I called Walter Goodkind and asked him if he could assemble his family at his home that afternoon. His reaction, too, was to bombard me with questions. I deflected all of them, telling him I'd answer them later. Finally, he agreed, and we set the meeting for one o'clock that afternoon. That done, I called Kate and asked her to join me there, too.

"You just left me," she said, sounding put out. "Why didn't you tell me?"

"Because I didn't want to talk about it, any of it. I'll see you there at one." And I hung up, knowing I'd probably pissed her off, big time.

It wasn't until I arrived at my offices that I was able to carefully read the email Tim had sent me. As I digested the information, I was even more certain that I had what I needed to solve the case.

Finally, I leaned back in my chair and smiled, then I went to Tim's office to congratulate him on a job well done and was somewhat surprised to find Bob already there.

"What's going on?" I asked. "Something I should know about?"

Bob grinned and said, "Harry, I was just coming to find you. I had a hunch last night, so I came in early this morning and asked Tim to help me figure it out."

I raised my eyebrows. "Really? What kind of hunch?"

"Well, see... Since you gave me the evening off, I gave Zoe a call and we met for drinks. She was... well, different. She asked a lot of questions about the case... and, well, she was a little too interested, if you ask me."

"Maybe she's interested because of what you do for a living," I said. "Let's face it, Bob, being a PI is... unusual. Maybe she's tickled to be dating the local Mike Hammer."

"I don't think so, Harry. I don't have your instincts, but I do know when I'm being pumped, so I asked Tim to run her background. You're not going to believe what he found. Zoe is not who she claims to be... Well she is, but she isn't, if you know what I mean."

"No, I don't know what you mean. Who the hell is she?" I suddenly had that awful feeling that everything was about to fall apart again.

"Zoe Mullins legally changed her name, in 2005," Tim said, "when she was nineteen. Before that her name was Flagg, Denise Flagg."

I was stunned... No, I was shattered.

"Son of a bitch," I said quietly. "That's a frickin' game changer, if ever there was one. How the hell did we not see it, Bob?"

Bob rubbed his temples. "Why would we?" he said. "There was no reason to think she was anyone other than who she said she is. It was only when she began asking questions last night that I started to wonder. She asked a lot of questions about Walter Goodkind. She wanted to know if we thought he was the murderer. At first, I thought she just wanted to make sure she wasn't working for a killer, but, when I made it clear to her that we were looking at all the options and that we weren't targeting any one particular person, she looked at me kind of funny, went real quiet, then said it was getting late and she wanted to go home. It wasn't late. It was only fifteen 'til ten. Anyway, I dropped her off. Now, this morning, she won't answer her phone."

I looked at him and shook my head. "You're not saying she could've killed her own brother, are you? Good God, Bob. She was only twelve."

I couldn't even imagine a kid, much less a twelve-year-old girl, toting that heavy Colt 45, never mind trying to fire the damn thing... and how the hell would she have gotten herself out to Sailmaker? No, it was impossible. There had to be another answer.

Bob shook his head and said, "Not hardly. No, I think she wants to see Walter Goodkind behind bars. In fact, that's probably why she got the job at Legacy in the first place."

Now that made a whole lot more sense. What must she have felt when she lost her older brother to a nasty homicide? Add to that the fact that just about everyone was certain Walter Goodkind was the perp, and you could understand how the kid might grow up hating the man.

"I just called Legacy Health," Tim said. "Zoe didn't show up to work today. Do you think she's planning something?"

I shook my head. "I don't know, Tim. But we better go and find out. What's her address?"

"I have it," Bob said.

I looked at him and nodded. "Then let's go, partner. I have a feeling we need to hurry!"

And we did.

43

"I just can't believe it, Harry," Bob said as I drove to Zoe Mullins' address. "But you were right. I shouldn't have gotten personally involved. But then, I never could resist a pretty face."

"Quit beating yourself up," I said. "You had no way of knowing who she is. I do think she played you right from the beginning, though. I also think she has a plan, and that she's sticking to it. I just hope we can get to her before she does something really stupid. It would also be nice if we could include her in the meeting this afternoon."

"What meeting?"

"Oh yeah. I forgot to mention that, didn't I?" And I proceeded to fill him in, leaving out my reasoning, of course.

Bob smiled. "Geez, Harry. I can't believe you're going to have an Inspector Clouseau moment... Should be kinda fun, though."

"Maybe. Maybe not!"

The address where Zoe Mullins lived was an apartment above a double garage with a separate entrance in a quiet, working-class neighborhood. All was quiet... and yet, when Bob knocked on her door, I had a weird feeling in the pit of my stomach that something wasn't quite right.

"She's not here," I said. "Let's go."

We were about halfway down the stairs when my phone rang. It was Tim.

"What's up, Tim?"

"I hope you're not gonna get mad at me," Tim said, "but I did a little creative... searching?"

It wasn't really a question. He was just letting me know he'd been hacking again.

I sighed, put him on speaker and said, "Tell me, Tim. What did you find?" By then I was down the stairs and almost at the car.

"Well, I did an extended background check on Zoe Mullins. Harry, she has a concealed carry permit."

Bob and I exchanged glances, and he looked as worried as I felt.

"Oh crap. You're sure about that?" I asked.

"Oh yeah. And she's a member of the Chattanooga Rifle Club. I bet the girl knows how to shoot."

Yes, I bet she does.

"Okay, Tim. Nicely done. We'll take it from here."

We ran to the Maxima, then headed west toward Lookout Mountain.

"Where d'you think she is?" Bob asked.

I looked at the clock on the dash. It was a little after twelve noon. I had a gut feeling I knew exactly where she was, and I stepped on the gas.

I was hoping to get there in time to stop Zoe from becoming a murderer—and catch the real killer.

44

It took us almost thirty minutes to get to the Goodkind residence on West Brow Road up on Lookout Mountain, and I wasn't surprised to see that we weren't the first to arrive. Three vehicles were parked on the circular drive in front of the porch. Two of them I recognized as belonging to Todd Young and Christopher Goodkind. The other, a Ford Focus, I'd never seen before, but I would have bet money on who it belonged to.

So, Walter kept his promise, I thought as we exited the car. *They're all here, and early, too. How long before the Flaggs arrive, I wonder?*

It was still early, and I figured the Flaggs wouldn't arrive much before one o'clock, if at all. One member of the Flagg family, though, was already there. I was sure that the Ford belonged to Zoe.

We ascended the steps to find Todd Young standing at the open front door.

"Thank God you're here," he said. "I was just about to call the police when I saw you arrive. One of Walter's secretaries has locked herself in his study with him. She has a gun and is threatening to kill him!"

"Just take it easy, Mr. Young. It will be all right. We'll handle it." I pushed past him and went to Walter's study, where I found the rest of the Goodkind family outside the door, clamoring to get inside.

As soon as Jennifer Young spotted me, she turned and said, "You must do something, Mr. Starke. That crazy young woman has my father at gunpoint. She says he's a murderer. Can you break down the door or something?"

I looked at the door: three inches of solid oak. I looked at the lock: sturdy. But with a little extra effort, I figured I could hit it hard enough to rip it out of the door frame. Bob, thirty pounds heavier than me, would find it easier, but smashing the door wasn't the answer.

"If we do that," I said, "she'll shoot him."

Jennifer's eyes filled with tears. "Oh, no! Then don't do it. But how can we get them out of there? Can you call the SWAT team?"

Jennifer obviously didn't have a clue what she was talking about. I couldn't order up a SWAT team even if I wanted to, and I didn't. I did, however, call Kate and asked her to get her butt in gear and get there ASAP.

Of course, she wanted to know what the hurry was all of a sudden. I told her I had an emergency and that I had to go, and I hung up. Not a good idea, but what the hell. I was already in way over my head. What else could happen?

I looked around the group, then said, "Just to confirm, there's no one else in there other than Zoe Mullins and Walter?"

They all shook their heads.

Stacy Hudson's face was twisted in anger and fear. "She

isn't Zoe Mullins. Her name is Zoe Flagg. She said so before she slammed the door in our faces."

They all looked at me. "Yes. That's who she is," I said with a sigh.

Christopher Goodkind's face was pale, totally devoid of color, his eyes wide. "So she's the murderer? She killed Hunter and Sam?"

I shook my head slowly. "Look, I need y'all to calm down. Everything's going to be fine. No, she did not kill her brother and your sister. She was only twelve years old in 1998, and besides... Oh, never mind. First things first. Let's see if we can get your father out of there in one piece."

I went to the door, put my ear to one of the panels, and listened. Nothing. All was quiet.

"Zoe?" I called. "Can you hear me?"

There was a pause.

"Go away!" Zoe shouted. "You had your chance to get him. Now it's too late. Now it's my turn."

"Zoe," I shouted. "You need to listen to me. If you hurt him, you'll go to prison for a very long time. It doesn't have to be that way. Come on out and let's talk about it."

"I told you, it's too late for that," she screamed. "You had your chance, Detective Starke."

"Zoe!" Bob called from behind me. "It's me, Bob Ryan. Listen to Harry. He can help you."

Another pause.

"No one can help me now. I know he killed my brother. I always knew. Everybody knew. They just couldn't prove it. I thought you and Mr. Starke would get him and put him behind bars, but you told me last night that you didn't know who killed Hunter. I can't wait any longer. He has to pay for what he did."

"Zoe, listen to me," I said. "You don't have any proof that Walter killed your brother, do you?"

She didn't answer.

Christopher Goodkind tapped me on the shoulder and said, "I think my sister's right. I think we should break the door down and get them out of there before she hurts him. I would've tried to do it myself, but I hurt my wrist mountain biking this morning." He held up his right hand. It was bandaged.

"No one's breaking the door down. Get that idea right out of your head."

I turned my attention back to the door.

"You didn't answer my question, Zoe. Do you have any evidence that Walter Goodkind killed your brother?"

After another long pause, she finally spoke up. "I don't need any evidence. I know it's true."

"Well, that's a shame, because I do have evidence. I know exactly who killed your brother. You wouldn't want to kill the wrong man, now would you? You said you wanted justice, so why don't you open the door and let's talk about it?"

"I'll be delivering justice today, Mr. Starke."

"She has a gun to my head, Harry," I heard Goodkind call. He didn't sound well, and no wonder.

"If you pull that trigger, Zoe, it won't be justice you deliver. It will be murder. I'm telling you, Walter Goodkind did not kill your brother. Now come on out before you do something stupid. What do you say?"

"Zoe," Bob shouted. "Your parents are on the way. So's Danny. So is Lieutenant Gazzara. Harry knows who killed your brother. So let's let him do his job, okay?"

There was another long pause. Everybody on my side of the door was holding their breath. I bet Walter was too.

Finally, Zoe answered. "Okay, but you have to promise you won't hurt me."

I smiled. "No one is going to hurt you, Zoe. Just put the gun down and unlock the door."

And she did!

As soon as the lock on the office door clicked, I turned the knob and pushed the door open slowly. Walter came out first, his face ashen. I figured the experience had probably robbed him of a good ten years. And, when you're as old as Walter Goodkind, you don't have ten years to spare.

Zoe came out next, tears streaming down her face. It was at that moment that Kate arrived with two uniformed officers. One of them started forward, handcuffs at the ready. I put my hand on his arm, looked at him and shook my head. He turned and looked at Kate. She shook her head too, and he backed off.

"Thanks, Kate," I said. "I think it would be a good idea if she stays. She needs to know who really killed her brother. Besides, I don't think Walter will press charges when he hears what I have to tell him."

Kate nodded, smiling. "I don't think anyone wants to miss your big reveal, Harry. You've been teasing us all day!"

I nodded, looked at the old man, who seemed to be feeling somewhat better, and said, "How about it, Walter?"

"You really think you know?" he asked skeptically.

"I do!"

"About damn time! Let's do it."

45

Steve, Wendy, and Danny Flagg arrived just a few minutes after we had sat down in the living room, lounge, whatever. Me? I decided that, if I was going to do dramatic, the best place for me to do it would be to stand by the fireplace.

Kate and the two officers stood together at the other end of the room with Zoe seated just in front of Kate, and she cried when she saw her parents.

"Denise?" Steve said. "Why is she here?"

"Please just sit down," I said. "I'll explain later."

I paused and waited for everyone to settle down. All eyes were on me.

I must admit, I did feel a little like Inspector Clouseau, especially as I was about to drop a "bem" on them, as he put it in his funny French accent. Joking aside, though, it isn't often that I get the chance to solve a case in such a dramatic manner. And, let me tell you, it's pretty cool having everyone looking at you, waiting for answers. That kind of thing could easily go to your head!

But it wasn't about me. It was about catching a killer, one who'd already killed three times and, I was sure, wouldn't hesitate to kill again.

"I have to admit," I began, "that this investigation took us places I never expected. But let's begin at the beginning.

"One dark night in 1998, Hunter Flagg and Samantha Goodkind were murdered, shot to death with a large caliber revolver, a 45, and were then stripped of their clothes and left on the roadside."

"From the very beginning, Walter Goodkind became the prime suspect. Now, fast forward to last Sunday, when DA Larry Spruce asked me to look into the case. I went into it with an open mind. Yes, Walter was still the prime suspect, but we had to prove it. We also had to look at all the possible angles. And that's when the investigation stalled. Someone was working against me, and my team."

I looked around the room. "First, we discovered that someone stole the physical evidence from the Chattanooga Police Department's evidence room, along with the original case files. No one knows exactly when, but Deputy Chief Finkle is of the opinion that it must have been several years ago, possibly even ten or more.

"Then, on Monday last, someone hired a computer geek to delete the digital case files. So nothing was left. It was as if the murders had never happened. We found the geek—it was a young woman—and we talked to her, but she didn't know who hired her."

I looked at the faces around the room, wondering if I'd triggered a reaction. I hadn't. So I continued.

"And then, early last evening, someone murdered Samantha's ex-boyfriend, Jack Sloan, and staged it to look like he committed suicide. It didn't work. The staging was clumsy, obvious. I believe the person who killed Sloan also killed Hunter and Samantha..."

I paused, then continued, "There are three guilty people here in this room. One of them is a killer."

I turned to Goodkind and said, "How about you, Walter? You publicly expressed hatred toward Hunter and his family. You hated that Samantha was in love with Hunter, and you publicly threatened both of them in front of witnesses. You even slapped your daughter when she threatened to run away."

Walter didn't flinch. "You've already said that I didn't kill anyone, Detective Starke. I didn't. I'm innocent. So please cut the theatrics and get to the point?"

"Oh, I know you didn't kill anyone, Walter, but you're not innocent, are you? It was you who arranged for the files and the physical evidence to be stolen from the police department. You're the only person in this room that had the resources and connections to make it happen."

Walter Goodkind's stare was ice cold. "I deny it, of course."

I smiled. "You can deny it all you want. And you're going to get away with it because I can't prove it, but that doesn't change anything, does it, Walter?"

He couldn't help it. He looked away, at the floor between his feet. I smiled. I had him and he knew it.

"I don't believe it," Todd Young said angrily. "Why would he do such a thing? If he didn't murder them, why hide evidence?"

Jennifer Young shot him a nasty look.

I cocked an eyebrow in her direction. "It's a legitimate question, isn't it, Mrs. Young. You know why he did it, don't you? Walter Goodkind stole the evidence for the same reason you did."

Jennifer feigned shock and surprise, quite convincingly, too.

"How dare you?" she said angrily. "I did nothing of the sort, and neither did my father. You're barking up the wrong tree, Mr. Starke."

I shook my head. "Your pretentious outrage isn't going to work, Jennifer. You see, it's simply a process of elimination. We figured you both out early in the investigation. Walter thought you were responsible for the murders and arranged for someone to steal evidence, probably many years ago, to protect you. You, on the other hand, thought your father was responsible for their deaths and hired the Iron Maiden... Sorry, the Iron Crusader to delete the digital files for precisely the same reason. Kind of ironic, don't you think? Each of you trying to protect the other for crimes neither one of you committed."

Bob was grinning, looking back and forth between Jennifer and Walter Goodkind. "We figured that one out early, didn't we, Harry?" he said. "It's just a matter of family protecting family."

"Unfortunately, there's no way to prove it either way," I said. "You, Walter, are home free, as are you, Mrs. Young, thanks to your very deep pockets. I doubt the state cybercrime unit in Nashville will be able to track your hacker down, so you get to walk too."

"Not that it would do any good if they did find her," Kate said. "I doubt she'd snitch. It would be bad for business." She gave me a knowing little wink.

I nodded to Kate and then continued. "But, as I said, although neither of you committed the murders fourteen years ago or killed Jack Sloan last night, you are both guilty; your lack of trust for one another caused you both to commit a litany of lesser crimes, including obstruction of justice."

I looked around the room at the faces. The reactions ranged from total shock to mild surprise to indifference. Zoe Mullins, or should I say Zoe Flagg, looked as if she'd found a spider in her underwear.

Steve Flagg was the next to speak, "So who did do it? Who killed my boy?"

I glanced at Steve and smiled. "Yes, let's get to that detail now."

Again, I paused and looked around the room, studying each face. I was already certain who it was, but the look I received from one of them confirmed it. I knew who the killer was, and the killer knew it.

"Do you want to tell them about what you did, or should I?" I said.

There was a gasp as all eyes turned to...

46

Christopher Goodkind looked up at me and smiled sadly. "I told you justice was overdue, detective, and even when I panicked and tried to get out of it, you saw through everything I did."

I nodded at him and said, "I had my suspicions almost from the beginning. They were just little things, attitude, odd looks, questions. You couldn't look me in the eye, could you, Chris?"

I cocked my head to one side, narrowed my eyes, and stared at him. Sure enough, he looked away.

"But that isn't much to go on, is it? Then you said something to me yesterday, in Jennifer's office. You said you lived in Pittsburgh at the time of the murders. Well, I already knew that. Then you said you visited your family every couple of weeks, ostensibly to keep your father happy. Reasonable enough, so I thought. Actually, I thought you were probably tapping him for money. But that's beside the point. You also said that you rode down to Chattanooga every two weeks... and that was the kicker.

"It didn't dawn on me, not at first. I imagined you driving

home in some rich kid's car to ask daddy here for more money to blow on partying up in Pittsburgh with your writer friends. It wasn't until later that I realized you said, and I quote, that you *rode* down, like on a motorcycle. Actually, you said ride, but that's neither here nor there."

I looked over at Danny Flagg. "At first, I was convinced that Danny, here, had killed Jack Sloan—and the two youngsters back in the day—but he provided me with irrefutable proof that he couldn't have killed them. Thus he had no reason—no motive—to kill Sloan. But then, Danny, you reminded me that all kinds of people own motorcycles these days, both rich and poor."

Danny Flagg nodded at me.

"No, no." Stacy Hudson stood up, shaking her head, her tight black curls dancing back and forth, her eyes full of tears. "You can't blame any of this on my Chris. He didn't do it! It had to be one of them." She pointed across the room where the three Flaggs were sitting.

"Your fiancé does own a Harley motorcycle, doesn't he, Ms. Hudson?"

She nodded. "Yes, but that doesn't mean anything. That isn't enough evidence to convict somebody. Someone can't be guilty just because they own a motorcycle."

"That's true, Ms. Hudson," I said. "But you see, this morning my computer expert messaged me confirming that Christopher actually owns three motorcycles, including a 1996 Harley Fatboy and a... 1994 Honda 250 Nighthawk. But, as you say, that's not enough to convict anyone of anything. However, it is enough for the police to get a warrant to search his home, and that Harley motorcycle. And I'm willing to bet that the Harley's rear tire will match the tire tracks we found at the scene of Jack Sloan's murder, putting you right there at the scene, Chris."

Again, he looked away and didn't answer.

"You killed Jack Sloan and staged it to look like a suicide. You just about blew the top of his head off with the same .45 caliber revolver you used to kill Hunter and Samantha. Then you left it in his hand—big mistake—the idea being to divert suspicion of the earlier murders from you to Sloan. But it wouldn't have worked anyway. Thanks to your father, the physical evidence was gone, so there was no way to match the bullet that killed Samantha to the weapon. You killed the poor guy for nothing, and horribly, too. How does that make you feel, Chris?"

I looked at him. "That bright idea was a last-minute effort to cover the murders you felt you had to commit, and because you thought Jack Sloan knew who you really were."

Walter Goodkind looked at his son with both fear and sadness in his eyes and said, "Did you do this, my son? Did you murder your sister and that boy, and this other person? If you did, why, and what the hell does he mean, who you really are?"

It was Bob who answered his question. "He was Hunter's contact."

"That's right, Bob," I said. "Good old Chris here was helping Hunter and his brother steal medical supplies from Legacy Health's business partners."

Goodkind stared at his son, slowly shaking his head, obviously in shock. Jennifer had her arms crossed tightly over her chest, her eyes cold, chips of ice. The most relaxed member of the Goodkind family was Christopher himself. It was almost as if he wanted to get caught, which actually made a lot of sense.

I looked at him and said, "Chris, you told me justice was overdue, and I think you really meant it, didn't you?"

He nodded, slowly. "In fact, I came close to confessing last night. If I'd had just a little more to drink, I probably would have told you everything. Remember, out in the driveway? I was so tired of it all, you know?"

Stacy got up from the couch and stepped away from him, sniffing loudly.

Christopher continued. "Yes, I was giving tips to Hunter. I needed the money, you see? Sam knew about it, too. In fact it was she who suggested it. We... she and I, were just so tired of being a part of this... family. Tired of all the unreasonable expectations you laid on us." He looked at his father. Walter's face was the color of week-old oatmeal. "We were tired of our so-called friends. All they wanted was money. We just wanted out, to be left alone."

"But you couldn't do that without money, could you, Chris?" I said. "You said that you were ready to confess, but then you killed Jack Sloan? What made you change your mind? Why the last-ditch effort to throw it off onto him?"

Christopher gave a little shrug. "It was yesterday afternoon, after I talked to you in my sister's office. I'd been thinking about my family all day. I do love them, you know. I'd wanted to get some lunch, you see, with Jennifer... I really did. But then, when she couldn't go, I went to talk to my father." He shook his head, then continued. "It probably sounds implausible, but after chatting with him, I suddenly realized I didn't want to let him down. I thought if I could tie up a couple of loose ends, I could put it all behind me... and move on... for Stacy, and for the rest of my family."

"But you didn't have to kill Jack Sloan," Bob said. "Jack didn't know you. He had no idea you were Hunter's contact."

Christopher shook his head. "But I didn't know that, you see. I did know he used to be Sam's boyfriend, and that Hunter was trying to enlist him to do one last job... You see, I had information about a shipment of expensive drugs. The payoff would have been enormous. I thought Sam had told Sloan about me. I couldn't risk it. Besides, he was the perfect... what d'you call it? Fall guy? The perfect fall guy. I did what I had to do, and I did what I had to with Hunter and Sam, too."

"But why?" This from Zoe Mullins. "Why did you have to kill them?"

"They wanted out. They wanted to get away from here, and fast. After Jack Sloan chickened out, they decided to black-mail me instead. Hunter wanted a hundred thousand dollars. I would have gladly given it to him, but I didn't have it, not even a fraction of it." Again he looked at the old man. "And I couldn't ask you for it, could I?"

I nodded, looked at Danny Flagg and said, "You told me that Hunter had expected to come into a lot of money. That he was going to split it with you and then start a new life with Sam in California."

Danny nodded angrily.

"So you arranged to meet Hunter and Samantha out on Sailmaker Drive, didn't you, Chris? I'm thinking you told them you had the money. But you didn't. You killed them."

Chris looked down at his lap. "Hunter was a little shit, so ungrateful. After all I had done for him. And Sam, she was no better than he was. She chose that nasty little turd over her family... And I'd supported them. I'd already given Hunter everything I could. And now he was asking for cash. He said he would tell my father that I'd betrayed him and his company. I just couldn't believe they'd do that to me... I couldn't let them do it to me. So, yes, I killed them, and I've regretted it every minute since." He continued to stare down at his lap.

"So," I said, "you arranged to meet them. You rode out there on your Honda Nighthawk. You parked back around the bend where they couldn't see you. You approached Hunter's truck on foot, under cover of darkness. Then you shot them both, and then you left them among the trees at the side of the road." I paused and looked around the room. Everyone was staring at me with rapt attention, even Kate. I winked at her and continued.

"You knew that Hunter often carried his bike in the back of his truck, and that he kept a ramp in the bed to load it. So it was easy enough for you to load the lightweight Honda into the truck and then drive away... Then you off-loaded the bike and dumped the truck, probably in the river. I get all that, but what I don't get is why you had to strip them of their clothes?"

"Isn't it obvious?" Steve Flagg said. "He wanted to make it look like some sick freak had done it. A serial killer like them they show on TV."

Chris shook his head, still unable to look at anyone. "No, that wasn't it at all. A week or so earlier I'd watched an episode of the Forensic Files on TV. It said something about wild animals—wolves and coyotes and especially wild hogs—and we do have those around here, you know. It described how they can eat a body, even the bones. All they leave is the clothing... so I thought that if I took their clothes, Hunter and Sam would just... disappear. Everyone would think they'd run away together, like they'd intended to. I had no idea someone would find them the very next morning."

And there it was. All the questions were answered. This young man, this rebel, hated his family so much, and yet he'd felt betrayed when his own sister tried to blackmail him. I couldn't help but look at him and shake my head.

In fact, all eyes were on Christopher as he sat there, studying his hands in his lap, obviously feeling sorry for himself. And because everyone was looking at Christopher, no one noticed Stacy Hudson until they heard the click as she cocked the hammer of her revolver.

47

The room went quiet. It seemed as if everyone had stopped breathing. Every pair of eyes were focused on Stacy and the .32 Smith & Wesson in her trembling hands.

Tears streamed down her face, but there was murder in her eyes!

Murdering someone in cold blood when there are at least five armed people in the room—two police officers, Kate, Bob, and myself—is about the dumbest thing someone can do. But, as I could see from Stacy Hudson's face, twisted in anger, she wasn't exactly in her right mind.

I took a step toward her, my left hand extended to try to calm her. My right hand was at my side. If I had to, I knew I could draw my gun in less than half a second. I also knew that Bob, Kate and her two officers were thinking the same.

"Give it to me, Stacy," I said quietly, trying to keep my voice as calm and reassuring as possible. "This is not what you want to do."

Stacy shook her head and said, "You don't understand.

None of you understand. First, I marry a deadbeat drunk who beat the shit out of me every time he staggered home—I promised myself I'd never go through that again—and then I fell in love with Chris." The tears ran in rivulets down her cheeks. "He was perfect, honest and decent and caring. He had dreams, ambitions. And now this? He's a fricking cold-blooded killer? Are you fricking kidding me?"

I took another step toward her. She sniffed loudly.

"He fooled everybody, Stacy," I said. "I can't imagine how you must feel, but you can't kill him. He's not worth what will happen to you if you do. I mean, look at him. He's pathetic. He's thrown away his future. He'll spend the rest of his life in prison because he did what you're about to do right now."

I took yet another step forward. I was closing in on her. "You don't want to end up like him, do you? It would be like... you'd be paying for his crimes."

Another step.

Stacy broke down, sobbing violently, and the barrel of the gun dropped a few inches.

I took a final step forward, placed my hand on the gun, and gently pushed it down toward the floor.

Stacy collapsed in my arms, sobbing. I took the weapon from her and eased the hammer down, and then everyone was moving at once.

Kate and the two uniforms stepped quickly forward, cuffed Christopher Goodkind, read him his rights, and Kate watched as they took him away.

Walter Goodkind stood up unsteadily, stumbled over to the fireplace and leaned against the mantle, his forehead against his arm, a tired, broken old man. Jennifer and Todd remained sitting silently where they were. God only knows what was going on inside their heads.

Zoe Flagg jumped to her feet, ran to her family and threw

her arms around her father's neck, hugging him fiercely. She was crying almost as hard as Stacy, whom I handed off to Kate, along with the little revolver, and asked her to give me a moment. She nodded, put an arm around Stacy's shoulder and tried to comfort her.

Me? I sat down beside Bob. "You look blue," I said. "Are you still beating yourself up about going out with Zoe?"

"No, I'm over that, Harry... What a frickin' mess, though, huh?"

"You can say that again," I said. And he did.

"What a frickin' mess."

I smiled and said, "Yep, but it's over. Hunter and Samantha now have the justice they... Well, knowing what we now know, I'm not so sure they do deserve it."

"I just wish we'd have been quick enough to save Jack Sloan, poor guy. What a way to go, Harry."

I nodded. What could I say? I said nothing. Sloan's death was on my conscience, and I didn't know which was worse: the fact that I felt somewhat responsible for his death, or that it didn't bother me as much as it once used to.

But at least it was over... Finally over.

48

I t was a few weeks later, on a Saturday afternoon, after a round of golf with Judge Strange, Larry Spruce and my father, when the subject of the Goodkind-Flagg murders came up. Kate was there, too. She'd joined us for lunch.

"I still can't believe how it turned out," Larry said. "All this time, we were so sure it was Walter Goodkind that we never looked at his son. There has to be a lesson in that, somewhere, I think." He looked at Kate and winked.

"Hey, don't look at me," she said. "It was before my time."

I nodded, stared down into my drink, and said, "Yes, things certainly weren't as they seemed, were they? But, judging by what I've seen in the papers and on TV, the case is really ramping up. And that Amanda Cole on Channel 7 is really giving Henry a hard time over it."

Spruce nodded. "Thanks to you and your team, we have more than enough to put young Goodkind away for life."

"Hey, I helped too, you know," Kate said, laughing.

"That you did, my dear," Strange said, tapping her gently

on her knee. He always did have a soft spot for her. In fact, she could just about twist him around her little finger.

"Oh, and I have some news," Larry said.

We all looked at him expectantly.

"The TBI cybercrimes division is bringing charges against Jennifer Goodkind. It appears they have proof it was she who arranged the hack."

I frowned. "Really? You mean the hacker's talking?"

Larry shook his head. "No, not exactly. She remains anonymous. It turns out, though, that she held onto the original digital files, and the emails back and forth between her and Jennifer Goodkind, and they prove that Jennifer hired her to do the job."

I leaned back in my chair and smiled. Good old Iron Britches. She must have seen the headlines and decided to do something about it. Well good for her!

I took a sip of my drink. "How's Zoe Flagg doing, by the way. I haven't heard a word from her or the Flaggs since that afternoon. Anybody know?"

My father looked up, smiling, and said, "Yes, I have. She's doing fine."

"*You* have?" Kate asked. "How do you know her?"

"Yes," I said. "How the hell would you know her?"

Again, he made with the smile and said, "Well, I should. She works for me."

"She... *What?*" I was stunned.

"She works for me. She's a paralegal. I needed another one. She applied. I interviewed her and then I hired her. She is one sharp kid... I know you know that, Harry, but what you don't know is what she was really doing working at Legacy Health."

"She was trying to get the goods on Walter," Kate said. "She thought he killed her brother."

"That she did, but that's not the only reason she infiltrated

Legacy. Zoe was investigating Walter Goodkind because she believed he had orchestrated the scandals that almost bankrupted American Flagg. In fact, when I hired her, I also agreed to take the Flagg's case. She really is a smart young lady; make a fine attorney one day. Anyway, I'll be filing suit against Goodkind before the end of the month. I think I can get the Flaggs a very significant settlement."

I shook my head and said, "Well, that's one for the books. Zoe Flagg. Who would have thought it? You old dog, August."

Henry Strange laughed, and so did Larry Spruce. In fact, we all laughed, especially my father. I looked at my watch. It was almost two-thirty.

"One more for the road, Harry?" August asked.

"No. Thank you. I've had enough, in more ways than one, and I'm tired. C'mon, Kate. Let's go home."

*****

Thank you for reading One Dark Night, Book 6 in the Harry Starke Genesis series. Would you like to read more?

Harry Starke Book 1 is the first book in continuing Harry Starke series of 14 more novels... so far. You can grab a copy at the discounted price of just $3.99, a 35% saving. CLICK HERE!

CPSIA information can be obtained
at www.ICGtesting.com
Printed in the USA
BVHW091450230221
600894BV00028BA/2755/J

9 780578 859781